The Haunting of Eldermoor

By K.W.Krieger

©2024

Table of Contents

I.
Unsettling Inheritance

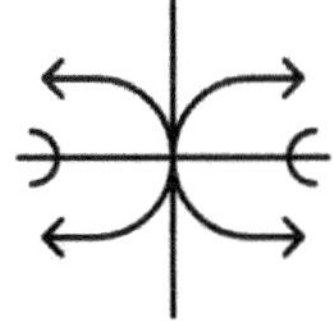

Amelia sat alone in her small, dimly lit apartment, where the air felt perpetually stagnant. The walls, a weary shade of beige, seemed to absorb the faint light from the single, flickering overhead bulb, casting a dull glow that barely reached the far corners of the room. The sparse furniture—a threadbare couch with frayed edges that she had picked up from a garage sale some time ago, and a coffee table marred by scratches—was arranged with clinical precision but lacked any hint of personal touch or comfort.

In one corner, an old, battered bookshelf leaned precariously, its few books collecting dust like forgotten relics. A tattered rug lay in the centre of the room, its once-vibrant colours faded to a dreary grey. The window, covered with heavy, unadorned curtains, allowed only a narrow strip of sunlight to sneak through, adding to the oppressive gloom.

The apartment's only decorations were a couple of faded, generic prints hanging crookedly on the walls, their colours as muted as the atmosphere around them. The kitchen area, visible through an open archway, was no better—a small, worn-out table with mismatched chairs and a collection of chipped mugs and plates that spoke of years of neglect.

Everything about the space seemed to reflect a life devoid of inspiration or excitement, a place where motivation had long since abandoned its occupant. The distant hum of the city outside, muffled by the thick walls, seemed almost like a distant, indifferent observer to the monotony within.

A sense of dullness had settled over her life, like a heavy fog that refused to lift. Amelia's job was as unremarkable as her apartment, a reflection of her current state of mind. She worked as an administrative assistant in a nondescript office building located in the heart of the city. Her days were consumed by monotonous tasks: processing paperwork, answering phone calls, and scheduling meetings for her overburdened manager. The work was routine, a cycle of repetitive motions and droning tasks that required little more than mechanical efficiency. Her desk, surrounded by stacks of unfiled documents and outdated office equipment, felt like a prison of mundane duties.

Her mornings began with the blare of an alarm clock at an ungodly hour, the sound cutting through the heavy silence of her apartment. She would drag herself out of bed, her movements slow and deliberate, and prepare a hasty breakfast of bland cereal or toast. The small kitchen offered no solace, its utilitarian design devoid of the warmth that might have once made mornings enjoyable.

As she stepped out of her apartment, the city greeted her with its predictable, droning symphony. The streets were lined with identical grey buildings and crowded with faceless commuters; each one trapped in their own cycle of routine. The once-thrilling cacophony of the city—the honking of taxis, the murmur of bustling crowds, and the distant clamour of construction—had become a monotonous backdrop to her life, no longer holding the allure it once had.

The subway ride to work was another exercise in drudgery. Packed into a crowded car, Amelia would cling to a metal pole, staring blankly at the grimy advertisements plastered on the walls. The flickering lights and the rhythmic clatter of the train on the tracks were a dull drumbeat that underscored the tedium of her daily commute.

Her office environment mirrored the dreariness of her home and commute. The fluorescent lights buzzed incessantly, casting a sterile glow over the sea of grey cubicles and the drone of keyboards. The occasional chat with colleagues was polite but superficial, lacking any genuine connection or warmth. Lunch breaks were spent in the nearby, uninspired cafeteria, where the food was as bland as the conversations.

Evenings were a continuation of the monotony. Amelia would return to her apartment, often too exhausted to do anything more than collapse onto the couch and watch the same old TV shows or scroll aimlessly through her phone. The city outside, bathed in the dim glow of streetlights and the occasional flash of neon signs, seemed to mock her with its ceaseless activity, a world she once yearned to explore but now found indifferent and alien.

Her weekends, once a respite from the grind, had become predictable as well. Errands and chores filled the days, with brief escapes to the same old coffee shop or a solitary walk through the same tired streets. The parks and cultural spots she once found enchanting now felt like stale remnants of a forgotten dream.

Amelia's life had settled into a rhythm that felt both unchanging and suffocating, a series of small, monotonous moments that blurred together into a single, unremarkable existence. The city, with all its promise and potential, had become a backdrop to her daily grind, a reminder of the dreams that had slipped away one by one, like fallen dominoes.

One evening, as twilight cast long shadows across her room, the quiet was suddenly interrupted by a soft, deliberate sound—the rustle of paper sliding across the floor. Amelia's gaze shifted from the half-lit television to the source of the sound, and she saw a single envelope slip beneath her door. It came to a stop just inside the threshold, its presence a stark contrast to the stillness that enveloped her.

The envelope itself was a relic of a bygone era. Its paper, a warm, creamy off-white, was slightly yellowed with age, giving it a timeless, antique quality. The edges were uneven and slightly frayed, suggesting it had been handled numerous times before reaching its destination. The envelope had a slight texture, its surface faintly embossed with a pattern of subtle, intricate designs that hinted at its journey through the years.

Across the front, Amelia's name was written in an elegant, looping script that seemed to dance across the paper. The handwriting was both graceful and precise, its curves and flourishes betraying a personal touch that felt oddly intimate and unfamiliar. It was as if the letters had been crafted with a careful, deliberate hand, each stroke imbued with meaning.

Amelia's curiosity piqued, and she reached down to retrieve the envelope, her fingers brushing against the slightly roughened surface. She turned it over, noting the absence of a return address—just a plain, unmarked back that did nothing to reveal the sender's identity. Her heart quickened slightly as she carefully broke the seal, her movements cautious yet eager.

As she opened the envelope, the crisp sound of paper unfolding filled the room. Inside were a few sheets of parchment, folded neatly. Amelia hesitated for a moment, her breath catching in her throat as she unfolded the letter. The paper inside was of a finer quality, smooth and slightly heavier, hinting at something more significant within.

She began to read the letter, her eyes tracing the elegant, flowing script that seemed to carry an air of mystery and anticipation. Each word seemed to resonate with a strange familiarity, yet it was the kind of familiarity that made her feel as though she was stepping into a world she had long forgotten or perhaps never fully known.

The room around her—the faded, threadbare furniture, the dim, flickering light—seemed to fade into the background as she focused entirely on the letter, her mind racing with questions and possibilities. The envelope, once a simple object of curiosity, had now become a symbol of change, a tangible connection to something beyond the confines of her droning existence.

The letter read.

Dearest Amelia,

By the time this letter reaches your hands, I will have departed from this world, and my journey will have come to an end. It is with a heavy heart that I pen these final words, for my passing is not merely the end of a life but the passing of a duty that has been entwined with our family for generations. It is now my solemn responsibility to pass on a truth that has been hidden and guarded for many years.

To you, my dear Amelia, I bequeath the Vandercliffe Manor, an ancestral estate nestled within the remote and enigmatic town of Eldermoor. This mansion, with its grand yet faded splendour, has fallen into a state of disrepair over the years. Its walls, though weathered, hold within them secrets that have remained untouched, waiting for the arrival of someone with the right heart and mind to uncover them. Though the mansion may appear forlorn and neglected, it is rich with history and mystery, and you may find something of great value within its confines.

However, I must caution you about Eldermoor itself. The town is a place shrouded in mystery, where time seems to have come to a standstill. The locals, though they have their own peculiar charm, are not particularly welcoming to outsiders. They harbour their own secrets and are wary of strangers. Should you encounter difficulties or feel out of place, simply mention my name—Eleanor Vandercliffe. My name will grant you a measure of respect and perhaps even aid, for I have lived among them all my life and they have come to know me well.

I am acutely aware of the hardships you have faced, particularly following the passing of your mother. It is my sincerest hope that this letter finds you in good health and a spirit ready to embrace what lies ahead.

Your inheritance extends beyond the mere possession of the mansion. It comes with the weighty responsibility of uncovering the truth about our family's connection to secrets that many generations have fought to conceal, even with their lives. There is a dark shadow that looms over our family history, and I fear that by the time you read these words, it may already be too late for me to offer you more guidance. There are mysteries surrounding your mother's passing that may find their answers within the manor.

I implore you to embark on a journey to Eldermoor. Let the winds of fate guide you as you delve into the heart of the unknown and seek out the truths that have eluded us for so long.

With all my love and hope for your journey,

Eleanor Vandercliffe

Amelia's heart raced as she finished reading the letter, the gravity of its message settling heavily upon her. As she folded the letter and set it aside, a sudden, unexpected clank interrupted the silence. She looked down to see an old, rusty key lying on the floor of her room, having fallen from the envelope.

It struck Amelia as peculiar that the envelope, which had felt almost weightless in her hands, had concealed such a substantial object. The key was indeed substantial, its iron frame heavy and worn with age.

The key was an ornate piece of craftsmanship, its design both intricate and imposing. It had a large, elaborate bow—its shape reminiscent of a gothic arch—engraved with swirling patterns and symbols that seemed almost arcane. The shaft was sturdy, with an array of notches and ridges, culminating in an old-fashioned bit with four serrated teeth, each one meticulously fashioned to fit a specific lock. The key's surface was mottled with patches of rust, lending it an air of ancient mystery and neglect.

As she reached down to pick it up, Amelia noticed a faint, almost imperceptible hum emanating from it, a sound so subtle it was barely perceptible. It was as if the key held within it a whisper of its own existence, resonating with a hidden energy. She picked it up, her fingers wrapping around its cold, coarse surface. The hum ceased the moment her fingers made contact with the key, and for an instant, she could have sworn she felt a slight vibration coursing through her fingertips.

The sensation was brief but unsettling—a fleeting tremor that seemed to ripple through the metal and into her own body. It was as though the key had been awaiting her touch, reacting to her presence in a way that defied logical explanation. The sudden silence that followed the cessation of the hum seemed almost eerie, amplifying the key's mysterious aura.

Amelia examined the key closely, her mind racing with questions about its significance and what secrets it might unlock. The key, despite its age and rust, felt alive in her hand, as though it carried a weight far greater than its physical form. The contrast between the key's heavy, iron presence and the envelope's near weightlessness only deepened the paradox of the moment.

 As Amelia reread the letter, its words seemed to penetrate deeply into her soul, stirring emotions she had long forgotten. The letter's message ignited within her a flicker of hope—an exhilarating sense of possibility that reached beyond the confines of her mundane existence. It was as though a dormant part of her, buried under layers of routine and disillusionment, was awakened by the promise of something greater, something filled with purpose. Yet, alongside this newfound hope was an equally powerful sense of fear. The prospect of confronting hidden truths, the eerie anticipation of what might lie ahead, and the weight of responsibility felt overwhelming. The dichotomy of hope and fear wove together, creating a tapestry of intense, conflicting emotions.

Amelia's gaze fell upon a small, enigmatic symbol in the bottom corner of the letter. It was an intricate array of lines and arrows, forming a design that seemed both complex and deliberately obscure. The symbol was reminiscent of an elaborate signature or perhaps a cryptic mark meant to convey a deeper meaning. The lines were meticulously drawn, their precision suggesting they were more than mere decoration.

For a brief moment, as she scrutinized the symbol, she noticed something unsettling. The lines and arrows appeared to shift ever so subtly, as though they were alive, writhing and moving in a barely perceptible dance. The sensation was fleeting, and Amelia blinked, wondering if her eyes were playing tricks on her. The motion was so slight that it could easily be dismissed as a trick of the light or a figment of her imagination. Yet, the brief appearance of movement imbued the symbol with an unsettling quality, as if it held a secret that was just beyond her grasp.

The realization that Great Aunt Eleanor, known for her eccentricities and enigmatic nature, might have used this symbol for a purpose only she could fully understand, added to Amelia's sense of wonder and apprehension. The symbol, though seemingly innocuous, now felt like a key to unravelling the mysteries of her inheritance, deepening her curiosity and unease about the journey that lay ahead.

As the city's noise faded into the background, Amelia's mind was consumed by thoughts of the Vandercliffe Estate. The mansion, with its imposing and mysterious presence, seemed to loom larger and larger in her imagination. The more she considered it, the more she felt the weight of her newfound knowledge settling upon her like a heavy mantle. The mansion was no longer just an old building but a repository of her family's hidden secrets, its very walls echoing with untold stories and long-buried truths.

In the quiet solitude of her apartment, Amelia made her decision with a sense of both resolve and trepidation. She would journey to Eldermoor, to the decrepit mansion that awaited her, determined to uncover the unsettling truths that lay beneath its shadows. The prospect of leaving her predictable life behind for the unknown was daunting, yet it also promised a glimmer of purpose and discovery.

That night, as she drifted into sleep, the weight of her decision clung to her dreams. She fell into a vivid and unsettling dreamscape that transported her directly to the Vandercliffe Estate. In her dream, she stood before the grand entrance of the mansion, the key from the envelope clutched in her hand. The key seemed almost to hum with a strange, palpable energy, and she felt an inexplicable pull toward the door.

She inserted the key into the lock with a feeling of both anticipation and trepidation. The heavy, iron key turned with a slow, creaking motion, and as the door swung open, Amelia stepped into the mansion's grand foyer. The air inside was thick with dust and the scent of age, the grand chandelier above her hanging like a forgotten relic from another era.

She walked through the expansive hallways, each step echoing off the high, shadowy walls. The grandeur of the mansion was evident even in its decay—ornate mouldings, faded tapestries, and long-abandoned furniture whispered of a once-great opulence now shrouded in neglect. The hallways stretched out before her, branching off into dark, mysterious corridors that seemed to beckon her deeper into the mansion's depths.

But as she continued her exploration, the dream began to take on an unsettling quality. The once-familiar hallways seemed to twist and elongate, their dimensions shifting in a disorienting way. Shadows flitted just beyond her vision, and the air grew colder, heavy with an oppressive, almost palpable sense of foreboding. The details of the mansion, once intriguing, now seemed to conspire against her, weaving a sense of dread that she couldn't quite comprehend.

The dreamscape grew increasingly disorienting, and Amelia struggled to make sense of the shifting rooms and whispering shadows. The sense of unease deepened, and just as she was on the brink of understanding the source of her discomfort, the dream abruptly fractured. She awoke with a start, her heart pounding and her breath coming in short, sharp bursts.

The vividness of the dream lingered in her mind, leaving her with a mix of apprehension and curiosity about what awaited her in the Vandercliffe Estate. The dream had given her a glimpse of the mansion's grandeur and its hidden mysteries but had also underscored the eerie, unsettling atmosphere that seemed to pervade its very essence.

II. Whispering Woods

The journey to Eldermoor was a long and winding one, stretching across miles of forgotten backroads and mist-shrouded valleys. As Amelia ventured further from the city's familiar, bustling streets, the landscape around her began to change, taking on a quality that felt almost otherworldly. The sleek, modernity of the urban environment gradually gave way to a more ancient, untamed wilderness, where the trees grew taller and denser, their branches intertwining like the fingers of old, gnarled hands.

With each passing mile, the sense of detachment from the outside world grew stronger. Her phone, once a reliable connection to the world beyond, began to lose its signal. The bars of reception dwindled from full, to one, and finally to none, leaving her cut off from the modern conveniences she had always taken for granted. Something was disconcerting about the sudden isolation, the feeling of being truly alone in a place that seemed untouched by time.

The route to Eldermoor became more archaic with every turn. At first, she travelled by bus, the vehicle rattling along the crumbling roads that wound through small, forgotten towns. These towns were relics of a bygone era, their buildings old and weathered, with peeling paint and sagging roofs. The few people she saw seemed as though they, too, belonged to another time, their faces etched with lines of hard-earned wisdom and weariness.

As the bus journey ended, Amelia transferred to a small, antiquated train, its carriages built of polished wood and brass fixtures that gleamed faintly in the dim light. The train chugged along at a leisurely pace, its rhythm steady and unhurried as if it had all the time in the world. The passengers were few, their silence heavy with the same sense of solemnity that had settled over the landscape. The countryside outside the windows seemed to roll by in slow motion, revealing fields of overgrown grass and ancient stone walls that crisscrossed the land.

Finally, the train reached its last stop, a lonely platform in the middle of nowhere, surrounded by dense forest on all sides. There was no station building, just a simple wooden sign that read "Eldermoor." As Amelia stepped off the lonely train platform, the mist curling around her ankles, her gaze fell upon the solitary horse-drawn carriage waiting in the dim light. The carriage itself was an imposing sight—its dark, weathered wood adorned with iron accents, barely visible in the thickening fog. The only source of illumination came from two flickering lanterns affixed to the sides, their warm, golden glow casting long shadows across the gravel path.

The driver, a stoic figure wrapped in a heavy coat that seemed almost as old as the carriage itself, stood silently beside it. His face was largely hidden beneath the brim of a wide, worn hat, casting his features into deep shadow. Only his eyes, sharp and discerning, caught the faint light, watching her approach with an intensity that sent a shiver down her spine.

As she drew nearer, the driver tipped his hat slightly in a gesture that might have been one of respect or mere formality. His voice, when he spoke, was low and creaky, like the groan of ancient wood under strain.

"Miss Vandercliffe," he said, the name rolling off his tongue with a weight of familiarity and perhaps even a hint of reverence. The way he addressed her sent a chill through her, as if her identity was already known in this strange, isolated place.

Without another word, he stepped forward and opened the carriage door with a creak that echoed through the silent night. He then extended a gloved hand, ushering her toward the carriage with a gesture that was both deferential and insistent.

The interior of the carriage was shrouded in shadow, the only light coming from the lanterns outside, which barely penetrated the gloom within. The seats were upholstered in dark, faded fabric, and the air inside was heavy with the scent of old leather and faint traces of smoke from the lanterns.

Amelia hesitated for just a moment, her eyes darting to the driver's obscured face. There was something unsettling about the entire scene—the fog, the darkness, the man's creaky voice—but she knew there was no turning back now. With a deep breath, she took the driver's hand and climbed into the carriage.

As soon as she settled into her seat, the driver closed the door with a soft, final click. A moment later, he was back in his place, taking up the reins with practiced ease. With a gentle flick, the horse began to move, the carriage lurching forward on the gravel path that led deeper into the mist-shrouded woods.

The journey continued in silence, the lanterns swaying gently with the motion of the carriage, casting flickering light that danced across the surrounding darkness. Amelia could feel the weight of the driver's presence just beyond the door, his creaky voice still echoing in her mind as the carriage carried her further into the unknown.

As the carriage set off, the road narrowed even further, transforming from a paved path to a rough, gravel trail that crunched under the weight of the carriage wheels. The trees grew thicker and closer, their branches forming a dense canopy overhead that blocked out much of the fading daylight. The mist that had clung to the valleys now enveloped the carriage, swirling around it like a ghostly shroud, obscuring the path ahead and adding to the growing sense of unease.

Amelia could feel the weight of the past pressing in on her from all sides. The air itself seemed to grow heavier, thick with the scent of damp earth and decaying leaves. The sound of the outside world was muffled, reduced to the rhythmic clatter of the carriage wheels and the occasional distant call of a bird or the rustle of unseen creatures in the underbrush.

It was as if time had slowed to a crawl, the modern world left far behind, replaced by an ancient, almost forgotten realm. The journey into Eldermoor felt like a passage into another era, a place where the past lingered in the shadows and the present held little sway. As the carriage continued its slow, deliberate progress, Amelia couldn't shake the feeling that she was crossing a threshold, leaving behind everything she knew for a place where time itself seemed to stand still.

The town of Eldermoor emerged from the mist like a spectral apparition, its presence both unsettling and mesmerizing. The buildings were a patchwork of weathered wood and crumbling stone, their facades bearing the scars of time and neglect. The air hung heavy with an eerie stillness, broken only by the occasional rustle of leaves or the creak of a distant, unseen door. As Amelia took in her surroundings, a sense of isolation settled deep within her, as if the town itself were cut off from the world, existing in a realm of its own.

The trees that encircled Eldermoor stood tall and imposing, their ancient branches reaching out like shadowy fingers, swaying gently in the wind. Their gnarled trunks were covered in thick layers of moss and lichen, giving them an almost sentient appearance, as though they were watching her every move. The dense canopy overhead allowed only slivers of light to penetrate, casting dappled shadows on the cobblestone streets below. It felt as though the forest itself was alive, concealing secrets that only it understood—secrets that might never be revealed to human eyes.

As the carriage rolled to a stop in front of a small, decrepit inn, Amelia stepped out into the unsettling embrace of Eldermoor. The inn was a modest structure, its roof sagging under the weight of years, and its wooden beams darkened by countless seasons of rain and fog. The sign hanging above the door, barely legible through the grime, bore the name "The Weeping Willow." The inn's windows were clouded with age, and the dim light within barely seeped through the layers of dirt and dust that clung to the glass.

Amelia took a tentative step onto the narrow main street, her footsteps echoing softly in the quiet. The town seemed frozen in time, with buildings leaning into one another as if they needed the support just to remain standing. The cobblestones beneath her feet were uneven and worn, their once sharp edges now rounded by the passage of countless feet over the centuries. The air was thick with the scent of damp earth and decaying leaves, mingled with the faint, acrid odour of smoke from distant hearths.

As she walked, she noticed the townspeople going about their business, yet there was something distinctly off about them. Their movements were slow and deliberate as if they were operating on a different plane of reality, detached from the world she knew. Their faces were pale and drawn, with deep-set eyes that seemed to hold a perpetual weariness. They were dressed in outdated clothing, the fabrics faded and threadbare, as though the fashions of Eldermoor had not changed in decades, perhaps even centuries.

The people of Eldermoor moved through the streets like phantoms, their presence felt more than seen. They barely glanced in her direction, and when they did, their gazes were fleeting, as if acknowledging her existence was an effort they could scarcely afford. A shopkeeper swept the steps of his store with a slow, methodical motion, while a woman in a tattered shawl carried a basket of wilted produce down the street, her expression vacant. Children played in the shadows, their laughter subdued, as if even joy had been muted by the town's pervasive gloom.

The buildings that lined the street were a motley collection of forgotten times—some had been grand once, with elaborate carvings and ornate facades that had long since faded into obscurity, while others were simple, utilitarian structures that seemed to sag under the weight of their own history. Ivy and vines crawled up the sides of many buildings, their tendrils snaking into cracks and crevices as if reclaiming the town for the forest that surrounded it.

Everywhere Amelia looked, there was a sense of decay and abandonment, as if the town itself were slowly being swallowed by the encroaching woods. The trees at the town's edge seemed to merge into one another, forming a dense wall of green that enclosed Eldermoor in a tight, suffocating embrace. The forest was both a guardian and a prison, its secrets hidden deep within the shadows, waiting to be uncovered by those brave—or foolish—enough to seek them out.

As she continued down the street, Amelia couldn't shake the feeling that she was being watched, not just by the townspeople, but by the very town itself. It was as if Eldermoor were a living entity, its presence pressing in on her from all sides, whispering its ancient, unknowable truths. She felt both drawn to and repelled by the place, the duality of its allure and dread pulling her deeper into its fold.

Amelia approached a weathered market stall nestled at the edge of the narrow street. The stall was a haphazard collection of oddities: crooked roots and vegetables that seemed to twist unnaturally, dried herbs tied in bundles that hung like shrivelled talismans, and a scattering of curious trinkets that glinted dully in the weak light. Behind the stall sat an old woman with faded, milky eyes that seemed to see far beyond the present. Her face was a map of deep wrinkles, etched by time and countless worries.

"Welcome to Eldermoor," the woman muttered without lifting her gaze, her voice barely more than a rasping whisper carried on the wind.

"Thank you," Amelia replied, her tone cautious but polite. She attempted to engage the woman in conversation, hoping to learn more about the strange town she had just arrived in. "I'm new here, just arrived. Just trying to get my bearings of what's around."

The old woman's eyes flickered briefly, catching Amelia's with a glint of something—perhaps recognition, or perhaps something far more elusive. Her gaze was fleeting, like a shadow passing over the surface of deep water before she turned her attention back to her stall. She began to fiddle with a twisted root, her gnarled fingers tracing its knots and curves with a practised ease.

"Best be careful, stranger," the woman said, her voice dropping to an almost conspiratorial tone. "Eldermoor holds more secrets than it lets on. Those woods," she gestured with a bony finger toward the dense, looming forest beyond, "they whisper strange tales in an archaic tongue."

Amelia's brows knitted in confusion and intrigue. "Whisper? What do they say?" she asked, leaning in closer as if the answer might be hidden in the folds of the woman's tattered shawl.

The woman shook her head slowly, a nervous, almost eerie smile tugging at the corners of her thin lips. "No one knows for sure… not exactly. The words get lost in the mist, twisted by the wind, carried off to places where they change into something else—something you'd rather not hear. But it's best not to listen, not to try and understand." Her voice wavered, slipping into a murmur that was almost a chant. "Bad things happen to those who listen too closely, bad things in the night, where shadows don't always stay still."

Amelia felt a chill creep up her spine. The woman's words were like threads of an old, fraying tapestry—disjointed, but woven together with a meaning she couldn't quite grasp. "I'm only here to take care of some family business," Amelia said, trying to shake off the unease that had settled over her like the mist around the town. "I'll be on my way soon enough."

The old woman's hands stilled, and her eyes, clouded though they were, seemed to bore into Amelia's with an intensity that belied her age. "Family business, you say?" she croaked, her voice tinged with something akin to pity—or was it fear? "Eldermoor's no place for family. Not anymore. Too much blood in the roots, too many bones in the ground. You'd best be about your business here and then leave. Some of us don't take too kindly to outsiders… especially those who think they belong here."

Amelia felt a prickling sensation at the back of her neck as if the very air around her had grown colder. "What do you mean?" she asked, though she wasn't sure she wanted to hear the answer.

The woman let out a low, cackling laugh, her teeth—what few remained—gleaming like dull stones in the shadow of her hood. "Meanings get lost here, child, just like the people who come searching for them. Eldermoor doesn't give up its secrets without a price. It's a place that doesn't forget, even when it should. Remember that, Miss Vandercliffe." She spoke her name with an unsettling familiarity, as though it had been written in the dust long before Amelia's arrival.

Amelia recoiled slightly at the mention of her name, a jolt of fear mingling with her rising curiosity. The old woman was already turning away, her focus drifting back to the tangled mass of roots and herbs on her stall, as if the conversation had never happened. Amelia stood there for a moment, unsure whether to press for more or heed the warning she had been given.

Before she could decide, the woman muttered under her breath, barely loud enough for Amelia to catch, "Turn back while you can, before the shadows take you too. The forest remembers... and it's always hungry."

Amelia swallowed hard, her mouth suddenly dry. The old woman's words hung in the air like a curse, and as she turned to leave, the feeling of being watched—by the town, the trees, and perhaps something more—followed her, pressing in from all sides.

Amelia's unease deepened with every step she took through Eldermoor. The town, with its oppressive atmosphere and its inhabitants who seemed to move like shadows, felt more and more like a place out of time—a place that didn't welcome outsiders. The old woman's cryptic warnings echoed in her mind, and the air itself seemed to grow colder, heavier as if the town was closing in around her.

As she continued to explore, the people she passed avoided her gaze, their eyes fixed on the ground or on the tasks before them. They moved with a strange detachment as if they were sleepwalking through their daily routines, existing in a world that barely overlapped with hers. Amelia felt like an intruder, a stranger in a place that had forgotten how to recognize the living.

Then she noticed him.

Sitting on a weathered bench beneath a gnarled tree, an old man watched her with an intensity that sent a jolt of fear through her chest. His eyes, sharp and unnervingly clear, were locked onto hers, penetrating her with a look that seemed to see straight through to her soul. His face was deeply lined, the skin sagging and paper-thin, giving him an almost skeletal appearance. His lips twitched as if he wanted to speak, but the words refused to come.

There was something deeply unsettling about him—his stillness, the way his eyes never wavered from her, the unspoken message that seemed to hang in the air between them. Amelia felt a cold sweat begin to bead on her forehead, and her pulse quickened. She had the overwhelming sensation that the man knew something about her—something she herself had yet to discover.

For a moment, she considered approaching him, drawn by a strange mix of curiosity and dread. But the longer she stood there, the more her fear grew. The man's expression was a mask of silent torment, as though he was trying to warn her, to tell her something crucial—but he was unable to voice it, trapped by some unseen force.

The hairs on the back of her neck stood on end. She tore her gaze away from his, her heart pounding in her chest, and began to walk away, quickening her pace as she put distance between herself and the unnerving figure. But the feeling of being watched persisted, prickling at her senses like a thousand tiny needles.

Unable to resist, she glanced back over her shoulder.

The bench was empty.

The old man had vanished, leaving no trace that he had ever been there. Amelia stopped dead in her tracks, a cold wave of fear washing over her. She blinked, her mind racing to make sense of what she had just seen—or what she thought she had seen. The bench stood exactly as it had before, the tree overhead casting long shadows across the cobblestones, but there was no sign of the man. No footsteps, no lingering presence—nothing.

For but a moment, she questioned her own sanity. Had the old woman's ramblings infected her mind, making her see things that weren't there? Or was there something more to this town, something that defied explanation?

Amelia's breath caught in her throat as she tried to steady herself. The rational part of her mind told her that she must have imagined it, that the stress of the journey and the eerie atmosphere of the town were playing tricks on her. And to top it all off the crazy old lady's ramblings to ward off strangers while deeply unsettling meant nothing surely? But deep down, she couldn't shake the feeling that something was terribly wrong—that Eldermoor was a place where the line between reality and illusion was dangerously thin.

With trembling hands, she pressed on, trying to push the encounter from her mind. But the image of the old man's piercing eyes and his ghostly disappearance stayed with her, gnawing at the edges of her thoughts, casting a long, dark shadow over her resolve.

As the day wore on, the wind that swept through the dense forest surrounding Eldermoor began to take on an eerie, almost sentient quality. It wasn't just the typical rustling of leaves or the occasional groan of a tree branch under pressure; this wind seemed to carry with it a language all its own—a low, haunting murmur that threaded through the trees and mingled with the oppressive silence of the town.

Each gust of wind brought with it the creak and moan of ancient branches, their twisted forms bending and swaying as if in conversation with one another. The sound was unsettling, a discordant symphony that seemed to rise and fall like a whispered chant. At times, it almost felt as though the trees were speaking, their voices hidden within the rustling leaves and the groaning limbs, carrying secrets that had been buried deep within the woods for centuries.

Amelia found herself instinctively listening, her ears straining to catch words that hovered just out of reach, always on the edge of comprehension. The wind's whispers seemed to circle around her, tugging at her thoughts, filling her with an inexplicable unease. There was a rhythm to it, an ancient cadence that resonated with the town's aura of forgotten times and forbidden knowledge.

It felt as if the forest was alive with mysteries—ancient and forbidden—waiting for someone to decipher their enigmatic language. And as she walked, the wind's whispers grew more persistent, more insistent, as though the very trees themselves were trying to communicate with her, to warn her of something lurking just beyond her understanding.

The sensation that the woods were speaking, that they had a voice all their own, settled deep into her bones, heightening the tension that had been building within her since she first arrived in Eldermoor. Every creak of a branch, every rustle of leaves, felt like a message—one that she wasn't sure she wanted to understand.

Amelia stepped into the inn, the heavy wooden door creaking loudly in the oppressive silence of the evening. The interior was dimly lit, the dull glow of a few scattered oil lamps casting long, flickering shadows across the walls. The atmosphere was thick with an unwelcoming vibe, a stark contrast to the fleeting comfort the inn offered as the most inviting part of Eldermoor she had encountered so far. The air was tinged with the scent of old wood and something faintly damp, as if the building itself had absorbed the melancholy of the town over the years.

The innkeeper, a gaunt figure with a weary expression, barely glanced at her as he handed her a heavy brass key, his hand lingering just long enough for her to notice the tremor in his fingers. No words were exchanged beyond a brief nod, and Amelia was left to find her way to her room in near silence. The narrow hallway stretched out before her like a tunnel, the worn floorboards creaking underfoot, echoing the pervasive unease that seemed to permeate the very walls.

Her room was small and sparsely furnished, a single bed with a thin, faded quilt, a wooden chair, and a nightstand bearing a dimly flickering lantern. The window was covered with heavy drapes that blocked out the last light of the dying day, sealing her within the inn's cocoon of isolation. Despite the unease gnawing at the edges of her mind, Amelia felt an overwhelming exhaustion settle over her. The journey, the town, the unsettling encounters—all of it weighed heavily on her, pulling her down into the bed with a weariness that felt like it could swallow her whole.

As she lay down, the mattress sagged beneath her, and the dull creaks of the inn seemed to blend with the whispers of the wind outside. The forest's distant murmur followed her into her sleep, a strange, alien song that echoed through her dreams. Shadowy shapes flitted at the edges of her consciousness, indistinct figures that moved just beyond her grasp, their intentions unknowable and their presence deeply unsettling.

In the heart of the night, Amelia awoke with a sudden jolt, her heart pounding in her chest. The room was pitch black, the only sound the increasingly loud whispers that seemed to fill the air around her, more urgent now, more insistent. The words were just as elusive as before, slipping through her grasp like smoke, leaving behind a residue of anxiety that clung to her mind like a thick fog.

She lay there in the darkness, trying to shake the feeling of being trapped in a place where she didn't belong, a stranger in a world that held secrets she wasn't sure she wanted to uncover. The inn, the town, the whispering woods—it all felt wrong, as if she had stumbled into a dream that wasn't hers to experience.

But as she tried to convince herself that she was awake, something changed. The whispers grew louder, more rhythmic, like the beat of drums echoing from deep within the forest. The sound seemed to swell inside her head, pulsing with an intensity that made her temples throb. It was as if the forest itself was alive, trying to force its way into her thoughts, to take root in her very soul.

Suddenly, she felt a constriction around her limbs. Panic surged through her as she realized that the sheets had somehow wrapped themselves around her, tightening like vines. She tried to move, but the more she struggled, the tighter they became, as if the bed itself had become an extension of the forest, determined to ensnare her. The sensation of roots twisting around her ankles, branches curling around her wrists, grew stronger, and she could feel the rough bark pressing against her skin.

Her breath caught in her throat as something covered her mouth, silencing the scream that clawed its way up from the depths of her terror. Her vision blurred, and she could feel the forest closing in around her, the trees leaning in with their ancient, knowing presence, their whispers now a deafening roar in her ears. The weight of the branches, the roughness of the bark, the sense of suffocation—it was all too real.

And then, just as quickly as it had begun, it stopped.

Amelia shot upright in bed, gasping for air, her heart hammering in her chest. The room was quiet, the sheets tangled around her but no longer suffocating, the oppressive weight of the forest gone. She was alone in the darkness, the inn silent save for the distant creak of old wood and the faint rustling of the wind outside.

For a moment, she sat there, trembling, unable to shake the vividness of what she had just experienced. The lines between dream and reality had blurred in a way that left her questioning whether she had ever truly woken up. Had her arrival in Eldermoor been real, or was she still trapped in some nightmare conjured by the town's malevolent presence?

Amelia touched her face, her fingers brushing her lips, half expecting to feel the rough texture of bark or the cold grip of the branches that had silenced her scream. But there was nothing—only her own breath, ragged and shallow, as she tried to convince herself that it had been nothing more than a terrible dream within a dream.

But as she lay back down, the weight of dread settled over her like a shroud, and she knew sleep would not come easily again. The forest's whispers, though muted now, lingered in the back of her mind, a haunting reminder that whatever was happening in Eldermoor was far from over.

As she lay in the darkness, listening to the rustling echoes of the forest outside her window and the muffled footsteps of people below in the bar, she questioned her very motive for coming to Eldermoor, was it worth it? What if her Great Aunt was just a crazy old fool writing nonsensical ramblings on paper moments before her bitter end? "No there must be something more to this town, to these people and to this estate" What secrets lay dormant within the walls of The Vandercliffe Manor? What secrets waiting to be unearthed

III. The Curious Journal

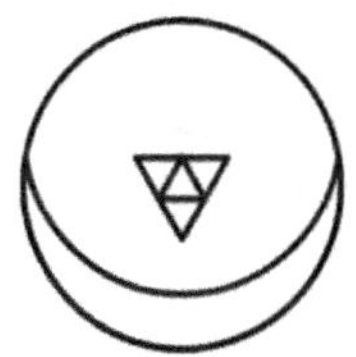

The very next morning, Amelia's fitful sleep left her feeling unrested and anxious. She hastened to dress and gather her things, her mind preoccupied with the haunting memories of her dreams and the unsettling atmosphere of Eldermoor. As she prepared to leave the inn and head towards Vandercliffe Manor, her thoughts were interrupted by an unexpected and chilling encounter.

As she hurried down the narrow hallway of the inn, her footsteps echoing softly against the worn wooden floor, she was abruptly halted by an unexpected presence. There, standing in the dim light of the early morning, was the old man who had so unnervingly stared at her the previous day. His appearance was both familiar and jarringly out of place. His face was ashen and weathered, with deep-set eyes that seemed to pierce through the very fabric of reality. His clothing was tattered and old-fashioned, suggesting a bygone era that had long since faded from the town's memory.

Before Amelia could fully process the sight, without warning, the old man grabbed Amelia's arm with a grip that was both weak and unnervingly firm. The touch was cold, his bony fingers like skeletal claws that sent a shiver up her spine. Amelia's heart raced as she looked up at him, her gaze meeting his. The intensity of his stare was piercing, his eyes wide and filled with a terror so profound it was almost palpable. It was a look she had seen before in animals cornered by predators—a desperate, helpless fear that seemed to freeze her in place.

The old man's eyes were filled with a kind of terror she had only seen in the wildest of nightmares—fear so intense that it left her momentarily speechless. His gaze was almost as if he were staring directly into an abyss, the look of a creature trapped in its final moments, helpless and resigned to its fate.

In a voice that seemed as if it hadn't been used in centuries, creaky and fragile like the rusted hinges of a forgotten door, the old man spoke a single, haunting word. "Beware." The word was delivered with such profound dread that it sent a shiver racing down Amelia's spine. It was not merely a warning; it was a foreboding, a statement drenched in the finality of a death sentence. The single syllable hung in the air, vibrating with a chilling finality that made Amelia's blood run cold.

The instant he spoke, the old man's demeanour shifted dramatically. The fear and intensity in his eyes seemed to drain away, leaving behind a blank, lifeless stare. He released her arm as if he were suddenly detached from his own actions and returned to his previous position—a rickety old chair in the hallway. He slumped back into the chair, his body appearing almost frozen, his eyes glazed over as though he had become a mere fixture of the inn. It was as if he had been suddenly possessed by an otherworldly force, his awareness of his surroundings and the encounter completely vanished.

Amelia stepped back, her heart pounding in her chest. "Excuse me?" she called out, her voice trembling with a mix of fear and confusion. She hoped for some kind of response, some sign that the old man was still aware of her presence. But there was nothing—no movement, no sound, no flicker of recognition in his eyes. He sat there like a forgotten statue, his entire being seemingly shut off from the world.

The eerie stillness that followed was suffocating. Amelia's mind raced as she grappled with the unsettling encounter. Had she truly witnessed this bizarre transformation, or was it a figment of her troubled imagination, distorted by the fears and anxieties that had plagued her since her arrival in Eldermoor?

With a final, fearful glance at the old man's unmoving form, Amelia quickly exited the inn. The encounter left her shaken and deeply unsettled, casting a long shadow over her resolve. As she made her way towards Vandercliffe Manor, the old man's chilling warning echoed in her ears, and she couldn't help but question whether venturing into the heart of the town and the mansion itself was an ill-fated decision. The haunting words and the old man's sudden, eerie transformation lingered in her mind, leaving her with a sense of dread that only deepened as she continued her journey.

Amelia hurriedly walked away from the inn, her steps quick and uneven as she navigated the narrow, winding streets of Eldermoor. The air was cold and thick with a sense of foreboding that seemed to press down on her chest, constricting her breath and making her heart pound with every step. The eerie silence of the town weighed heavily on her, broken only by the distant rustle of the trees and the occasional creak of old wood settling in the chill of the morning.

The forest loomed ever closer as she moved, its dark, gnarled branches stretching out like skeletal fingers, casting long, sinister shadows across her path. The trees seemed to close in around her, their ancient trunks and twisted limbs creating an almost tunnel-like effect, further amplifying the claustrophobic feeling that clung to her.

Every sound seemed magnified—each snap of a twig or rustle of leaves echoing with unsettling clarity in the quiet of the morning. Amelia's thoughts raced, a swirling hurricane of questions and fears. The old man's terrifying warning, the unsettling encounters of the previous day, and the ominous atmosphere of Eldermoor all converged into a singular, pressing anxiety that gnawed at her insides.

Despite the fear that clamped around her chest like an iron band, Amelia pressed forward with a steely resolve. She was desperate for answers, for some explanation that would make sense of the dread that had settled over her. Each step toward the Vandercliffe Manor was fuelled by a mix of trepidation and determination. She needed to know what lay hidden within the manor's decaying walls, to uncover the secrets that seemed to be entwined with her own fate.

The manor itself, still shrouded in mist and shadow, loomed ahead, its imposing structure partially obscured by the thickening fog. Its once-grand facade, now marred by time and neglect, stood as a stark reminder of the mystery she was about to confront. Amelia's resolve hardened with each step, even as her heart raced, and her mind churned with fear. The manor's dark silhouette against the cloudy sky seemed to beckon her forward, promising answers but also whispering of the dangers that lay ahead.

As she neared the gates of the Vandercliffe Manor, the weight of her fear seemed to lift slightly, replaced by a resolute focus. Amelia knew that whatever awaited her within those walls would be a crucial part of unravelling the tangled web of secrets and dread that had ensnared her since her arrival in Eldermoor.

The Vandercliffe Manor loomed before Amelia, an imposing relic of a bygone era. The wrought iron gate at the entrance was a masterpiece of Gothic design—its blackened metal twisted into intricate, arcane patterns that seemed to writhe and coil with a life of their own. The gate's sharp spires reached skyward, and curling tendrils of iron formed sinister, arching shapes that hinted at the mansion's dark past. Each time the wind whispered through the bars, the gate groaned in response, adding to the oppressive atmosphere that surrounded the manor.

Beyond the gate, the mansion itself stood as a monument to decay. Its once-grand façade was now a patchwork of peeling paint and crumbling stone, overrun by creeping ivy that seemed to strangle the very walls it clung to. The vines and moss formed a dense tapestry over the building, their tangled growth obscuring the intricate details that hinted at the mansion's former opulence. The roof was sagging under the weight of time and neglect, its tiles cracked and missing, exposing the wooden beams beneath.

The garden, too, was a testament to abandonment. Wilted flowers drooped listlessly from overgrown beds, their once-vibrant colours faded to muted hues of brown and grey. Bushes had grown wild, their tangled branches and leaves intertwining with the broken, ironwork of old garden structures. Trees, their branches gnarled and twisted, seemed to press in on the manor as if attempting to reclaim it from the encroaching wilderness. Some of the vines and branches even crept up to the base of the mansion, ensnaring parts of its lower walls in their grasp, creating an illusion of the manor being swallowed by nature itself.

Amelia approached the entrance with a mixture of trepidation and determination. The key, which had somehow appeared from the weightless envelope, was now a constant companion, its weight a solid reassurance against her side. She fumbled with the key in her pocket, her fingers trembling slightly as she pulled it out. The key was old, wrought from iron, and felt cool and heavy in her hand. Its surface was worn smooth from age, its once-clear engravings now faded and obscured by time.

She examined it closely, the cold metal catching the dim light of the overcast sky. The key was ornate, with delicate filigree designs that spoke of craftsmanship from an era long past. It seemed almost alive in her hand, its weight and texture a stark contrast to the almost ethereal lightness it had when it first appeared.

Amelia's gaze shifted to the massive front door of the manor. It was an imposing slab of dark wood, adorned with elaborate carvings that had become obscured over the years by dirt and grime. The brass door handles were tarnished and weathered; their once-lustrous sheen dulled to a grimy patina. The handles were large and ornate, their intricate patterns echoing the Gothic design of the gate.

With a deep breath, Amelia slid the key into the old, rusted keyhole. She turned it slowly, feeling the resistance of the ancient mechanism. An audible 'click' echoed through the still air as the lock finally gave way. She removed the key, its surface cold and heavy against her palm, and grasped the brass handles. They felt rough and uneven under her fingers, a testament to years of neglect.

As she pushed the large, ornate door open, the hinges let out a long, mournful creak, the sound reverberating through the silent garden like a mournful wail. The door swung inward with a groan, revealing the shadowed interior of the mansion and inviting Amelia into its dark, forgotten depths.

The interior of the Vandercliffe Manor was a haunting blend of faded grandeur and lingering decay. As Amelia stepped over the threshold, her breath caught in her throat at the sight before her. Despite the layers of dust and the unmistakable scent of age that permeated the air, the mansion's interior was a testament to the wealth and power that had once coursed through its halls.

The grand foyer stretched out before her, vast and imposing. The ceilings soared high above, their ornate plasterwork adorned with intricate designs that hinted at a time when the manor was the pinnacle of luxury. Faded gold leaf, though tarnished with age, still clung to the edges of the ceiling's decorations, catching the weak light that filtered through the grime-covered windows and casting a dim, almost ethereal glow across the room.

Massive pillars lined the edges of the foyer, each one carved from a rich, dark marble that had taken on a ghostly sheen over the years. The pillars were adorned with elaborate motifs—twisting vines, mythical creatures, and heraldic symbols—frozen in time, their details softened by layers of dust. These columns seemed to hold up the weight of the entire manor, their silent presence a reminder of the strength and influence the Vandercliffe family once commanded.

The floor was a sweeping expanse of polished stone, the intricate patterns beneath the dust revealing a meticulous attention to detail. The surface was cold and smooth underfoot, the echoes of Amelia's steps ringing out in the vast emptiness, magnified by the sheer scale of the space around her.

At the far end of the foyer, a grand staircase dominated the room, its wide steps sweeping upward in a graceful curve that led to the upper floors. The banisters were crafted from dark, polished wood, their surfaces intricately carved with scenes of myth and legend. Though covered in dust and the signs of neglect, the craftsmanship was unmistakable—a testament to the artistry and wealth of a bygone era. Each step was broad and deep, designed to convey a sense of importance and ceremony to those who ascended them.

The walls of the foyer were lined with large, ornate paintings, their once-vibrant colours now muted by time. Portraits of long-dead Vandercliffe ancestors stared down at Amelia, their eyes following her every move with an eerie intensity. The figures in the paintings were dressed in opulent garments, their faces a mix of pride and stern authority, as if they were silently judging the intruder who dared to step into their domain. The frames that held these portraits were as elaborate as the paintings themselves, gilded and decorated with intricate patterns that hinted at the family's vast wealth and influence.

Massive chandeliers hung from the ceiling, their crystal pendants dulled by decades of neglect, yet still managing to catch the faint light and refract it into a thousand tiny rainbows. The chains that held them creaked slightly as if the weight of time had finally begun to take its toll.

As Amelia ventured further into the manor, she could feel the echo of its past grandeur resonating through the walls. Every inch of the space spoke of opulence and power, of a family that once held sway over this remote corner of the world. Yet, beneath the beauty and the wealth, there was an undeniable sense of abandonment—a feeling that the glory days of the Vandercliffe Manor had long since passed, leaving behind only the ghostly remnants of what once was.

The air was thick with dust, yet it also carried a faint, lingering scent— something ancient and mysterious, as if the very stones of the manor had absorbed the secrets and stories of generations. Amelia felt a chill run down her spine as she imagined the lives that had played out within these walls, the power struggles, the whispered intrigues, and the dark secrets that still lingered in the shadows.

Despite the overwhelming sense of history that permeated the manor, there was something oddly comforting about it. The mansion, though neglected and forgotten by time, still held a beauty that was undeniable—a beauty that had endured through the ages, just as the secrets it guarded had endured. As Amelia stood in the grand foyer, she couldn't shake the feeling that she had stepped into a place where time itself had paused, waiting for her to uncover the truths hidden within its walls.

As Amelia ventured deeper into the mansion, her footsteps reverberated through the vast, echoing hallways, their sound magnified by the cavernous space. Each room she entered told its own story—a parlour adorned with faded, velvet-upholstered furniture; a grand dining room where a long-forgotten feast seemed to have once taken place, the table still set with tarnished silverware and crumbling porcelain plates; a ballroom with a cracked marble floor, where long-dead musicians might have played as the elite of a bygone era danced beneath glittering chandeliers.

In each room, the remnants of the past clung stubbornly to life, even as dust and decay gnawed at the edges. There were bedrooms draped in moth-eaten curtains, with grand four-poster beds that seemed to have not been disturbed in decades. The walls were adorned with faded wallpaper, once vibrant but now barely clinging to the plaster beneath, its patterns obscured by layers of grime. There were once-cozy sitting rooms with cold, blackened hearths and high-back chairs arranged as if awaiting occupants who would never return.

The history of the Vandercliffe family was etched into every corner of the mansion, but it was a history steeped in silence, in secrets that lingered like ghosts in the air. The grandeur of the mansion was unmistakable, yet it was as though a veil had been drawn over it, hiding the true nature of the place—a nature that was at once beautiful and unsettling, as if the house itself was waiting, watching, guarding its secrets with a jealous vigilance.

After what felt like hours of exploring, Amelia finally found herself standing before a door at the end of a narrow, dimly lit corridor. The door was slightly ajar, its worn wooden surface marred by time and use. She pushed it open with a creak, revealing a small, dimly lit study.

The room was a stark contrast to the grandiosity of the rest of the mansion. It was intimate, almost claustrophobic, with walls lined from floor to ceiling with bookshelves that sagged under the weight of countless volumes. The books themselves were a chaotic mix—some were leather-bound with gold-embossed titles, others were tattered, barely holding together by thin strands of string or brittle, disintegrating covers. The air was thick with the scent of old paper and ink, a heady mix that spoke of knowledge accumulated over centuries, of secrets documented and then forgotten.

The centrepiece of the room was a large, heavy desk, its dark wood polished to a dull sheen by the passage of time. The surface of the desk was cluttered with a bewildering array of items—dusty manuscripts and old books stacked haphazardly, their pages yellowed and brittle; ancient maps and charts that hinted at forgotten explorations or perhaps secret territories; inkpots that had long since dried out, their lids crusted with the remnants of black and blue ink; and quill pens, some broken, others still intact, lying across the desk as if abandoned in the middle of a thought.

Among the papers were scattered notes, some hastily scribbled and barely legible, others written in a meticulous hand, their contents mysterious and incomprehensible to anyone but their author. There were scrawled equations, fragmented sentences, and sketches of strange symbols that made no sense at a glance. The writings seemed to hint at something hidden, something that had driven the writer to the brink of obsession.

A single, flickering candle sat on one corner of the desk, its weak flame casting long, trembling shadows across the room. The candle was nearly spent, the wax pooling around its base in a thick, congealed mass. The light it provided was barely enough to pierce the gloom, but it lent the room an eerie, almost otherworldly atmosphere.

The walls of the study were lined with more bookshelves, each one crammed full of volumes that ranged from the arcane to the mundane. The spines of the books were cracked and faded; their titles barely legible. Some shelves were also filled with rolled-up scrolls and documents tied with fraying ribbons, their contents a mystery yet to be uncovered.

On a side table near the desk, a dusty globe stood, its surface marked with the passage of fingers that had traced the contours of long-forgotten lands. Nearby, an old leather-bound journal lay open, its pages filled with dense, cramped handwriting that trailed off abruptly as if the author had been interrupted mid-thought.

Amelia's gaze fell on an old, ornate mirror hanging on one wall, its surface clouded with age. For a moment, she thought she saw movement in its depths, a fleeting shadow that sent a shiver down her spine. But when she blinked, the mirror reflected only the flickering candlelight and the disarray of the study.

This was a room that had seen much and remembered everything. It was a place of study, of obsession, and of secrets that had been locked away for too long. As Amelia stood in the centre of the room, she felt the weight of those secrets pressing down on her, a palpable presence that seemed to fill the air with an almost suffocating intensity. Yet, amidst the fear and uncertainty, there was also a sense of purpose—a feeling that she was standing at the threshold of something important, something that could finally unravel the mysteries that had plagued her family for generations.

As Amelia carefully sifted through the scattered papers on the desk, her hand brushed against something unusual—an old, leather-bound journal. The journal's cover was worn and weathered, its once-rich brown leather now faded and cracked with age. It bore the marks of countless hands that had turned its pages over the years, the corners softened from use and time. The leather felt rough under her fingers as if it had been passed down through generations, each one leaving its own imprint on the fragile cover.

Intrigued, Amelia picked up the journal, feeling its weight in her hands. The aura of age and mystery surrounding it was undeniable. She could almost sense the years of history contained within its pages. As she hesitated for a moment, a strange rush of anxiety coursed through her as if the journal itself was warning her not to open it. But the pull of curiosity was too strong to resist.

With a deep breath, Amelia slowly opened the journal, the creak of the leather filling the quiet room. The pages inside were yellowed and delicate, some corners folded over from years of use. The handwriting was elaborate and graceful, reminiscent of a bygone era, with each letter carefully formed as if the writer had taken great care in recording their thoughts.

On the title page, written in the same elegant script, were the words: "*Journal of Percival Darrow*." The name meant nothing to Amelia, but the significance of the journal was undeniable. It was a piece of the puzzle she was trying to solve, a glimpse into the past that could hold the answers she sought. As she turned the pages, the feeling of being watched returned, but she pressed on, unable to tear herself away from the secrets that awaited her within the journal's ancient pages.

As Amelia flipped through the journal, her eyes were drawn to the cryptic drawings that seemed to haunt every other page. The images were unlike anything she had ever seen—grotesque and mesmerizing in their impossibility. Twisted figures with far too many limbs crawled and slithered across the pages, their forms contorted in ways that defied natural anatomy. Some appeared to be humanoid but with elongated torsos, multiple sets of arms and legs, and faces that lacked eyes yet seemed to stare back at her, full of malevolent intelligence.

The geometries in the drawings were even more unsettling. Shapes that should not have been able to exist in three-dimensional space twisted and merged, creating impossible structures that seemed to bend reality itself. Triangles overlapped to form paradoxical figures, circles looped back into themselves, and spirals twisted infinitely inward. The lines of these shapes did not adhere to any known mathematical principles; they were chaotic, bending and warping as if they were alive, pulsating with a hidden energy. Looking at them made Amelia's head ache as if her mind was struggling to process a concept beyond human understanding.

Among these unnatural forms were symbols—arcane sigils that seemed to pulse with a dark power, drawn with a hand that trembled with fear or madness. Some resembled ancient runes, others were completely foreign, their meaning lost to time. They were scrawled haphazardly in the margins, sometimes overlapping the main drawings, as though the writer was desperate to communicate something but couldn't quite grasp what it was. The symbols seemed to shift as Amelia looked at them, making her question if they were static at all.

The landscapes in the journal were equally disturbing, depicting realms that twisted her perception of space and time. Jagged mountains rose at impossible angles, their peaks bending toward each other as if conspiring against the sky. Oceans of ink-black water churned beneath the weight of unseen forces, their surfaces disturbed by waves that moved in patterns she couldn't predict. In some drawings, the land itself seemed to breathe, the ground rippling as though alive, and the sky bled into the horizon, a sickly hue that defied the natural order of colours.

The final pages were a chaotic blend of symbols, distorted figures, and illegible scrawls, all blending into one another in a nightmarish tapestry. Some of the drawings appeared to have been scratched into the paper with a sharp object, the ink smeared as if the author's hand shook uncontrollably. These final, frantic sketches seemed to depict creatures emerging from within the very walls of the mansion—beings of shadow and smoke, with limbs that twisted and coiled around themselves, their faces a mass of writing tendrils. The very act of looking at them filled Amelia with a sense of vertigo as if she were being pulled into the drawings themselves, into the madness that had consumed the author.

Amelia could feel her own sanity fraying at the edges as she continued to stare at the pages, the images seared into her mind. The journal was not just a record of one man's descent into madness; it was a portal to something far more terrifying, a glimpse into a reality that defied all logic and reason. As she closed the book, the symbols and shapes seemed to linger in her vision, their twisted forms burned into her consciousness, leaving her questioning the nature of the world around her and the darkness that lurked just beyond the veil of reality.

As Amelia delved deeper into the journal, the world around her seemed to blur, fading into the background as the unsettling words consumed her attention. The entries began innocuously enough, recounting strange dreams and odd occurrences, but soon they took a darker turn.

"...the shadows dance at the edges of my vision, and I hear whispers that chill my soul. Shapes move within the walls, figures that defy the laws of nature. They beckon, always just out of reach. I am not alone here, though I am unsure if that is a comfort or a curse."

The writing was vivid, yet filled with a sense of unease, as if the author was teetering on the brink of something incomprehensible. Amelia could feel a knot tightening in her stomach, a growing fear that something within these pages was meant to remain hidden. She turned the page with trembling hands.

"...the veil between worlds grows thin. I have glimpsed the true forms that lurk beyond our understanding, unearthly and incomprehensible. Their eyes burn with knowledge that scorches my sanity. They are watchers, beings from places our minds cannot fathom. Their presence corrodes reality, bending it to their will, and I fear they will soon breach the barriers that hold them at bay."

The journal entries became more frantic, the once-elegant handwriting growing jagged and erratic. Amelia's breath quickened as she read on, her heart pounding in her chest. The room felt smaller, the air heavier, as if the walls themselves were pressing in on her, driven by the same malevolent force that had driven the author to madness.

"...I have seen their cities, sprawling in dimensions beyond perception. They are watchers, observers of our existence, their intentions unfathomable. I fear what will happen when they finally breach the barriers that hold them at bay."

The words on the page seemed to pulse with a life of their own, and Amelia's grip on the journal tightened as the sensation of being watched intensified. The drawings became more grotesque and impossible, depicting figures that twisted and contorted in ways that defied logic, as if they existed in a reality that obeyed different laws.

Amelia's mind struggled to grasp the horrors described within the journal, her thoughts growing as fragmented as the writings themselves. Her head pounded as the fear rooted deep within her consciousness took hold. The author's descent into madness was palpable, the final entries devolving into a chaotic scrawl of cryptic symbols, meaningless words, and wild ramblings that made no sense at all. She could almost hear the voice of the writer in her head, a voice filled with terror and desperation, echoing through the mansion's dark corridors.

"...they are here. They have always been here. The walls... they breathe. The eyes... oh, the eyes. They see everything. I cannot escape. They have taken my mind, my soul... I am lost..."

The final pages were nothing more than a jumble of ink, as if the author had descended into complete madness, their thoughts unravelling into a cacophony of fear and insanity. Amelia slammed the journal shut, her heart racing, the sound of her own breath filling the oppressive silence of the room.

She felt the weight of unseen eyes upon her, the presence of something ancient and malevolent lurking just beyond the edges of her perception.

For a moment, she questioned her own sanity, wondering if she too would succumb to the same madness that had claimed the journal's author. The mansion, once just a decaying relic of her family's past, now seemed alive with secrets that were better left undiscovered.

As Amelia closed the journal, her thoughts churned with a chaotic mix of fear, doubt, and an overwhelming need for answers. Her hands trembled as she placed the journal back on the desk, the weathered leather cover still warm from her touch. The words and images within its pages had burrowed deep into her mind, gnawing at the edges of her sanity. Was Percival Darrow merely a madman, lost in his own delusions? Or had he glimpsed something far more sinister, something that now threatened to pull her into the same abyss?

Amelia felt a tug-of-war within her. Part of her wanted to flee, to leave this cursed mansion and never look back. But there was another part—a stronger, more insistent voice—that urged her to stay, to dig deeper, to uncover the secrets that had ensnared her family. The thought of walking away now, after coming so far, was unbearable. She needed to know why her family was connected to all of this madness, why she had been drawn to this place. The fear that gripped her was real, but so was the pull of the unknown, the allure of forbidden knowledge that whispered promises of understanding.

She stood in the study, her thoughts swirling, as if the very air around her was charged with the energy of the journal's revelations. The mansion, once merely a decaying relic, now felt like a living entity, its corridors and rooms holding secrets that beckoned to her, promising both enlightenment and doom.

In a daze, Amelia began to walk, her feet moving almost of their own accord. The mansion seemed to close in around her as she wandered through its labyrinthine halls. Doors appeared and disappeared, leading her into rooms that seemed to shift and change as soon as she stepped inside. Some were grand, with high ceilings and ornate chandeliers, while others were small and cramped, filled with dusty furniture and shadowed corners. She passed by rooms filled with forgotten relics, portraits of stern-faced ancestors whose eyes seemed to follow her every move, and long-forgotten family heirlooms cloaked in dust.

The mansion's layout twisted and turned, a maze that defied logic. Hallways stretched on endlessly, their walls adorned with faded tapestries and peeling wallpaper. Each turn led her deeper into the heart of the mansion, yet it felt as though she were moving in circles, trapped in an unending loop. The further she went, the more her sense of time and space seemed to blur, her surroundings warping and shifting like the impossible geometries she had seen in the journal.

Her mind teetered on the edge of reality, caught between the tangible world and the horrors described within the journal. She could feel the mansion's oppressive atmosphere pressing down on her, the weight of its secrets almost suffocating. Yet, she couldn't stop herself. The pull was too strong, the need to understand too powerful to resist. She was like a moth drawn to a flame, aware of the danger but unable to turn away.

As she continued her aimless walk, Amelia's thoughts became increasingly fragmented, her focus slipping in and out like a flickering candle. The mansion whispered to her, its voice a low murmur that she couldn't quite understand. The corridors seemed to stretch on forever, a never-ending labyrinth that led her deeper into the unknown. Every door she opened revealed another room filled with shadows and silence, yet none offered the answers she sought.

She wandered, lost in the mansion's twisting maze, her mind pulled in all directions—by fear, by doubt, by a desperate need to uncover the truth. The journey seemed endless, the mansion's secrets just out of reach, as if mocking her efforts. Yet even as her thoughts threatened to unravel, she couldn't stop. She had to know. She had to understand why her family was tied to this place, and what it all meant. Even if the truth lay hidden in the darkest corners of the mansion, she would find it—no matter the cost.

IV. Descent into Dreams

Amelia's nights became a descent into a waking nightmare, where the lines between her dreams and reality dissolved into a murky, indistinguishable haze. Each time she closed her eyes, she was plunged into a labyrinthine version of the mansion, where the halls stretched endlessly, and doors led to places that defied logic and reason. The walls seemed to pulse with a life of their own, shifting and warping as she passed, trapping her in a maze that felt alive, as though the mansion itself were toying with her.

During the day, Amelia wandered through the same halls, yet she could never quite shake the feeling that she was still dreaming. The mansion seemed to conspire against her, its corridors twisting and turning in ways that made no sense, leading her in circles, always back to where she started. Every room she entered felt like a part of the dream she couldn't escape, a continuation of the nightmare that had begun the moment she stepped foot in Eldermoor.

The whispered voices that haunted her dreams bled into her waking hours, filling her mind with an incessant, unintelligible murmur that set her nerves on edge. Sometimes, she would hear them clearly, as if they were right beside her, only to realize that she was alone in the room. The sensation was unnerving—like being watched, pursued, yet never being able to catch a glimpse of her tormentors. She would spin around, expecting to see a shadow or figure, but there was nothing. Just the empty, dusty rooms of the mansion, silent and still, yet teeming with an unseen presence.

Amelia's sense of time began to fracture. She could no longer tell where one day ended, and the next began. The dream world bled into her waking life so seamlessly that she questioned whether she had ever truly woken up at all. Was she still trapped in some terrible dream, unable to escape, or had the dream seeped into reality, corrupting it beyond recognition? The mansion was a prison, its corridors winding endlessly, its rooms a jumble of forgotten memories and ancient horrors.

As she walked through the mansion, she would sometimes find herself in a room she had never seen before, filled with strange objects that seemed to pulse with an otherworldly energy. Other times, she would walk through a door and find herself back in a place she had just left, as though the mansion were playing tricks on her, leading her deeper into its labyrinthine depths. She began to dread each turn, each doorway, unsure of what she would find on the other side.

The fear grew, a suffocating presence that weighed down on her chest, making it hard to breathe. She was trapped in a nightmare she couldn't wake from, a dream that had no end. She would pinch herself, dig her nails into her palms, anything to feel something real, but the pain only confirmed that she was awake—or was she? The mansion seemed to shift and warp before her eyes, the walls undulating like the surface of a disturbed pond, and she felt herself slipping further into madness.

There were moments when she would pause, her heart pounding, convinced that she had found the way out, only for the hallway to twist and morph, leading her deeper into the bowels of the mansion. The overwhelming sense of dread grew with each step, as if she were walking toward something unspeakable, something that lay in wait for her in the deepest, darkest corners of the manor.

Every time she tried to retrace her steps, the paths seemed to change, leading her back to rooms she had never seen before, or places she was certain she had just left. The mansion was alive, its very architecture conspiring against her, trapping her in a dream from which there was no escape.

Amelia's mind raced with fear, confusion, and a gnawing doubt that perhaps she was no longer truly awake. Perhaps she had never been. The thought chilled her to the core, but she couldn't stop. She had to keep moving, had to keep searching for answers, for a way out of this waking nightmare. But with every step she took, the mansion pulled her deeper into its clutches, its labyrinthine halls echoing with the whispers of ancient secrets, and she feared she might never find her way back to reality—if reality even existed anymore.

Amelia's existence had become a waking nightmare, where shadowy figures haunted her every step, mocking her with their mere presence. These beings were more than mere phantoms—they were twisted manifestations of darkness itself, with forms that defied logic and reason. Their bodies were as black as the void, amorphous and ever-shifting, sometimes appearing as grotesque, half-formed shapes that twisted in impossible angles. Their limbs elongated unnaturally, fingers tapering into points that seemed to claw at the very fabric of reality.

But it was their eyes that were the most terrifying of all. Burning like twin embers, they blazed with an intensity that seemed to bore into Amelia's very soul. The flames flickered and danced within those hollow sockets, a cruel mockery of life, and wherever she turned, those eyes followed, unblinking and relentless. It was as if they could see through her, stripping away her defences, leaving her exposed and vulnerable.

These shadowy figures never fully entered her line of sight, always remaining just at the periphery, teasing her with their presence. They would flicker in and out of existence, sometimes vanishing when she tried to focus on them, only to reappear a moment later, closer, their fiery eyes gleaming with malevolent intent. They whispered to her in voices that seemed to come from everywhere and nowhere at once, a cacophony of incomprehensible words that sent shivers down her spine. The whispers were a torment, an incessant reminder that she was never alone.

Every step she took, every room she entered, every corner she turned—she felt their gaze upon her, a constant weight pressing down on her chest. The mansion had become a prison, and these figures were its jailers, watching her with a sadistic glee as she stumbled through its endless corridors. The sense of being hunted was overwhelming, a primal fear that gnawed at her sanity. She was never safe, never truly alone; the figures were always there, lurking just out of sight, waiting for her to let her guard down.

The feeling of entrapment was suffocating. Amelia felt as though she were caught in a paradox, trapped between two worlds—a dream from which she could not wake, and a reality that no longer made sense. She was lost in a maze of shifting walls and endless hallways, with no way to tell where one nightmare ended, and the other began. The mansion's architecture seemed to warp and bend around her, leading her in circles, and all the while, the figures closed in, their eyes burning brighter, their whispers growing louder.

There were moments when she questioned her own sanity, wondering if she had ever truly left Eldermoor, or if she was still wandering through the forest, lost in some twisted dream. The line between reality and nightmare had blurred beyond recognition, and she no longer knew which was which. Was she still asleep, caught in the throes of some terrible vision, or had the horrors of her dreams seeped into the waking world, tainting everything with their darkness?

The figures seemed to sense her confusion, her fear, and they fed off it, growing more bold, more terrifying. They mocked her with their silence, their presence a constant reminder that she was trapped, with no escape. Amelia could feel their eyes on her even when she closed her own, their burning gaze searing into her mind. She was never alone, never at peace, always being watched, always being hunted.

The mansion had become a living nightmare, a place where time had no meaning and reality itself was twisted beyond recognition. The figures were her constant companions, haunting her every step, mocking her attempts to escape. They were the embodiment of her deepest fears, and no matter how fast she ran, no matter where she hid, they were always there, waiting for her in the shadows. Amelia's world had become a prison of terror, and there was no waking from this nightmare, no escape from the relentless gaze of those burning eyes.

In her dreams, Amelia was thrust into realms that defied all logic and comprehension, where the very fabric of reality seemed to unravel and reweave itself into a chaotic tapestry of madness. The landscapes before her were twisted and distorted as if moulded by an unseen hand with a mind bent on creating something utterly alien and incomprehensible.

She stood on the edge of a precipice that seemed to float in a void of swirling chaos. The ground beneath her feet was neither solid nor liquid, but a strange, shifting substance that pulsed with a life of its own, sending tremors up through her legs. Below, an ocean stretched out in all directions, but it was not an ocean as she knew it—this was a sea of impossible colours, a churning mass of hues that defied description. The waters shimmered with iridescent tones that bled into one another, creating a cacophony of colours that no human eye could fully grasp. It was as if the ocean itself was alive, constantly shifting and morphing, its waves crashing silently against the shore in patterns that made no sense, the edges dissolving into the void beyond.

Above her, the sky was a swirling maelstrom of impossible geometries, where angles and shapes twisted and folded in on themselves, creating a dizzying array of forms that defied all understanding. The skies were not the blue expanse she knew but a tumultuous cascade of colours that bled into each other—fiery reds melding into deep purples, which in turn faded into sickly greens and eerie blues. The sky and ocean were indistinguishable as if the

horizon had been erased and the heavens had merged with the sea, creating an endless loop of colour and chaos. Clouds moved in unnatural patterns, their forms ever-changing, merging and splitting apart with a life of their own, their undersides glowing with an unsettling, otherworldly light.

Amelia found herself walking through forests where the trees reached up to the sky, their branches intertwining with the stars themselves. The bark was smooth and metallic, and the leaves shimmered with a cold, unnatural light. These trees seemed to grow both upwards and downwards at once, their roots disappearing into the sky while their branches sank deep into the earth. The paths she followed wound through impossible landscapes where the ground shifted beneath her feet, tilting and warping as if refusing to be bound by the laws of gravity. Mountains rose at impossible angles, their peaks spiralling into the sky, while valleys seemed to sink into the abyss, their depths hidden by a thick, swirling mist that obscured everything.

Time was meaningless in these places. One moment, she stood at the edge of a cliff, gazing out over an endless expanse of stars that stretched across the ground like a river; the next, she was plunged into a dense, fog-covered jungle where the trees whispered secrets in languages long forgotten. The sky above was not constant, sometimes dark and filled with stars that blinked in strange patterns, other times ablaze with shifting auroras that danced across the heavens in a rhythm that defied any sense of order. The sun, when it appeared, was a blazing orb that seemed to pulse with a malevolent life of its own, casting shadows that writhed and twisted as if alive.

Amelia's senses were overwhelmed by these impossible places. The sounds were a dissonant symphony of noises that did not belong—whispers that cut through the air like shards of glass, the rustling of leaves that sounded like screams, the distant rumble of thunder that seemed to emanate from the very ground beneath her feet. The smells were equally alien, a mixture of decay and sweetness, of burning metal and blooming flowers, all swirling together in a way that made her head spin.

As she moved through these planes of existence, she caught fleeting glimpses of things—creatures, or perhaps structures, that existed just at the edge of her vision. They were always moving, shifting in and out of existence, never fully seen but always felt, a constant reminder that she was not alone in these worlds. The sense of being watched, of being hunted, was overwhelming, and with each step, the fear grew, a cold, creeping dread that threatened to consume her entirely.

In these moments, the line between dream and reality blurred even further. Amelia could no longer tell where the nightmare ended and where the waking world began, or if there was even a distinction to be made. The landscapes she traversed in her dreams seeped into her waking hours, infecting her thoughts, her vision, and her very sense of self. She was trapped in a paradox of existence, caught between worlds that made no sense, with no way to escape, no way to wake up from a dream that might never have been a dream at all.

As Amelia wandered through these impossible landscapes, she found herself slipping not only between worlds but also through the fragmented remnants of her own past. The boundaries of time and space dissolved, and she was dragged into memories that no longer felt like her own. These memories, once familiar and comforting, had been twisted, altered in ways that made them feel alien and unsettling. It was as if she were watching scenes from someone else's life, moments that she should have recognized but now felt distorted and distant.

In one such memory, Amelia found herself standing in the kitchen of her childhood home. The smell of freshly baked bread filled the air, and the warm light from the afternoon sun streamed through the window, casting a golden hue over everything. But something was off—details that should have been clear were blurred as if seen through a foggy lens. Her mother stood at the counter, humming a tune that Amelia had heard countless times before, but the melody was wrong, twisted into something unfamiliar. When her mother turned to face her, the features of her face were indistinct, like a painting smeared by careless hands. Amelia felt a pang of recognition, but it was dulled, muted, as if she were watching a stranger go through the motions of a memory that was supposed to be her own.

She reached out to touch the counter, to ground herself in something real, but her hand passed through the wood as if it were made of mist. The scene shifted abruptly, and she was no longer in the kitchen but in her old bedroom, surrounded by the faded pastel colours of her youth. The room was exactly as she remembered it—or almost. The walls seemed to breathe, the paint pulsing in time with her heartbeat, and the furniture was subtly distorted, the angles all wrong. Her bed, which had always been a place of comfort, now loomed large and ominous, its shadow stretching across the floor like a gaping maw.

Amelia saw herself as a child, sitting on the bed, clutching a worn stuffed animal to her chest. But the child's face was obscured, the features indistinguishable, and as she watched, the figure flickered, like an old film reel burning up under the heat of a projector. The stuffed animal's eyes seemed to glow with an unnatural light, and when the child looked up, the face was gone, replaced by a blank, featureless void. Amelia recoiled, a scream caught in her throat, but no sound came out. The scene dissolved into darkness, and she was thrown into another memory, this one even more fragmented and bizarre.

She was in the park where she used to play as a little girl, the sun bright in the sky, children's laughter echoing around her. But the colours were wrong—the grass was a sickly yellow, the sky a deep, oppressive gray. The swings creaked with a rhythm that set her teeth on edge, and the faces of the other children were twisted into grotesque caricatures, their laughter a cacophony of mocking voices. Amelia watched herself run through the park, but she couldn't recognize the child she had seen. The movements were jerky, and unnatural, as if her younger self were a puppet being manipulated by unseen strings. The faces of the children around her began to blur, melting into a swirl of colours and shapes that made no sense.

The park scene morphed into a memory of her first day of school, but the building was a twisted labyrinth of corridors that stretched on forever, doors leading to nowhere, and teachers with faces that were half-formed, their eyes hollow pits of darkness. Amelia could barely recognize herself in the sea of children, her own form flickering in and out of focus as if she were being erased from existence. The memory was familiar, yet alien, like a dream that was slipping through her fingers, impossible to grasp fully.

As these disjointed memories played out before her, Amelia felt a deep sense of unease, a gnawing fear that she was losing herself, that the person she had been was slipping away, replaced by something else. The faces of people she once knew faded into blurs, their voices a distant echo that she could no longer place. She was a spectator in her own life, disconnected from the events that had shaped her, watching a stranger's memories unfold in a distorted and nightmarish theatre.

The more she tried to focus, to anchor herself in these memories, the more they twisted and changed, slipping through her grasp like sand. Even the most mundane moments—sitting at the dinner table, walking to school, laughing with friends—were tainted by this pervasive sense of wrongness. The scenes looped and overlapped, details shifting with each repetition until she could no longer tell where one memory ended and another began. Faces she had once known intimately became unrecognizable, fading into nothingness, leaving her isolated and adrift in a sea of forgotten moments.

Each time she awoke, Amelia was left with the unsettling feeling that she had never truly woken up at all. The mansion's halls stretched before her, a labyrinth of doors and corridors that mirrored the twisted paths of her mind. She wandered through them in a daze, her thoughts muddled, unsure if she was awake or still trapped in the nightmare of her memories. Every corner she turned, every door she opened, led to more questions, more uncertainty, and the nagging fear that she might never find her way out—never escape the labyrinth of her own fractured reality.

The townspeople of Eldermoor appeared almost as spectres to Amelia—distant, alien, and imbued with a strange, unsettling energy that made her skin crawl. Their faces were blank, devoid of warmth, with eyes that seemed to pierce through her, their gazes lingering just a moment too long. Whenever she tried to engage them, they would either look away or offer curt, dismissive responses, as if she were an outsider who didn't belong in their world. The townsfolk moved with a strange, disjointed rhythm, their actions synchronized in a way that felt unnatural, like puppets on invisible strings.

The more Amelia tried to interact, the more she felt the town's collective consciousness pushing her away. The marketplace, once lively, now seemed muted; the colours dull, the air heavy. Conversations stopped abruptly when she approached, and the villagers would slowly turn their heads to stare at her with vacant expressions, their eyes reflecting an eerie, unspoken knowledge. The warmth and solace of human connection were absent;

instead, there was only the cold, suffocating presence of something unknown and hostile.

Fear and isolation wrapped around Amelia like a shroud. The walls of Eldermoor seemed to close in on her, the once quaint town now a prison with no means of escape. The ground beneath her feet felt unsteady, the air thick with an oppressive silence. She wandered through the narrow streets, searching for anything familiar, anything that could anchor her to reality, but the faces she passed were hollow, as though drained of life. Every interaction left her more disconnected, more certain that she was losing her mind.

As the torment continued, Amelia found herself contemplating the unthinkable. The nightmares had grown unbearable, their relentless assault on her psyche leaving her broken and desperate for a way out. The idea of escape, of ending the torment once and for all, began to take hold of her thoughts. In a moment of utter despair, she decided to end her life, convinced that it was the only way to free herself from the hellish existence that had consumed her.

She found herself standing on the edge of the town's old stone bridge, the churning waters of the river below calling to her. The night was cold, the wind howling around her as she looked down into the dark abyss. Her heart pounded in her chest, each beat a reminder of the life she was about to leave behind. Trembling, she closed her eyes and took a deep breath, then stepped forward into the void.

But instead of the cold embrace of the water, she felt nothing. When she opened her eyes, she was back in her bed at the inn, the sheets damp with sweat, the shadows in the room stretching out like claws. It had all been a dream—yet it felt so real, the terror, the desperation, the finality of her decision. The realization left her hollow, devoid of any sense of escape. Even death, it seemed, was not an option. She was trapped, bound to this nightmare world with no way out, forced to carry on in the face of overwhelming fear and despair.

The failure to escape only deepened her sense of hopelessness. She wandered through the town and the manor, her movements robotic, her mind numb. The shadows lengthened around her, the darkened corners of her mind expanding into every facet of her existence. Yet, despite the crushing weight of it all, a small, flickering ember of determination remained within her. With no other choice but to keep moving forward, Amelia steeled herself against the darkness, resolved to uncover the truth behind the horrors that haunted her.

Her body moved through the town and manor as if on autopilot, her mind detached, floating in a haze. She passed through the winding streets of Eldermoor, the eyes of the townspeople following her every step, their gazes a constant reminder that she was utterly alone. The mansion loomed in the distance, its dark silhouette a beacon of the unknown, calling to her with its secrets and lies. And so, with no other path to take, Amelia pressed on, driven by a need to understand, to find answers, even if they led her deeper into the abyss.

Time became meaningless for Amelia. Days stretched into weeks, and eventually, she lost all sense of how long she had been trapped in the nightmare that was the Vandercliffe Manor. The hours blended together, each moment as indistinguishable from the next as the dreams and reality that bled into one another. Was it weeks? Months? Years? The world outside the mansion seemed to fade away, leaving her alone with the dark secrets she was slowly uncovering.

In her relentless search for answers, Amelia stumbled upon an ancient tome buried beneath layers of dust in a forgotten corner of the manor. Its leather cover was cracked and brittle, the pages yellowed with age, and the symbols etched into its spine were both alien and familiar. The tome seemed to pulse with a dark energy as if it were a living thing waiting to be awakened.

As she read, the words whispered of forgotten rituals, of beings that existed beyond the comprehension of man, and of a veil that separated reality from the madness that lurked in the spaces between. The text spoke of the "thinning" of this veil, where dreams and nightmares could spill over into the waking world, and where ancient, eldritch entities could infiltrate the minds of those who dared to look too closely into the abyss.

The deeper Amelia delved into the tome, the more she felt her grip on reality slipping. The lines between her waking life and the nightmarish visions that plagued her dreams grew thinner and thinner, until she could no longer distinguish one from the other. The words on the pages seemed to twist and warp as she read, shifting like the landscapes of her dreams, bending the very fabric of her sanity.

She began to question everything—her memories, her identity, her very existence. The tome suggested that the nightmares were not merely figments of her imagination, but glimpses into other planes of existence, where the laws of time and space were meaningless, and where beings of unimaginable horror waited in the shadows. The fear that had been gnawing at her since she arrived at the mansion now took root deep within her soul, threatening to consume her entirely.

But there was no escape, no waking from this nightmare. The only option left was to continue, to push forward through the madness, to unravel the mystery that had ensnared her—no matter the cost.

V. The Forgotten Cult

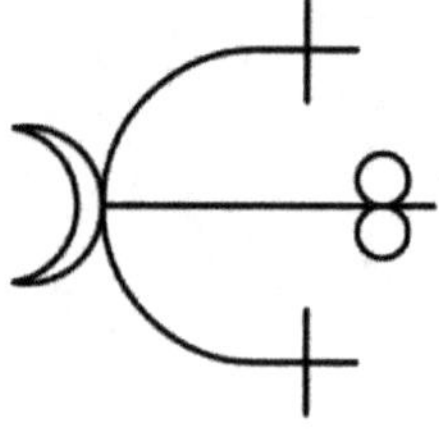

Amelia's search for answers became an obsession. She spent endless days and nights shifting through countless books and manuscripts, her hands trembling as she turned page after page in her desperate quest to uncover the truth. Every corner of the mansion's dusty library was explored, every forgotten nook and cranny probed in her unrelenting pursuit of knowledge. The once-imposing shelves, filled with ancient texts, now seemed to close in around her as she unearthed secrets buried by time.

It was during one of these fevered research sessions, surrounded by the smell of aged parchment and the musty scent of long-neglected books, that she found it—an old, weathered manuscript that seemed to beckon her from its hiding place. The manuscript was bound in cracked leather, its cover darkened by the passage of countless years. The edges of the pages were frayed and brittle, stained with the yellowing of age and the faint scent of mildew. It felt heavy in her hands, as though it carried the weight of the horrors contained within.

The title, embossed in faded gold lettering, read: "*The Chronicles of Eldermoor: A History Unveiled.*" As Amelia carefully turned the pages, she could feel the texture of the ancient paper beneath her fingertips, rough and fragile, as though it might crumble to dust at any moment. The faint scent of old ink and forgotten knowledge filled her nostrils, mingling with the oppressive atmosphere of the mansion.

The manuscript revealed a history that sent chills down her spine—a history overshadowed by the presence of a long-forgotten cult. The pages spoke of a secretive group known as the "Order of the Obsidian Veil," a cult that had once thrived in the shadows of Eldermoor. Their existence had been systematically erased from the collective memory of the town's inhabitants, their deeds buried in obscurity.

Within the pages of the manuscript hastily scrawled notes and incoherent ramblings were smattered across the pages, few passages of text were translatable and comprehensible, As Amelia sat in the forgotten shadows of the old library, whispers drifted through the musty air. "*The gate,*" one page read, "*is veiled in darkness, lost between the realms of time and space.*" The ancient book described "*dropping*," as if in a trance, "*where the rath—*" interrupted by a smudged ink blot—"*is a curse bound by the obsidian veil.*"

"*Ga, perhaps,*" another fragment stated, "*the rituals are a reflection of forbidden knowledge, draped in ancient symbols. The world's edges are—*" a scribbled note disrupted the text—"*rath, the truth lies in unravelling the shadows.*"

A torn page displayed an incomplete sentence: "*Through the rath, one might glimpse the—*" a faded corner held the elusive word "*dro.*" Near it, "*ga,*" seemingly unrelated to the preceding words, was inscribed in hurried script.

Elsewhere, a yellowed manuscript revealed a cryptic line: "The veil, shadowed by myths, conceals the forgotten dro—" the rest of the text faded away, leaving only hints of unfinished thoughts.

Scattered notes provided glimpses of fragmented revelations: "*The cult sought dro,*" and "*ga, ancient rites. The boundary of rath—*"

In a marginal scrawl, "*dro*" appeared next to "*ga, hidden truths,*" while another page had "*rath*" lingering in the margins beside the words "*arcane secrets, lost to time.*"

The air around her grew thick as she spoke the words, a summoning, an incantation meant to draw forth an entity from beyond the veil of reality. But the words came out wrong—"*DRO, GA, RATH*"—a slip of the tongue that echoed with a haunting resonance. The sound of those three words reverberated through the air, growing louder and louder until they seemed to pierce the fabric of existence itself.

As the echo of her voice twisted through the endless dimensions, reality itself seemed to buckle under its weight. Amelia clutched her head, a sudden jolt of pain radiating through her skull like lightning. The mispronunciation of the phrase hung in the air, a reverberation that clawed at the very fabric of her sanity.

The moment the words left her lips, a splitting headache surged forth, each throb pulsating like a drumbeat of chaos. It felt as if something deep within her mind had fractured, splintering her thoughts into jagged shards. The pressure mounted, her temples throbbing rhythmically, each heartbeat amplifying the agony. She stumbled backward, vision blurring as the world around her warped in response to her blunder.

A nauseating wave washed over her, and she fought to steady herself, the walls of the mansion closing in as if they were alive, mocking her.

The once pristine whites of her eyes were marred by a vivid, fiery red that seemed to seep from beneath the surface. The blood pooled beneath the thin, transparent membrane that covers the white of the eye, creating a dramatic, striking effect.

 Amelia's eyes felt gritty and irritated, as if tiny shards of glass had embedded themselves in her corneas. The constant pressure of the headache made her feel as if her eyes were swelling, though no actual puffiness was visible. The discomfort was persistent and aching, a dull, throbbing pain that resonated with each pulse in her head. Bright lights and sudden movements exacerbated the irritation, causing her to squint and shield her eyes from even the faintest sources of illumination.

Tiny red veins spidering across the whites, a painful reminder of the toll this mistake had exacted. The fiery pain radiated, causing her vision to swim with crimson spots, blurring the line between reality and nightmare.

Amelia felt as if her head might implode, a cacophony of whispers and shadows mocking her. The very air around her vibrated, filled with sinister laughter that echoed the consequences of her misstep. She gritted her teeth, forcing herself to breathe through the haze of agony. Each inhalation sent a jolt of pain through her skull, yet she pressed on, determined to regain control, to silence the chaos that had erupted from her single mispronunciation.

In that moment, she realized that she stood on the precipice of something far greater than her own understanding—an abyss that demanded respect and precision. Desperation mingled with fear, and she swore she could hear the dark corners of the mansion whispering, warning her to tread carefully, for the words she wielded held more power than she could fathom.

The walls of the room twisted and warped, bending in on themselves as if the very world around her was being reshaped by forces beyond comprehension.

It was then that she felt it, the sensation of being watched, not by eyes of flesh and blood, but by something far more ancient and powerful. It was as though the universe itself had turned its gaze upon her, observing her with a cold, detached curiosity. The feeling was suffocating, as if she were a specimen under a microscope, every thought, every emotion laid bare for some unseen entity to dissect.

The implications of her error were vast, rippling through the dimensions like a stone cast into a still pond. She was no longer alone in her mind; the universe was there with her, scrutinizing her every move. The power she had invoked had gone terribly wrong, and now she was trapped in a moment of cosmic scrutiny, with no escape in sight.

The universe, once distant and indifferent, now loomed closer, its gaze fixed upon her like a teacher observing a pupil who had made a grave mistake. Amelia could feel the weight of that gaze pressing down on her, driving her to the brink of insanity as the echoes of "DRO, GA, RATH" continued to reverberate through the endless expanse of reality.

Days melted into an indistinguishable blur since Amelia had uttered that dreadful phrase. Time had become a mere illusion, with the sun rising and setting as if it were mocking her plight. The feeling of being watched never ceased, an oppressive weight that clung to her, amplifying the shadows that danced in her periphery. It was as if the very walls of the mansion held their breath, anticipating her every move, while the townspeople of Eldermoor wore knowing expressions that only deepened her sense of isolation.

Amelia scoured every inch of the mansion and the library, her fingers tracing the spines of ancient tomes and weathered manuscripts, searching for fragments of information relating to the cult that had once thrived in the shadows of Eldermoor. Each new discovery felt like a breadcrumb leading her deeper into a labyrinth of madness and dark history.

She analysed and read through countless manuscripts and journals each one as cryptic as the next in one manuscript she found titled *The Rites of the Obsidian Veil*

"The followers of the Order of the Obsidian Veil were said to commune with entities beyond our comprehension. Their rituals, performed under the light of the blood moon, sought to tear the veil that separates our reality from the realms of shadow and chaos. It is whispered that they sacrificed those deemed unworthy to appease the ancients, their blood used to strengthen the bond between worlds."

Another manuscript read

"In the year of the Veil's Thinning, the townspeople reported seeing strange figures in the woods, their eyes like embers, haunting the edges of reality. The cult's gatherings grew more frequent, their chants echoing through the night, invoking names long forgotten. Eldermoor changed—its very essence tainted by the whispered secrets of the Obsidian Veil."

Amelia's relentless search through the mansion's library had become almost ritualistic, each day blending into the next as she poured over the musty tomes and dishevelled manuscripts. It was during one particularly fruitless afternoon, as she was rifling through a stack of old journals and ledgers buried beneath dust and cobwebs in a forgotten corner of the library, that she stumbled upon it.

The journal had been wedged between two larger volumes, nearly invisible against the clutter. Its leather cover was cracked and faded, but the binding seemed sturdier than some of the other manuscripts she had handled. She gingerly pulled it from its resting place, feeling a peculiar chill as her fingers brushed the worn leather. The journal's spine creaked in protest, revealing its age and the secrets it had guarded.

Opening the journal, Amelia found the pages filled with elegant but hurried script. Some of the ink had smudged over time, but the words were still legible. She turned the pages slowly, skimming through personal notes and mundane details, until she came across a section that deviated sharply from the rest. It was a journal entry that seemed out of place, written in a frantic scrawl that contrasted with the otherwise orderly text.

"I have witnessed the dark rituals performed under the guise of secrecy. Tonight, as we gathered beneath the ancient oak, I felt the air crackle with a power that sent shivers through my spine. They spoke of the convergence, the merging of our world with the beyond. I am torn between fear and

exhilaration. The entities we invoke are ancient, and I fear they do not come without a price. The visions I have seen, the shadows that dance before my eyes... they are a promise of power, but at what cost?
- Alysander Thorne, 1887"

As Amelia read the entry, a cold shiver ran down her spine. The vivid descriptions of the ritual, the mention of the ancient beings, and the ominous warning resonated deeply with the fears that had plagued her. The journal entry was like a direct link to the past, shedding light on the sinister practices of the cult and their influence on the present. It offered a glimpse into the mind of someone who had been both a participant and a witness to the horrors Amelia was now experiencing.

Each passage Amelia read resonated with the visions that had tormented her dreams—the eldritch beings, the shadowy figures, and the landscapes that defied the laws of nature. It felt as if the very fabric of reality was fraying at the edges, allowing the cult's influence to seep through.

As she pieced together the cryptic bits of information, a chilling realization gripped her heart: the cult had aimed to merge the dimensions, and their dark endeavors were still felt in Eldermoor. The pervasive dread and the shadowy figures that followed her were not mere figments of her imagination; they were manifestations of a reality warped by the cult's rituals. Amelia now understood that the nightmares were not just her own but a collective memory of terror that haunted the very essence of Eldermoor.

With each revelation, the weight of the truth pressed down on her, a suffocating reminder that she was entangled in a history much darker than she had ever imagined. The cult's legacy was a curse, and Amelia found herself unwillingly caught in its web. The echo of that cursed phrase, "DRO, GA, RATH," lingered in her mind, a chilling reminder of the forces she had unwittingly summoned.

Amelia's discovery of the journal entry from Alysander Thorne marked a turning point in her investigation. As she continued to sift through the fragmented and cryptic historical records, she began to piece together a troubling connection between her own family and the shadowy history of the cult.

The dusty tomes and yellowed manuscripts she encountered often mentioned the Vandercliffe name in connection with high-ranking members of the Order of the Obsidian Veil. Her family, once prominent and influential in Eldermoor, had been deeply entangled in the cult's dark machinations. The texts described how the Vandercliffe family, through their wealth and influence, had played a crucial role in the cult's most significant rituals and ceremonies. They were not just participants but key architects in the rituals that sought to merge dimensions and bring forth the malevolent entities the cult worshipped.

Amelia's heart raced as she read through the disjointed passages and faded ink. It became clear that the Vandercliffes were central figures in this cosmic tapestry of horror. Her great-aunt Eleanor's enigmatic legacy, combined with the family's historic involvement, painted a chilling picture of a lineage that had been deeply enmeshed in occult practices. It was as if the strands of fate had woven her into this nightmarish narrative, drawing her into a web of ancient and forbidden knowledge.

The realization struck Amelia like a thunderbolt. She was not merely an outsider stumbling upon forgotten lore; she was a direct descendant of those who had once wielded power within the Order. The mansion, the town, and the dark forces she had been grappling with were all intricately linked to her heritage. The cosmic tapestry of her family's past had ensnared her, and she was now an integral part of this horrific legacy.

Overwhelmed by the gravity of her discovery, Amelia felt a profound sense of urgency. The knowledge of her family's involvement and the cult's actions filled her with a desperate need to act. She understood now that the nightmares and horrors she had faced were not mere coincidences but the consequences of the cult's ancient rituals coming undone. The veil between worlds, the creatures from beyond, and the disturbances in Eldermoor were all part of a larger, catastrophic plan that had been set in motion by her ancestors.

Determined to stop the malevolent forces that had been unleashed, Amelia resolved to confront the legacy of her family and the Order. She knew that she had to undo the damage wrought by the cult, unravel the dark magic that had been set into motion, and restore balance to the realms. Her path was fraught with peril, but she could no longer turn away from her fate. The need to rectify the wrongs of the past and to protect both the waking world and the dreamscape from the encroaching darkness drove her forward.

VI. Familiar Faces

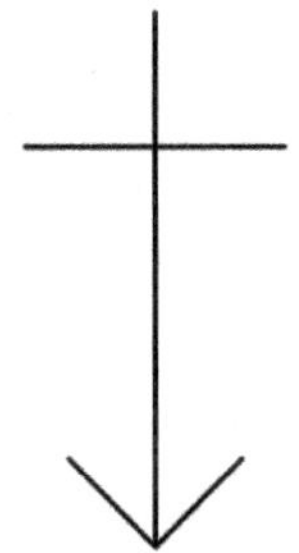

Since Amelia had uttered that dreadful phrase, everything around her had taken on a surreal and unnerving quality. The mansion, once a place of disorienting nightmares, now felt like a twisted reality she could no longer escape. The overwhelming sense of paranoia that had plagued her at every turn began to shift—whether it had eased, or she had simply become desensitized to the madness was impossible to discern. Perhaps, in a way, she had grown accustomed to the constant presence of something watching her, lurking just out of sight, and had begun to accept it as her new reality.

The town of Eldermoor, with its narrow streets and oppressive atmosphere, had changed too. The blurred faces of townspeople, once alien and distant, began to blend seamlessly with the shadowy figures that haunted her dreams. During her daily walks through the streets of Eldermoor, Amelia felt as if she were navigating a waking nightmare. The town, once merely unsettling, had become a twisted reflection of the horrors that plagued her sleep. The narrow, winding streets seemed to stretch endlessly, each turn leading her deeper into a maze that defied logic. The cobblestones underfoot were uneven as if the ground itself was shifting beneath her, conspiring to trip her up and pull her down into some unseen abyss.

The townspeople, with their blurred and indistinct faces, moved with a strange, disjointed rhythm. They no longer seemed fully human, their forms flickering in and out of focus like poorly tuned images on an old television screen. Amelia would catch glimpses of familiar features—eyes that burned with a strange intensity, lips that curled into unsettling smiles—but they would vanish as quickly as they appeared, leaving her questioning whether she had seen them at all.

The figures she had once relegated to her nightmares now walked openly among the living. Shadowy entities with elongated limbs and eyes like smoldering coals moved through the town as if they belonged there, their presence ignored by the townspeople, who went about their business as if nothing were amiss. These beings would brush past her in the narrow alleys, their cold touch sending shivers down her spine. Sometimes she would feel a skeletal hand lightly graze her shoulder, only to turn and find no one there, the air thick with the stench of decay.

The buildings themselves seemed to lean inwards, as if they were collapsing under the weight of some unseen force. The walls, once solid, now appeared translucent at the edges, with tendrils of darkness seeping through the cracks. Doors would creak open on their own, revealing rooms that shouldn't have existed, filled with impossibly old furniture and remnants of lives long forgotten. Windows, coated in grime, offered glimpses of otherworldly landscapes—skies that bled into oceans, and forests where the trees writhed as if alive.

Amelia's walks through Eldermoor were no longer simple errands or escapes from the confines of Vandercliffe Manor. They had become torturous journeys through a town that seemed to shift and change around her. The weight of the town's gaze was constant, a palpable pressure that bore down on her from all sides. She could feel the eyes of the townspeople—those blurry, undefined eyes—following her every step, watching her with a curiosity that was both alien and unnerving.

Even the familiar landmarks of the town—once comforting in their mundanity—had taken on a sinister aspect. The church steeple, which had once stood proudly against the sky, now loomed like a jagged tooth, its bell tolling at irregular intervals, the sound distorted and echoing in ways that made her ears ring. The market square, where she had once seen vendors and children playing, was now an empty void, a space where time seemed to stand still, the silence broken only by the distant wail of some unseen creature.

Amelia walked these streets in a daze, her mind teetering on the edge of madness. The boundary between dream and reality had dissolved entirely, and she felt as though she were trapped in a paradox, unable to wake from a nightmare that had somehow become her life. Each step was a battle against the pull of the darkness that seemed to seep from the very ground, and yet she kept moving forward, driven by a desperate need for answers, for some semblance of understanding in a world that no longer made sense.

But with each passing day, the sense of isolation grew. She was alone in this town of shadows and whispers, a stranger among the faceless masses, with no one to turn to and no refuge from the horrors that stalked her every moment. The once-vivid memory of her life before Eldermoor was fading, replaced by the twisted reality that had become her existence. And yet, despite it all, she couldn't stop. The darkness beckoned, and she knew that the only way out was to follow the path it had laid before her, no matter where it led.

Amelia would catch fleeting glimpses of them—elongated fingers reaching out from the edges of her vision, eyes like burning embers staring at her from the crowd. These figures, no longer confined to her nightmares, seemed to seep into her waking world, their presence inescapable.

At first, the sight of these spectres had filled Amelia with terror. Her heart would race, her breath would catch, and a cold sweat would break out across her skin as she struggled to distinguish between reality and illusion. The shadowy figures that lurked at the edges of her vision seemed to embody her worst fears—manifestations of the unknown, of the very nightmares that had driven her to the brink of madness. Each encounter left her shaken, her mind grappling with the impossibility of what she had seen.

But as the days bled into weeks, and weeks into an indeterminate stretch of time, the fear began to dull. It was as if her mind, battered by the relentless onslaught of horror, had reached a point of exhaustion. The initial terror that had gripped her with every glimpse of these phantasms started to fade, replaced by a weary acceptance. The abnormal had become her new normal. These once-alarming spectres, with their twisted forms and ember-like eyes, no longer sent her heart into a frantic spiral. Instead, they became a constant, almost mundane presence in her life, their appearance as expected as the rising of the sun.

Amelia's reaction to these figures shifted from outright terror to a numb acknowledgment. When they appeared, she no longer recoiled in fear; she simply noted their presence with a kind of detached resignation. Her mind, once sharp with panic, now responded with a muted indifference. The shadowy figures were no longer intruders in her world—they had become a part of it, woven so deeply into the fabric of her existence that she could scarcely remember a time without them.

In the beginning, she had fought against the madness, her mind straining to maintain a grip on reality. But the more she resisted, the more the shadows encroached upon her, until there was no clear distinction between the horrors of her nightmares and the reality she lived in. Eventually, her resistance crumbled. She no longer questioned whether these figures were real or the product of her fractured mind; she simply accepted them as a part of her world, as natural as the air she breathed.

The dulling of her fear was not a sign of strength but of surrender. Amelia had become desensitized to the horrors that surrounded her, her emotions numbed by the relentless exposure to terror. The shadowy figures, once the stuff of her darkest fears, now evoked little more than a weary sigh or a tired glance. They were no longer threats, but companions in her descent into madness—a constant reminder of the twisted reality she inhabited.

In this state of numbness, Amelia found a strange sense of peace. The fear that had once paralyzed her was gone, replaced by a grim acceptance of her fate. She no longer feared the spectres because there was nothing left to fear. They had become a part of her, and she of them, bound together in a reality where the lines between the living and the dead, the real and the imagined, had blurred beyond recognition.

In the end, it was this acceptance that kept her going. The shadowy figures were no longer enemies to be fought, but companions on her journey—a journey that had no clear destination, only the promise of more darkness ahead. And so, Amelia moved forward, not with the terror of the unknown, but with the resignation of one who has seen too much and survived, even if just barely.

Even the townspeople, who had once seemed distant and uninterested, now appeared to be watching her closely. Their vacant stares had transformed into something far more sinister—a cold, calculating gaze that followed her every movement. It was as if they were aware of the dark secrets she had uncovered, as if they knew she was unravelling the threads of a forbidden history that had been buried for so long. The silent judgment in their eyes was unnerving, and the weight of their scrutiny pressed down on her like an invisible burden.

Amelia's sense of isolation deepened. Every door she opened, every room she entered, every book she unearthed only served to confirm that she was inextricably linked to this madness. The connection between her family and the Order of the Obsidian Veil, the rituals, the nightmares—they were all part of a horrifying legacy that she was now entangled in. The mansion, with its endless labyrinth of hallways and hidden rooms, had become a prison of her own making, a place where time had no meaning, and escape was impossible.

Yet, despite the suffocating dread that surrounded her, there was a strange sense of acceptance. Amelia was no longer just a victim of the horrors that plagued her; she was a participant, a seeker of the truth, no matter how terrifying it might be. The madness that had once gripped her with fear had now become a twisted companion, guiding her deeper into the dark history of Eldermoor and the terrible legacy of her family.

In this new reality, where the line between the living and the dead, the real and the imagined, had all but vanished, Amelia knew that there was no turning back. The only path forward was through the darkness, through the veil that separated the waking world from the unearthly horrors beyond. And in the end, she realized, perhaps the greatest horror of all was the realization that she had always been a part of this—her fate woven into the very fabric of the nightmare she now lived.

Amelia's sense of unease deepened when a hooded figure appeared in her peripheral vision the hooded figure haunted Amelia's every waking moment, a dark spectre that seemed to materialize out of thin air. Cloaked in tattered velvet, obsidian robes with a deep purple inner lining visibly made out of satin the figure appeared to absorb the light around them, casting an unnatural shadow wherever they stood. The fabric of the robe looked worn as if it had weathered countless years, yet it moved with an eerie fluidity, almost as if it were alive. Beneath the heavy hood, their face was obscured in complete darkness, but Amelia could feel the weight of their gaze—a piercing, unsettling sensation that sent shivers down her spine.

It began with fleeting glimpses—a shadow at the edge of her vision, a quick movement just out of sight. She would turn, only to see the figure walking away, vanishing around a corner or behind a doorway, just as they were about to step out of view. It was as if they existed in the periphery of her world, always there but never fully visible. The figure never spoke, never made a sound, yet their presence was palpable, a constant reminder that she was never truly alone.

As days turned into a blur, the figure became a fixture in Amelia's life. Whether she was exploring the labyrinthine corridors of the mansion or walking through the unsettling streets of Eldermoor, the hooded figure was always near. Sometimes, she would catch a glimpse of them through a window, standing motionless in the courtyard below, their gaze seemingly fixed on her. Other times, she would feel their presence behind her, a cold sensation that crawled up her spine, compelling her to turn around, only to find the figure slipping out of sight once more.

The figure's appearances were not confined to any specific time or place. They could manifest in the dead of night or in the light of day, always lingering at the edges of her awareness. It was as if they were a visible splinter lodged in her mind, a dark stain that marred her reality. The longer she stared at them, the more she felt her sanity slipping away, as if their very presence was an affront to her understanding of the world.

This relentless observation eroded her sense of reality. Every time she tried to focus on something else, the figure would reappear, a constant reminder of the otherworldly forces at play. The more she tried to ignore them, the more persistent they became, until their image was burned into her mind, an inescapable part of her existence. No matter where she went, the figure was there—an unyielding, silent witness to her every move, their presence a dark omen that filled her with a deep, unshakable dread.

The feeling of being watched became suffocating. Every creak of the floorboards, every whisper of the wind through the old mansion's walls, every flicker of the candlelight seemed to carry the figure's presence with it. Amelia's once-steady resolve began to falter under the weight of this constant surveillance. She could no longer distinguish between her paranoia and the reality of the figure's existence. Was the figure real, or was it a manifestation of her own unravelling mind? She didn't know, and that uncertainty only deepened her fear.

One night, as Amelia lay in her bed, the weight of exhaustion pressing down on her, she awoke with a start. Her breath came in short, panicked gasps, the remnants of a nightmare still clinging to the edges of her mind. The room was dark, the only light coming from the faint glow of the moon filtering through the curtains. As her eyes adjusted to the dim light, she noticed a shape in the corner of the room—a silhouette that hadn't been there before.

Her heart skipped a beat as she recognized the familiar outline of the hooded figure. They stood in the deepest shadows, their form barely discernible, yet unmistakably there. The air in the room seemed to grow colder, and a suffocating sense of dread settled over her.

Amelia's mind raced with questions. What did it want? Why was it here, in the sanctity of her room? Was it an omen of her impending doom, or something far more sinister—a harbinger of the horrors she had unwittingly unleashed? Had she delved too far into the mysteries of the mansion, stirring forces that should have remained undisturbed?

The figure didn't move, didn't make a sound, yet its presence was overwhelming. Amelia's fear grew as she realized she had no way of knowing what it would do next. The stillness of the figure, its silence, was more terrifying than any threat it could have spoken aloud. It was as if the very fabric of reality had been breached, and this figure was a manifestation of the darkness she had been spiralling into.

Every instinct in her screamed to run, to flee from whatever nightmare this was, but she was paralysed with fear, her body frozen in place. Her eyes remained locked on the figure, half-expecting it to advance on her, to reveal whatever horror it concealed beneath that dark hood. Yet, it remained motionless, an unyielding sentinel that seemed to be waiting for something— perhaps for her to break, to succumb to the terror it represented.

Amelia's thoughts twisted in her mind, each more horrifying than the last. Was this figure the embodiment of the town's curse, or had she unwittingly called it into existence by uttering that dreadful phrase? The questions churned within her, but the figure offered no answers, only more questions, more fear.

Finally, unable to bear the tension any longer, Amelia blinked—just once. When her eyes opened, the figure was gone, as if it had never been there. But the chill in the room remained, as did the lingering sense that something had changed. She couldn't shake the feeling that the figure had left something behind—an invisible mark, a curse that would continue to haunt her.

The darkness in the corners of the room seemed to deepen, and Amelia knew that the figure would return. It was only a matter of time. She had crossed a line, and now, there was no going back. The figure was a constant reminder of the dangers she had invited into her life, a dark spectre that loomed over her, a silent warning of the horrors that lay ahead.

As Amelia wandered through the dimly lit streets of Eldermoor, the faint sound of her footsteps echoed against the cobblestones beneath her feet. Each step produced a sharp, rhythmic click, amplified by the stillness of the night. The cobblestones were old and uneven, their surfaces slick with a fine layer of moisture from an earlier rain, reflecting the muted glow of the few streetlights that still flickered along the path. The town itself was a relic of another time, its streets narrow and winding, lined with ancient, weathered buildings that leaned inwards as if conspiring to trap those who walked between them.

The air was thick with an unsettling calm, the usual murmur of life conspicuously absent. The only sound was the faint drip of water falling from the eaves of the surrounding buildings, punctuating the silence with an irregular rhythm. The sky above was a heavy, oppressive grey, the last remnants of daylight struggling to hold back the inevitable descent into night. The world seemed caught in a perpetual twilight, neither day nor night, a liminal space where time lost all meaning.

Her footsteps grew louder in the quiet, each one a reminder of her presence in a place that felt increasingly hostile, as though the very town was aware of her intrusion. The street itself was anything but modern, a winding path of aged cobblestones that seemed to have witnessed centuries of secrets and whispered conversations. The rain that had fallen earlier had left the stones dark and glossy, reflecting distorted images of the surrounding buildings. The few streetlights that still functioned cast long, wavering shadows, their light flickering as if on the verge of being snuffed out entirely.

As she approached the town square, a sense of foreboding washed over her. The square loomed ahead, shrouded in the eerie stillness of twilight. It was an open space, yet it felt suffocating, the buildings that surrounded it pressing in like silent, watchful sentinels. The oppressive silence was almost tangible, wrapping around her like a heavy shroud, amplifying the sound of her own breathing and the beating of her heart.

And then she saw him—out of the corner of her eye, the hooded figure, standing motionless in the center of the square. His form was draped in tattered, obsidian robes that seemed to drink in the surrounding light, rendering him a dark silhouette against the backdrop of the square. He stood perfectly still, an unnatural stillness that sent a shiver down her spine. His presence was like a void, an absence of light and life that drew her gaze and held it, compelling her to look even as every instinct screamed at her to turn away.

The figure made no move, no sound. He simply stood there, as if waiting, watching. The oppressive silence deepened, the echo of her footsteps fading into nothingness as she halted, her breath caught in her throat. The stillness of the square, the suffocating quiet, and the dark figure all combined to create an overwhelming sense of dread, as though she had stepped into a place where time and reality had unravelled, leaving behind only shadows and echoes of what once was.

Amelia's heart pounded in her chest as she stood frozen, her eyes locked on the figure in the centre of the square. The world around her seemed to fade, the dim light growing even dimmer, the air growing colder. She felt as if she were standing on the edge of a precipice, staring into an abyss that threatened to swallow her whole. The hooded figure remained motionless, a silent spectre in the twilight, and in that moment, Amelia knew that whatever lay ahead, it would not be something she could easily escape.

His sudden appearance sent a shiver down her spine. He was no longer a fleeting shadow in the periphery of her vision but a solid, undeniable presence. His face remained hidden beneath the dark hood, but Amelia could feel his gaze upon her, as if he were peering into the very depths of her soul. She froze, her breath catching in her throat, unsure of what to do or say.

The figure didn't speak; he merely raised a gloved hand, slowly and deliberately, and gestured for her to follow. The gesture was simple, almost gentle, yet it carried a weight of inevitability that Amelia couldn't ignore. Her instincts screamed at her to run, to flee back to the relative safety of the mansion, but something deeper, something more primal, urged her to follow.

Before she could make a decision, the figure turned and began to walk away, his movements fluid and deliberate. Amelia watched as he glided across the square, his dark robes brushing the ground with barely a whisper of sound. Then, just as he reached the edge of the square, he began to fade. His form grew less distinct, as though he were dissolving into the very shadows from which he had emerged. In a matter of moments, he was gone, leaving behind nothing but the lingering sense of his presence.

Amelia stood rooted to the spot, her mind racing. The crossroads before her was not just physical but mental, a choice between two paths that would shape her fate. Should she chase after the figure, delving deeper into the mysteries that had ensnared her? Or should she retreat, pull back, and try to regain some semblance of control over her life, to reestablish a grip on reality that was slipping away like sand through her fingers?

The fear that had gripped her for so long was still there, gnawing at the edges of her sanity. But now, it was mingled with something else curiosity, perhaps, or a sense of destiny. She couldn't shake the feeling that this figure, this spectre of darkness, held the answers she so desperately sought. Yet the thought of following him into the unknown filled her with dread.

For what felt like an eternity, Amelia wrestled with the choice, her mind teetering on the brink of both paths. The shadows of the town square seemed to close in around her, as if urging her to decide. And all the while, the figure's absence was a haunting reminder of the direction her life had taken. She knew that whatever path she chose, there would be no turning back.

In the end, the decision was hers alone to make—whether to surrender to the pull of the darkness or to fight against it, to reclaim her sanity and her life. And as she stood there, caught between the past and the future, she realized that the path ahead, whichever she chose, was fraught with peril. The journey into the heart of the unknown was not just a physical one; it was a descent into the very essence of fear, madness, and fate.

VII. Tainted Waters

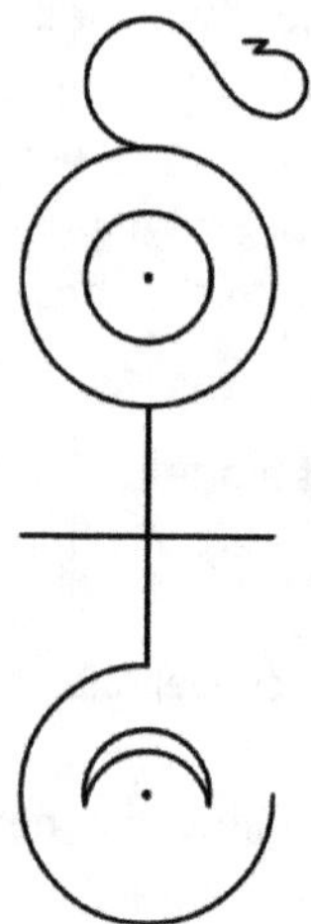

Days passed, and the hooded figure continued to haunt both Amelia's thoughts and her reality. Its presence, though silent and unmoving, was impossible to ignore. Each time she ventured into the town, the figure would appear, pointing towards the dark and foreboding forest at the edge of Eldermoor, as if urging her to follow. Despite the gnawing sense of dread that accompanied each encounter, Amelia felt a strange compulsion—a pull that she couldn't shake, as though the figure held the answers to the questions that tormented her.

The resistance to follow was strong at first, an instinctual fear that warned her against venturing further into the unknown. But as the days blurred together, that resistance weakened. The oppressive atmosphere of Eldermoor, the mounting terror, and the growing sense of inevitability began to erode her resolve. Curiosity, desperation, and a strange sense of duty warred within her, each pushing her closer to the decision she had been avoiding.

Finally, one evening, she could resist no longer. The figure's silent beckoning felt like a magnet pulling at the very core of her being. Determined to unravel the mysteries that had consumed her life, Amelia took a deep breath and stepped onto the path that led towards the forest.

The journey was surreal, each step feeling both real and dreamlike. The cobblestone streets of Eldermoor gave way to a narrow dirt path, overgrown with wild grass and lined with gnarled trees. The further she walked, the darker the surroundings became, as if the forest itself sought to swallow her whole. The air grew colder, biting at her skin, and the dense canopy above blocked out the last traces of daylight, leaving only a dim, silvery glow from the rising moon.

As she followed the figure, her emotions were a tumultuous blend of fear, curiosity, and determination. Her heart raced with anticipation, but there was also a deep-seated terror that gnawed at her insides. The figure moved soundlessly ahead of her, its form a shadow among shadows, always just at the edge of her vision. It never looked back, never slowed its pace, as if it knew that she would continue to follow regardless of her fears.

The path grew narrower and more treacherous as she walked deeper into the forest. The trees here were ancient, their twisted branches reaching out like skeletal hands, and the underbrush was thick and unyielding. The oppressive silence was broken only by the occasional rustle of leaves or the distant call of a nocturnal bird, sounds that seemed unnaturally loud in the stillness of the night.

Eventually, the trees began to thin, and the path opened into a small clearing. At the centre of the clearing stood an abandoned well, its stone walls weathered and covered in creeping moss. The well was ancient, a relic from another time, its stones worn smooth by centuries of exposure to the elements. The wooden frame that once held the bucket and rope had long since rotted away, leaving only a dark, gaping hole that descended into the earth.

The air around the well was thick with an unsettling energy, a palpable sense of wrongness that made Amelia's skin prickle with unease. As she approached, the feeling of being watched intensified, as if countless unseen eyes were trained on her every move. A single beam of moonlight pierced through the thick canopy of trees, casting a ghostly glow over the well and the surrounding clearing. It was as if the moon itself had singled out this place, illuminating it for her alone.

Amelia's breath caught in her throat as she peered down into the well. The darkness within seemed to swallow the light, rendering the bottom invisible. The air that rose from the well's depths was cold and damp, carrying with it the faint, earthy scent of decayed leaves and something far older, something that sent a shiver down her spine.

As Amelia approached the ancient well, an overwhelming sense of unease settled over her. The closer she got, the heavier the air seemed to become, as if the atmosphere itself was thick with dread. Her skin prickled with the sensation of being watched, though she knew the hooded figure had vanished. Each step felt laboured as if an unseen force was urging her to turn back, but something stronger—perhaps curiosity, perhaps a fatalistic acceptance—propelled her forward.

Reaching the well, she hesitated, her breath catching in her throat. The cold, rough stone beneath her fingertips was a stark contrast to the warmth of her hand, grounding her in the reality of the moment. Slowly, she leaned over the edge, peering into the depths below.

The water at the bottom of the well was eerily calm, its surface like a polished black mirror reflecting the dim light of the moon and stars. For a moment, it seemed almost tranquil, as if the darkness held no secrets. But as Amelia stared deeper, something began to shift. The water's surface, once smooth and serene, started to ripple as if disturbed by an unseen hand.

The ripples grew, distorting the reflection of the sky above. At first, the changes were subtle—a slight warping of the stars, a gentle bending of the moon's light. But then, the water seemed to come alive, churning and twisting, as though the very fabric of reality was unravelling before her eyes.

Within the shifting surface, the well began to reveal something far more sinister. The reflection of the night sky dissolved, giving way to impossible landscapes that defied logic. Oceans merged seamlessly with the heavens, their waters a deep, otherworldly hue that seemed to stretch endlessly in all directions. Trees, grotesquely twisted and gnarled, grew upside down from barren earth, their roots reaching skyward like skeletal hands grasping at nothingness.

Amelia's breath quickened as the visions became more vivid, more disturbing. The once still water now teemed with life, though not of any kind she had ever known. Shadowy figures began to coalesce beneath the surface, their forms grotesque and unnatural. They writhed in the dark water, their elongated limbs twisting and contorting as they struggled against some invisible force that kept them trapped below.

These figures were nightmarish, their bodies distorted and incomplete, as though they had been pieced together from fragments of different beings. Their eyes—if they could be called eyes—were dark voids, yet they seemed to pierce through the water, through the darkness, through Amelia herself. She could feel their gaze, cold and unrelenting, as if they were searching for something within her, something they could claim as their own.

The figures moved with a terrifying fluidity, their forms constantly shifting, merging, and separating as they writhed beneath the surface. They seemed desperate to escape, to break free from their watery prison, and for a moment, Amelia felt an overwhelming sense of empathy for them—a connection to their plight. But just as quickly, that empathy was replaced by a profound terror, a deep, instinctual fear that whatever these beings were, they were not meant to exist in her world.

The ripples in the water grew more violent, the images within more chaotic, as if the well itself was a portal to some other realm—a realm where the natural order of things had been upended, where the laws of time and space no longer applied. The grotesque figures reached out, their elongated limbs straining towards her, and for a brief, horrifying moment, it seemed as if they might actually break through the surface.

Amelia stumbled back, her heart pounding in her chest, unable to tear her eyes away from the unsettling scene below. The well had shown her something—something ancient and malevolent, something that defied all understanding. And yet, she knew deep down that this was only the beginning, a mere glimpse into the horrors that awaited her.

The unease that had settled over her had now become a living thing, crawling beneath her skin, whispering in her ear, urging her to leave this place before it was too late. But even as she recoiled in fear, a part of her was drawn to the well, to the dark water that had shown her these visions. The answers she sought were there, buried deep within the abyss, and she knew that she could not turn back now.

As Amelia stood by the well, the hooded figure materialized beside her, silent and imposing. Their presence sent a cold shiver down her spine, intensifying the sense of dread that had settled over her. The figure's face remained hidden in the shadows of their hood, but the weight of their gaze was palpable, pressing down on her with an almost tangible force.

Without a word, the figure extended a gloved hand towards the well, its obsidian surface glinting faintly in the moonlight. The gesture was unmistakable—an invitation, or perhaps a command, to immerse herself in the dark depths below. Amelia's heart raced as she hesitated, caught between the overwhelming fear that gripped her and the undeniable pull of the mysteries she had come so far to unravel.

She glanced down at the water, its surface deceptively calm, reflecting the twisted landscape of her surroundings. The fear gnawing at her mind clashed with the burning need to uncover the truth, and for a moment, she wavered. But the figure's silent insistence was unrelenting, and with a deep breath, she steeled herself for what was to come.

Slowly, she reached out, her fingers trembling as they brushed against the cold stone of the well. The air around her seemed to grow heavier, laden with the weight of centuries of secrets and eldritch forces. As her hand dipped into the water, a jolt of icy cold shot through her, but what startled her more was the way the water reacted. It clung to her skin, not like normal liquid, but as if it had a will of its own, wrapping itself around her fingers with an unnatural viscosity.

The water began to crawl up her hand, creeping along her wrist and forearm in thick, oily tendrils. It moved with a slow, deliberate purpose, as if seeking to consume her entirely. Panic surged within her, but even as her instinct screamed at her to pull away, she found herself unable to do so, transfixed by the sight of the water's sinister behaviour.

The tendrils of liquid climbed higher, snaking up her arm and wrapping around her like the tightening grip of a constrictor. The cold seeped into her bones, numbing her skin and leaving her breathless with fear. She watched in horrified fascination as the water spread, creeping over her shoulder, up her neck, and across her chest. It clung to her clothes and skin with a malevolent intent, as though it were a living thing, eager to claim her as its own.

The sensation was beyond anything she had ever felt—an overwhelming pressure that seemed to crush her beneath its weight as if the water sought to drag her down into the depths of the well. Her breathing grew shallow, her heart hammering in her chest as the water enveloped her, inch by inch. It was not just cold; it was suffocating, oppressive, and she could feel it probing, seeking to invade her very being.

As the water climbed higher, reaching her throat, she began to struggle in earnest, the primal urge to escape finally overriding her curiosity. But it was too late. The water had her in its grasp, and it would not let go. It slithered up to her chin, then her mouth, cold and slick against her skin, threatening to pull her under.

And all the while, the hooded figure stood beside her, a silent witness to her torment, offering no help, no respite, only the relentless pressure to continue. The water, like the figure, seemed to be alive, an extension of the dark forces at play in Eldermoor, intent on claiming her for its own.

As the water crept up towards her eyes, Amelia's panic surged into raw terror. This was not a test or a trial—there was no choice, no resolve to be mustered. The water was alive, relentless, and it was consuming her against her will. She could feel it dragging her down, pulling her closer to the well's unseen depths, and there was nothing she could do to stop it.

Her heart pounded as she tried to resist, to pull herself free, but the water's grip only tightened, wrapping around her like a vice. It surged over her face, muffling her screams as it covered her mouth and nose, choking off her air. The cold, wet darkness filled her vision, the weight of the water pressing her down, down, into the well's suffocating embrace.

Fear consumed her as she realized she was helpless, completely at the mercy of this malevolent force. The water pulled her under, dragging her into the abyss with a terrifying finality. She thrashed and struggled, but it was no use—the more she fought, the more the water enveloped her until all that remained was darkness.

As Amelia descended into the water's murky depths, the distorted reflections around her twisted and contorted, creating a nightmarish kaleidoscope of shifting forms and shadowy figures reaching out with spectral hands. Her heart raced, terror, flooding her mind as the cold darkness closed in. The hooded figure remained by her side, an unsettling witness to her plunge into the unknown, its presence a silent testament to the dread that enveloped her.

Without warning, a grotesque tendril, emerging from the depths of the reflections, snaked out from beneath the water. It was a sinuous, elongated appendage, writhing with an otherworldly life of its own. The tendril coiled around her arm with a vice-like grip, its cold, slimy surface sending shivers through her. Amelia's initial shock left her paralysed, her attempts to scream muffled by the water's embrace.

It felt like the world above was being torn away in an instant. The initial tug was sharp and relentless, pulling Amelia down with a force that left no room for resistance. The water rushed over Amelia in a frigid torrent, its icy grip stealing the breath from her lungs as it enveloped her entirely. She barely had time to gasp before she was yanked downward, the world above slipping away as the murky depths closed in around her. The tendril that coiled around her body was a sinister thing—cold, sinewy, and undeniably alive. It constricted her with an unrelenting force, dragging her deeper into the abyss with a purpose she could neither comprehend nor resist.

Her vision blurred, the faint light from the surface quickly swallowed by the darkness below. Panic surged through her as her lungs screamed for air, burning with a desperate need that went unfulfilled. The pressure intensified with every passing second, the water crushing in from all sides, making her movements sluggish and futile. Amelia's heart thundered in her chest, a wild, erratic rhythm that echoed in her ears, amplifying the terror that clawed at her mind.

The cold seeped into her bones, a numbing chill that spread through her body as the darkness thickened, growing more oppressive with each pull of the tendril. She was being dragged into the unknown, where light and hope could not reach. The deeper she sank, the more distant the surface became—a mere memory, fading into the shadows of her mind.

Every instinct screamed at her to fight, to thrash against the tendril's hold, but it was as if the water itself was conspiring against her, sapping her strength and will. The sensation was nightmarish, a horrifying blend of helplessness and inevitability as if she were trapped in a dream where escape was impossible. The tendril was relentless, pulling her down, down into the depths where no light could follow, where the air was a distant memory, and the crushing weight of the water threatened to snuff out the last flicker of hope within her.

Amelia's thoughts began to fragment, her mind splintering under the mounting terror. The world above seemed unreal, a distant, fading dream, as the tendril dragged her further into the void. The darkness was complete now, an all-consuming blackness that pressed in on her from all sides, choking, suffocating, drowning her in its merciless grasp. The cold was unbearable, the pressure suffocating, and as the last vestiges of her strength ebbed away, Amelia could feel the final spark of hope dimming within her, teetering on the edge of oblivion.

The tendril dragged her violently downward, pulling her through the distorted reflections and into the well's deeper, more ominous depths. The world above vanished, and she was submerged in the murky, pitch-black water. The pressure intensified, squeezing her senses, and the water around her felt like an oppressive force, crushing her body and mind.

Amelia's thoughts raced in a whirlwind of fear and confusion. She knew that whatever awaited her at the bottom of the well was beyond anything she could fathom—a reality where nightmare and truth intertwined. Her insatiable thirst for answers had led her here, to a realm where the waters held secrets capable of reshaping her understanding of everything she knew. As she sank deeper, the world around her seemed to dissolve into a swirling abyss of darkness and dread, her fate now entwined with the unfathomable forces lurking below.

VIII. Cryptic Revelations

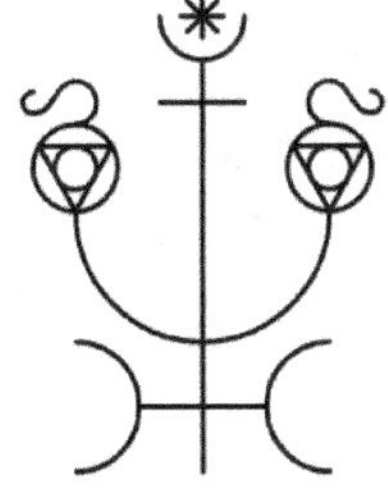

Amelia's descent through the water's depths brought her into a realm far removed from the tangible world she knew—a place where reality unravelled, and the boundaries of perception twisted into the grotesque and the bizarre. As she floated weightlessly through the dark, it was as if gravity had been suspended, and she was adrift in an endless void of swirling, suffocating blackness.

Abruptly, the sensation of weightlessness ceased, and Amelia found herself abruptly standing on what felt like a precarious surface. The ground beneath her feet was neither solid nor liquid but an unsettling amalgamation of both. With each step, the surface responded with a strange, unsettling crunch and squish, as if it were a grotesque mixture of gelatinous matter and brittle shards. The sensation was alien and disorienting, each movement accompanied by a nauseating squelch that seemed to echo through the oppressive silence.

The landscape stretched out before her in a surreal and incomprehensible array. The sky above was an otherworldly canvas of shifting, indescribable colours—vivid hues blending and swirling in patterns that defied natural laws. It was as if the heavens themselves were in a state of perpetual, chaotic flux, casting an eerie, undulating light over the terrain.

The air was thick with an acrid scent, a blend of decayed matter and something metallic as if the very essence of this realm was tainted with an ancient rot. Every breath was a struggle, the oppressive atmosphere making her lungs burn.

Amelia's eyes scanned the horizon, and she noticed the hooded figure standing before her. Their presence remained constant; their form seemingly unaffected by the bizarre transition. The figure's gaze, hidden beneath the shadow of their hood, seemed to pierce through the very fabric of her being. For the first time, Amelia sensed a peculiar blend of curiosity and empathy emanating from them—a stark contrast to the malevolent silence that had pervaded her previous encounters.

In this strange, fractured world, Amelia's sense of reality had been irrevocably shattered, and she was left grappling with the disorienting truth that her quest for answers had led her into the heart of an unfathomable, nightmarish domain.

"You've ventured deep into the waters, into the realm of Amlagrar," the figure's voice resonated, chilling and sinister, its echo twisting through the murky void. The words seemed to hang in the air, heavy with an ominous weight.

Amelia stared around in shock, her voice trembling. "Amlagrar? What is this place? Where am I?"

The figure remained motionless, their presence a dark silhouette against the swirling, unnatural landscape. "Amlagrar is the abyssal cradle of forgotten truths, where the boundaries of reality dissolve into madness. This is where seekers of forbidden knowledge find themselves—lost in the labyrinth of their own fears and desires."

Amelia's heart raced, her breath coming in short, panicked bursts. "I'm searching for answers... I need to understand what's happening to me. I have to escape this nightmare."

The figure's voice grew colder, more menacing. "Many have sought the truth, only to be consumed by it. The truth does not yield easily; it has its own will, capable of twisting and tearing at the very fabric of your mind. It devours the sanity of those unprepared, leaving only fragments of the self behind."

A dark glint seemed to flicker in the figure's hidden eyes. "You are part of an ancient prophecy—a lineage destined to confront forces far beyond mortal comprehension. This path was not chosen for you; it was your birthright."

Confusion and terror clawed at Amelia's insides. She felt the ground beneath her pulse with a nauseating rhythm, and the figure's words felt like a cold, unrelenting vice tightening around her mind. "What prophecy? What are you talking about?"

The figure's voice, though muffled, resonated with an unsettling certainty. "The prophecy speaks of a descendant who will uncover the cosmic threads binding Eldermoor and Amlagrar, awakening the slumbering horrors that dwell within. Your journey has only just begun, and the truth awaits, shrouded in darkness."

As the figure shifted slightly, Amelia could almost sense a hidden grin beneath the shadows of the hood. "The Ebon Watchers, beings of insidious power and ancient knowledge, are stirring. They exist beyond the boundaries of reality, quietly observing and manipulating the mortal realm. It was foretold that a descendant of the Vandercliffe bloodline would possess the power to confront them—a power you unknowingly carry within."

Amelia's mind raced, her heart pounding with disbelief and dread. "But how? What do they want?"

"Eldermoor is a nexus, a thin place where the veil between dimensions wears perilously thin. The cult you uncovered sought not to merge the realms but to contain the Ebon Watchers and prevent them from awakening. They tore a rift through reality, but it remains only a fraction, a mere splinter. The prophecy speaks of one who can wield the essence of Amlagrar's forces, someone who can seal the rifts the cultists have opened and keep the Ebon Watchers from manifesting fully in our world."

Amelia's head spun under the weight of this revelation, a mixture of purpose and dread washing over her. "But how can I stop them? How can I close the rifts?"

The figure's shadowy form shimmered with a sinister intensity. "You must confront the Ebon Watchers within the realm of Amlagrar. They can be bound by the symphony of your will—the melodies that weave through the fabric of existence. Only by awakening the power that lies dormant within you can you hope to seal the rifts and keep their influence at bay. If they break through, it would surely spell the end of your reality."

Amelia's mind whirled with the enormity of what she had just learned. The weight of the prophecy pressed heavily upon her; each revelation more staggering than the last. The figure's cryptic answers and ominous warnings only deepened her sense of dread. The truth was more intricate and far-reaching than she had ever imagined when she first received the letter from her grandmother. What began as a quest for understanding had transformed into a perilous journey into the unknown.

Taking a shaky breath, she gazed into the dark void beneath the hood. "I need to know more," she said, her voice trembling with both determination and fear. "Who are you? What is your role in all of this?"

The figure's silence stretched like an eternity, the shadows shifting as if reluctant to reveal their secrets. When it spoke again, its voice was as enigmatic as ever. "In the tapestry of fate, some threads are obscured by shadows. I am but a guide, a fragment of the greater design. My name is not yours to know, but my purpose is clear: to lead those who are fated to face the darkness."

Amelia's heart pounded, the uncertainty gnawing at her resolve. "How can I confront the Ebon Watchers without losing myself? How do I avoid the madness that consumed the cultists?"

The figure's voice took on a rare softness, a hint of what might be considered compassion. "You possess a strength they lacked—a rare balance between the realms of Amlagrar and the mortal world. By seeking understanding and maintaining equilibrium within yourself, you can channel their power without succumbing to their influence. Yet the path ahead is fraught with peril. You must be prepared for the trials that await you beyond the veil."

The figure's words reverberated in the strange, shifting realm around her, and Amelia felt a mix of fear and determination solidifying within her. The enormity of her task began to crystallize, and the reality of confronting the Ebon Watchers loomed before her like an insurmountable wall.

She took a hesitant step forward, her heart racing with each echoing footfall. "I... I have to do this. I must confront them and close the rifts. But how can I be certain I am not walking into my own doom?"

The figure's form seemed to waver as if acknowledging the gravity of her question. "Certainty is a luxury that may not be afforded to you. You must trust in your strength and resolve, for the journey will test every facet of your being. Proceed with caution and let the symphony of your will guide you through the darkness."

Amelia's breath came in shallow, ragged gasps. The strange, undulating ground beneath her feet seemed to reflect her turmoil, shifting and squelching with each step she took. The uncertainty of the path ahead weighed heavily on her, and she hesitated, feeling the cold fingers of fear tighten around her heart.

Finally, with a deep, shuddering breath, she gathered her courage and steeled herself. The decision to step forward felt like plunging into an abyss, but she knew she had no choice. The prophecy, the Ebon Watchers, and the fate of both worlds now hinged on her actions. With a mixture of dread and determination, Amelia prepared to face the horrors that awaited her within the realm of Amlagrar.

As Amelia took another hesitant step forward, the world around her seemed to warp and shudder. The ground beneath her feet felt less like a surface and more like a pulsating mass of darkness, shifting unpredictably with each movement. Her breath quickened, each inhalation coming in ragged, shallow bursts. The weight of her task felt like an unbearable burden pressing down on her chest.

The strange realm of Amlagrar seemed to close in on her, the swirling skies above darkening and twisting with grotesque colours that defied logic. She stumbled, her vision swimming with distorted shapes and eerie reflections that blurred the lines between reality and nightmare. The ground felt as though it were turning to liquid beneath her, the sensation of walking on a surface that was both solid and intangible driving her further into panic.

Suddenly, shadowy figures began to materialize around her, their forms grotesque and shifting, merging with the nightmarish landscape. Their eyes glowed with an eerie light, and their elongated limbs reached out as if to drag her into their darkness. She saw creatures with writhing tendrils and gaping, toothy maws that seemed to consume the very light around them. Her heart pounded so violently it felt as though it might burst from her chest.

Amelia's breaths came in rapid, panicked gasps. Her vision tunnelled, the edges of her sight darkening as she felt an overwhelming sense of vertigo. Her hands trembled uncontrollably, fingers clutching at her sides as if trying to hold onto some semblance of reality. The cold sweat dripped down her face, mixing with the tears streaming from her eyes.

Her knees buckled, and she collapsed to the ground, her body curling into a tight foetal position as she tried to block out the nightmarish visions. Her chest heaved with each laboured breath, and her body shook with violent spasms as though she were being wracked by an invisible force. The panic was all-consuming, leaving her feeling as though she were drowning in a sea of fear and confusion.

Amelia's thoughts raced in a chaotic frenzy. "I can't do this," she thought desperately, the words repeating in her mind like a mantra. "It's too much. I can't... I can't..."

Her senses were overwhelmed by the cacophony of whispers and murmurs that seemed to rise from the depths of the realm itself. The voices were garbled and indistinct, but the underlying menace in their tone was unmistakable. The ground beneath her seemed to pulse in sync with her racing heart, the sensation both nauseating and terrifying.

In her fractured state, Amelia felt as though the very fabric of reality was unravelling around her. The fear and anxiety gnawed at her, leaving her unable to distinguish between the horrors within her mind and those manifesting in the darkened realm. The shadowy figures and monstrous entities continued their relentless dance, each vision more disturbing than the last.

Desperation clawed at her insides. Amelia reached out with trembling hands, grasping at the ground as if trying to anchor herself to some semblance of reality. Her cries for help echoed into the void, swallowed by the encroaching darkness. Her mind teetered on the edge of collapse, the boundary between sanity and madness blurring with every passing second.

As the panic attack raged on, Amelia felt herself slipping further into the abyss. Her resolve seemed to dissolve, leaving only a raw, exposed vulnerability in its wake. The horrors of Amlagrar had become an inescapable nightmare, and the weight of her task felt like an unbearable shackle, tightening around her with each breathless gasp.

She was lost, utterly consumed by the darkness that surrounded her, and in that moment, the enormity of her journey seemed insurmountable. The world spun into a chaotic blur, and Amelia could only cling to the faint hope that she might find a way to rise from the depths of her despair and confront the looming terror that awaited her.

Amelia's screams pierced the oppressive silence of Amlagrar, her voice cracking with the jagged breaths of her panic. "Help! Someone, please! I can't... I can't...!" Her cries reverberated through the twisted landscape, but the only response was the haunting echo of her own voice mingling with the distorted whispers that clawed at her sanity.

The shadowy figures and grotesque entities closed in, their forms shifting and writhing with malevolent intent. Amelia's mind felt as though it were being torn apart, each vision more horrifying than the last. Her hands gripped the ground with a desperation born of pure terror, but the pulsing, shifting surface offered no solace.

Just as the darkness seemed to swallow her whole, a soft touch landed on her back. The sensation was startlingly gentle amid the chaos, and Amelia's eyes, wide with fear, turned to see the hooded figure standing beside her. His presence, though still cloaked in shadow, exuded a sense of calm that contrasted sharply with the torment around her.

"Amelia," the figure's voice was soothing, almost tender, despite the eerie undertone. "You're safe. I am here."

She gasped for breath, her vision blurring and her body trembling uncontrollably. "Please... help me... I can't..."

The hooded figure placed a reassuring hand on her back, his touch warm and oddly comforting. "I can keep the maddening forces at bay for a time, but you must hold on. They are consuming, but not forever. You have strength within you. Let me guide you."

As his words washed over her, the oppressive weight of her fear seemed to lift. The ground beneath her stopped its unsettling pulsing, and the nightmarish visions began to fade. The figures that had loomed so threateningly around her dissolved into wisps of shadow and smoke. Amelia's frantic breaths began to slow, and the chaotic whispers receded into silence.

She blinked, and the once grotesque and shifting landscape of Amlagrar began to dissolve, melting away like a dark mist. The swirling skies and disturbing ground vanished, leaving only the familiar and comforting woods of Eldermoor. The well stood before her, its stone surface still and undisturbed, and the trees around her swayed gently in the breeze.

The hooded figure's touch remained a gentle presence as he guided her back to the edge of the well. Amelia's heart still raced, but the terror had ebbed, replaced by a profound sense of relief. She looked around, realizing with a mixture of astonishment and gratitude that the maddening visions and the feeling of being watched were gone. The oppressive atmosphere had lifted, and for the first time since her arrival, she felt a semblance of normalcy.

Amelia sank to her knees beside the well, her breaths coming in deep, steadying gulps. She glanced up at the hooded figure, who regarded her with an inscrutable gaze.

"Thank you," she managed to whisper, her voice hoarse but filled with genuine appreciation.

The figure nodded slightly, a gesture of acknowledgment. "This is but a respite. The path ahead remains fraught with danger and revelation. But for now, you are safe. Gather your strength, and when you are ready, the journey will continue."

With that, the figure began to fade into the shadows, his presence slipping away as if he were part of the night itself. Amelia watched him disappear, her mind still reeling from the ordeal but grateful for the brief moment of peace. She was alone once more, but the normalcy of her surroundings offered a fragile comfort amidst the uncertainty of what lay ahead.

As she stood up and steadied herself, Amelia knew that the journey was far from over. But in that moment of calm, she allowed herself a brief respite, her resolve strengthened by the experience and the eerie reassurance of the enigmatic figure.

IX. Veil of Madness

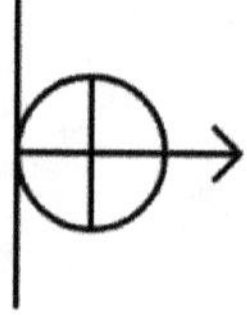

Days had passed since Amelia's breakdown, and Ezekiel had become a nearly constant presence in her life. He was often found in the library of the Vandercliffe manor, engrossed in ancient texts and cryptic manuscripts. His hooded figure, now a familiar sight, seemed to absorb the dim light of the library, adding to the aura of mystery surrounding him. Amelia had caught a rare glimpse of his face one evening—an encounter that left a lasting impression. Ezekiel was an older gentleman with a rugged, yet refined appearance. His silver hair framed a face marked by wisdom and age, with deep-set, piercing blue eyes that seemed to hold the weight of countless secrets. He was strikingly handsome, with a certain magnetic allure that belied his advanced years.

One crisp morning, Ezekiel guided Amelia through the winding paths leading to the outskirts of Eldermoor. The forest, with its gnarled trees and thick underbrush, seemed to close in around them as they walked. The air was charged with an unsettling quiet, broken only by the crunch of leaves underfoot and the distant calls of unseen creatures. The landscape shifted subtly as if the woods themselves were shifting to accommodate their passage.

They emerged into a secluded clearing, where a circle of ancient stones lay in the heart of the forest. The stones were weathered and moss-covered, each one etched with cryptic symbols and runes that seemed to pulse with a faint, eerie light. The circle was a stark contrast to the surrounding wilderness, an otherworldly anchor in the midst of nature's chaos.

The clearing was shrouded in an otherworldly atmosphere, encircled by towering trees whose branches twisted like skeletal fingers against the twilight sky. The air was thick with the scent of damp earth and moss, and a palpable energy hung in the atmosphere, charging the space with an unsettling yet exhilarating tension.

In the center stood the circle of ancient stones, each one a towering monolith, rough-hewn and weathered by the ages. Their surfaces were covered in a tapestry of cryptic symbols, intricately carved and worn smooth by time. Some resembled spirals and swirling patterns, while others depicted creatures that seemed to writhe and twist as if alive. Amelia could feel the energy pulsing from them, a low hum that resonated deep within her chest.

The stones appeared to have been arranged with great intention, their positioning creating a nexus of energy that beckoned her closer.

"The ritual we are about to perform," Ezekiel's voice was low and grave, resonating with the weight of ages, "will allow you to glimpse the Amlagrarian realm. It is a realm of shifting realities, of truths that defy human understanding. But be warned, Amelia, for the visions you will witness can drive even the strongest minds to the brink of madness."

Amelia's heart raced as she gazed at the sigil-baring stones, their presence radiating ancient power. The weight of her responsibility pressed heavily upon her, yet a thrill coursed through her veins. Steeling herself for what lay ahead, she nodded firmly, indicating her readiness.

Ezekiel stepped into the circle, his demeanour shifting from sombre to purposeful. He began the preparations with an efficiency that belied his age, his movements deliberate and practised. As he worked, he carefully removed his dark robes, revealing his torso.

His body was reminiscent of a silver fox—muscular yet lean, with a rugged handsomeness that commanded attention. His torso was a study in contrasts: lean, sinewy muscles rippled beneath the weathered skin, and scars crisscrossed his body like maps of battles fought and survived. These marks told stories of close encounters and victories earned through hardship, each one a testament to a life lived on the edge.

His chest was broad and powerful, each muscle finely defined and tapering to a set of chiselled abs that spoke of physical endurance and strength. His shoulders were wide and strong, leading down to arms that were both muscular and flexible. The veins beneath his skin were like rivers, tracing a path across his arms and chest, hinting at the potent energy and vitality coursing through him.

Despite the ruggedness of his physique, there was an undeniable grace to his movements, a fluidity that spoke of both experience and control. His torso was marked by an intricate web of scars, some faded, others still vivid, each one a silent testament to the trials he had faced. His skin, though weathered and tanned, held a striking contrast against the stark white of his hair and beard, creating a figure of both formidable strength and undeniable allure.

Amelia's gaze lingered, captivated by the contrast between his aged face and the youthful vitality of his form. The sight was both mesmerizing and unsettling, a reminder of the strange, enigmatic nature of the world she had been drawn into. The moment hung in the air, heavy with unspoken tension, as she marvelled at the man before her.

"Focus your thoughts, Amelia," Ezekiel urged, snapping her back to the gravity of the moment. "This is not the time for distractions. The energies we will harness demand your full attention."

With a deep breath, Amelia steeled herself for the ritual. She stepped into the circle, aligning herself with the stones and their ancient power, her resolve fortifying as she prepared to confront the mysteries that lay ahead.

Ezekiel began the ritual with a series of meticulous movements, his actions precise and deliberate. He carefully arranged various arcane symbols and ancient relics around the circle, his hands moving with practiced ease. The air crackled with an almost tangible energy, and the stones seemed to pulse with a rhythm that matched the beat of her racing heart.

As Ezekiel raised his arms, he began to chant in a language that seemed to echo from the void itself. His voice was deep and resonant, each word vibrating with an otherworldly cadence:

"Dro'ga'rath na'khul i'gar,

Zeph'rel amn'delith z'syeth,

K'rag'thon el'mirath dar'shul,

Am'lag'rar z'na'dralith v'eth."

The words flowed like a dark melody, their sounds twisting and turning in the air. The chants wove a complex tapestry of sound, each phrase building upon the last. The language was alien and rhythmic, its very essence unsettling yet mesmerizing.

Amelia watched as Ezekiel's movements became more fluid, his gestures tracing intricate patterns in the air. He approached the center of the circle, where the ancient runes were etched into the ground, their lines glowing faintly as if imbued with a hidden power.

With a final, resonant chant, Ezekiel produced a dagger from within his robes. The blade was ancient and ceremonial, its surface etched with cryptic symbols that seemed to shift and shimmer in the dim light. He held it high, invoking a final, guttural phrase:

"Thy'mar z'kraal'deth, el'na'tor,

Y'lu'vieth ra'thul'mar."

The air seemed to thicken with anticipation as Ezekiel cut his palm open with the dagger. Blood welled up from the wound, its dark crimson hue stark against his pale skin. He carefully smeared the blood across the runes on the floor, the red liquid soaking into the ancient symbols. Each rune absorbed the blood as if it were a living entity, its glow intensifying and spreading outward, merging with the pulsating energy of the circle.

Amelia's senses were overwhelmed by the ritual's intensity. The air grew thick with the scent of iron and earth, mingling with the acrid tang of old magic. The vibrations from the chants seemed to reverberate through her bones, making her feel as though she were caught in a maelstrom of unseen forces.

As Ezekiel completed the final incantation, the runes began to glow with an eerie light, casting strange shadows that danced across the clearing. The energy in the circle reached a crescendo, and Amelia felt a profound shift in the atmosphere, as though the very fabric of reality was being stretched and reshaped.

The ritual reached its climax as Ezekiel finished the last of the chants, his voice echoing with a final, powerful resonance:

"Dro'ga'rath el'na'kthar v'zor Am'lag'rar"

The clearing seemed to pulse with the energy of the ritual, and for a moment, everything felt suspended between realms. Amelia's heart raced as she braced herself, knowing that the true test of the ritual's power and its implications for her journey into the Amlagrarian realm was yet to come.

Amelia closed her eyes as a sensation of vertigo gripped her. The ground
seemed to dissolve beneath her, and she was abruptly pulled into a spiralling
vortex of light and shadow. The very fabric of reality warped and twisted, her
surroundings melting into a chaotic maelstrom of colours and shapes.

Visions exploded in her mind, each one more bewildering and disorienting
than the last. She saw cities that defied all known geometry, their spires and
towers stretching into impossible angles, blending and merging with the sky
in a dizzying dance. Streets coiled and looped into themselves, creating
endless labyrinths of shifting walls and impossible structures. The buildings
appeared to breathe and pulse, their surfaces alive with shifting patterns that
writhed like sentient entities.

Landscapes morphed in surreal and disturbing ways. Oceans of ink-black
water flowed upward, cascading like liquid shadows into twisted skies where
thunderous tempests of neon light clashed with swirling dark clouds.
Mountains rose and fell like the undulating curves of a grotesque heartbeat,
their peaks stretching into voids that seemed to swallow the stars. Forests of
gnarled, skeletal trees reached out with limbs like grasping fingers, their
leaves shimmering with an eerie, phosphorescent glow.

Beings beyond human comprehension lurked within these chaotic vistas.
Enormous entities with countless eyes and writhing appendages drifted
through the scenes, their forms constantly shifting and morphing as if they
were made of liquid darkness. Their presence exuded an aura of malevolent
curiosity, watching Amelia with a hunger that seemed to pierce through the
very fabric of her soul.

The air was thick with an oppressive, vibrating energy, and whispers echoed
incessantly in her mind. These whispers were a cacophony of alien tongues,
their sounds incomprehensible yet hauntingly familiar. Phrases like
"Zeph'ral'i'gar" and "A'kthar'ma'lor" echoed through her consciousness, each
word dripping with a sinister, otherworldly cadence. The whispers seemed to
claw at her sanity, their meanings elusive but carrying a palpable sense of
foreboding and chaos.

The visions continued to assault her senses, a relentless barrage of
incomprehensible imagery and sound that threatened to overwhelm her. The
boundaries of her reality shattered, leaving her adrift in an endless storm of
cosmic horror. The sense of time and space dissolved, and she was left

suspended in a state of disorientation and dread, struggling to cling to any semblance of reality as the maelstrom of chaos raged around her.

Amelia's breath quickened as the visions intensified, revealing the Ebon Watchers—cosmic entities of indescribable horror. These beings existed beyond the boundaries of human understanding, their forms a nightmarish confluence of writhing shadows and sickening distortions.

The Ebon Watchers appeared as amorphous masses of shifting darkness, their shapes constantly fluctuating and merging in ways that defied natural laws. Tendrils of inky blackness undulated and writhed from their bodies, curling and twisting with an unnerving fluidity. These tendrils seemed to have a life of their own, extending and retracting with grotesque grace, reaching out as if to ensnare and consume anything within their grasp.

At the centre of each Watcher was a single, enormous eye—an eye of such vast and terrible dimension that it seemed to gaze through the very fabric of reality. This eye was a churning vortex of malice and curiosity, its surface a swirling maelstrom of shifting colours and patterns that defied coherent description. Within this colossal eye, countless smaller eyes were embedded, each one a glistening, pupil-less orb that blinked and stared with a disturbing, synchronized rhythm. The miniature eyes moved in eerie harmony, their gazes darting and shifting, creating an unsettling illusion of being perpetually watched from every conceivable angle.

The skin of the Ebon Watchers was an ever-changing mosaic of textures, ranging from slick and oily to rough and scaly. It seemed to pulse with an inner light, an eerie, bioluminescent glow that cast sickly shadows across their forms. These shadows twisted and flickered, further distorting the already grotesque shapes of the Watchers.

The very air around them seemed to warp and shudder in their presence as if the physical laws of the universe bent and cracked under the weight of their existence. The sensation was one of deep, profound dread—a feeling that reality itself was teetering on the edge of collapse.

Amelia felt a profound sense of insignificance and terror as she beheld these beings, standing on the precipice of cosmic forces that transcended all human comprehension. The Ebon Watchers were a living embodiment of the incomprehensible void, their grotesque forms a haunting reminder of the unfathomable horrors lurking beyond the veil of reality.

As the ritual's effects intensified, Amelia found herself ensnared in a relentless maelstrom of chaotic visions. Her attempts to cling to her sense of reality became increasingly futile as the world around her erupted into a kaleidoscope of distorted colours and shapes. The vibrant, seething hues twisted and spiralled in impossible formations, each flash of light and shadow threatening to tear her mind apart. The boundaries between the tangible and the ephemeral dissolved, leaving her in a frenzied state where every perception was a jagged shard of fractured reality.

The visions assaulted her senses with a torrent of incomprehensible imagery. She saw cities suspended in the void, their architecture contorting and reshaping in defiance of geometry. Landscapes flowed and merged in fluid, nightmarish transitions as if the very ground beneath her was an ever-shifting canvas of cosmic disarray. Strange symbols and patterns pulsed with a menacing energy, appearing and disappearing in rapid succession, their meanings elusive and alien.

Amelia felt her thoughts splintering, each fragment of her consciousness struggling to remain coherent amidst the swirling chaos. Her memories intermingled with the bizarre visions, creating a disorienting blend of past and present, reality and illusion. The edges of her sanity felt as if they were being frayed by the relentless assault on her mind, each wave of madness clawing at her thoughts, dragging her ever closer to the abyss of complete mental collapse.

Amidst the cacophony of swirling visions and the crushing weight of impending madness, Ezekiel's voice emerged like a beacon of clarity. His words cut through the chaos with a penetrating urgency. "Amelia, focus!" he urged, his tone unwavering and authoritative. "You must control the visions. Hold on to your will. Do not let it break! You are stronger than the madness. Fight to maintain your grip on reality!"

The sound of Ezekiel's voice provided a fleeting anchor in the tempest of her mind, a crucial reminder of her purpose amidst the turmoil. The stark contrast between his commanding presence and the enveloping chaos gave her a momentary respite, a lifeline that urged her to summon every ounce of her strength to resist the encroaching darkness.

Summoning every ounce of strength she had left; Amelia felt a primal scream rise from the depths of her being. Her voice erupted in a guttural, earth-shattering cry that reverberated through the maelstrom of visions. The sound seemed to pierce through the veil of chaos, cutting through the disorienting whirl of colours and shapes that threatened to overwhelm her. Each syllable of her scream was a desperate plea for control, a fierce declaration of her will against the cosmic forces assailing her mind.

As her scream echoed through the tumultuous realm, Amelia's resolve hardened. She channelled her sheer determination into focusing the visions, her mind straining to impose some semblance of order upon the chaotic torrent. She visualized the swirling, maddening images converging, willed them to coalesce into meaningful patterns, hoping for glimpses of truths that might aid her in confronting the Ebon Watchers.

Gradually, the once-unstoppable maelstrom began to relent. The fractal chaos that had engulfed her started to recede, and the jumbled fragments of vision began to align. The tumultuous vortex of colours and shapes shifted into a more coherent, albeit still alien, arrangement. The incomprehensible symbols and nightmarish landscapes began to form a narrative, their chaotic energy receding into something she could grasp—if only just.

Amelia's heart pounded fiercely against her ribcage, each beat echoing the effort of her mental struggle. Sweat poured down her brow, mingling with the tears that tracked her face. Her breathing was ragged, each breath coming in shallow, laboured gasps as she struggled to regain her composure. The weight of the visions' intensity had left her feeling drained and hollow.

As Amelia finally opened her eyes, she was greeted by a remarkable stillness. The clearing, once a chaotic storm of cosmic horror, had returned to its previous tranquillity. The ritual's effects had subsided, and the oppressive atmosphere that had gripped her was gone. The circle of ancient stones stood silent and unmoving; their power now dormant. The ambient light of the clearing seemed softer, and more welcoming, casting gentle shadows that offered solace after the tempestuous ordeal.

With the visions now at rest and her senses slowly regaining clarity, Amelia stood in the midst of the stillness, her body trembling slightly from the aftershocks of the ritual. The world around her had returned to normal, yet the echoes of her ordeal lingered, a reminder of the cosmic battle that lay ahead.

Ezekiel's gaze held a mixture of pride and concern as he looked upon Amelia, his voice filled with a tone of solemn awe. "You have witnessed the true form of the Amlagrarian realm, glimpsed the unfathomable truths within. It is a rare few who see the Ebon Watchers in their raw, unfiltered reality. But remember, the path you tread is fraught with peril. The line between sanity and madness is perilously thin when you confront the forces of the unknown."

Amelia nodded, her thoughts a tumultuous whirl. The profound horror of the Ebon Watchers had left an indelible mark on her psyche. The visions had not only pushed her to the brink but had also bestowed upon her a glimpse into the chilling reality of the cosmic entities she now faced. As she stood amidst the ancient stones, their aura still crackling with residual energy, she felt both a profound sense of awe and an unsettling dread. The weight of her new understanding settled heavily on her shoulders, a burden that seemed both immense and inescapable.

The revelations had left Amelia feeling both exhilarated and profoundly disturbed. Her mind felt like a battleground of fragmented thoughts, the intense imagery still vivid in her memory. The once-familiar world seemed altered by the dark truths she had seen, and she grappled with a deep sense of foreboding. The struggle against the Ebon Watchers and the rifts they had wrought was now a palpable reality, and she steeled herself for the challenges that lay ahead.

With a deep breath, Amelia attempted to regain her composure. The ritual's aftermath had left her disoriented, and she took a step forward, determined to continue despite the lingering disquiet within her. Yet, as she walked, a sudden wave of dizziness overcame her. The ground seemed to tilt beneath her, and the world spun in a disorienting blur.

Before she could react, her legs gave way, and she collapsed, her vision dimming as unconsciousness claimed her. Ezekiel was quick to react, his hand reaching out to catch her before she hit the ground. He held her gently, his expression a mix of concern and relief as he lowered her to the earth. The ancient stones around them seemed to pulse softly as if acknowledging the gravity of her sacrifice.

As Amelia slipped into darkness, the last thing she heard was Ezekiel's reassuring, yet sombre voice. "Rest now. The path is treacherous, and you have ventured far. You will need your strength for what is to come." The world faded to black, and the clearing, once vibrant with ritualistic energy, was left in a serene, almost mournful silence.

X. Fractured Reality

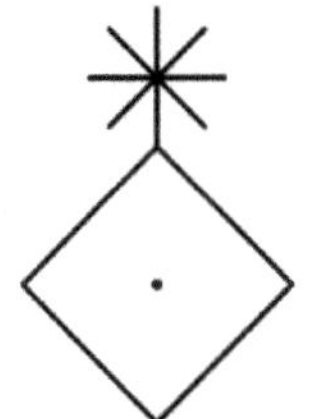

Amelia's unconsciousness was far from peaceful. As she lay in the depths of sleep, her mind was plunged into a twisted labyrinth of nightmares, each more harrowing than the last. The fragments of her memories, once clear and defined, began to blur and fade, slipping through her mental grasp like sand through her fingers. The comforting familiarity of her past—the echoes of her childhood, the warmth of her grandmother's voice, the life she once knew—became distant and obscure, as if they belonged to someone else entirely.

In the dark recesses of her mind, Amelia wandered through shifting landscapes that defied logic. The world around her twisted and contorted, morphing into grotesque, nightmarish visions that bore no resemblance to reality. She saw herself in countless forms—young, old, joyful, grieving—but none of these selves felt like her own. The faces of those she once loved appeared and disappeared like phantoms, their features distorted and unrecognizable.

Each step she took in these dreams pulled her further away from who she once was. The more she tried to hold onto her memories, the more they unravelled, leaving her with only a hollow sense of loss. It was as if the very essence of her identity was being stripped away, leaving behind nothing but a void where her past should have been.

Voices echoed through the darkness, speaking in languages she could not understand, their words laced with a malevolent intent that filled her with dread. Shadowy figures loomed at the edges of her vision, their forms shifting and writhing, always just out of reach but ever-present, watching her with eyes that gleamed like burning embers.

As the nightmares deepened, Amelia found herself standing on the edge of a vast, yawning abyss. The darkness below was endless, a chasm that seemed to devour all light and hope. She felt an overwhelming pull, a force that beckoned her to surrender to the void, to let go of everything she had ever known. The weight of it was crushing, suffocating, as if the darkness itself was alive, eager to consume her whole.

In that moment, Amelia felt her sense of self slipping away entirely. Her name, her past, her very soul—all seemed to fade into the blackness, leaving behind only a lingering question: Who am I?

The answer eluded her as the nightmares continued to swirl around her, a chaotic maelstrom of lost memories and fractured realities. She was adrift in a sea of madness, her mind splintered into countless pieces, each one further removed from the woman she once was.

And then, just as the darkness threatened to swallow her whole, a faint light appeared on the horizon of her consciousness. It was distant, barely more than a glimmer, but it was enough to give her the strength to resist the pull of the abyss. The light grew stronger, pushing back the shadows, and with it came a voice—a voice she recognized.

"Amelia," it called, cutting through the chaos. "Amelia, you must hold on."

The sound of her name, spoken with such clarity and urgency, anchored her to the last remnants of her identity. She clung to it, using it as a lifeline to pull herself out of the nightmare, away from the void that sought to consume her.

With a final surge of willpower, Amelia broke free from the darkness, her eyes snapping open as she gasped for breath.

Amelia stirred from the depths of unconsciousness, her mind struggling to piece together the shattered fragments of her thoughts. The world around her was a blur, a haze of unfamiliar shapes and shadows, but as her vision cleared, she found herself in a dimly lit room within the manor. The air was thick with the scent of aged wood and parchment, mingling with the lingering traces of incense from the ritual.

Across the room, seated in an old, weathered chair near the hearth, was Ezekiel. He was engrossed in a tome, his hood still pulled low over his face, casting a shadow that obscured his features. The soft flicker of candlelight danced across the pages of the book he held, revealing the ancient symbols etched within.

Amelia tried to sit up, but a wave of dizziness washed over her, and she fell back against the pillows. Her head throbbed with the aftershocks of the ritual, and her body felt heavy as if she were still submerged in that murky abyss.

Ezekiel's voice, low and calm, broke through the fog in her mind. "You're awake," he said, not looking up from his book. "The effects of the ritual can be... disorienting. It is best to take things slowly."

Amelia blinked, her thoughts still muddled. "What... what happened?" Her voice was hoarse, the words scraping against her dry throat.

"You glimpsed the Amlagrarian realm," Ezekiel replied, turning a page with deliberate care. "It is a place where the mind struggles to comprehend what it sees. The visions you experienced were only a taste of the truths that lie beyond the veil."

A shiver ran down Amelia's spine as the memories of the ritual began to resurface. The chaotic maelstrom, the grotesque forms of the Ebon Watchers, the whispers in alien tongues that threatened to unravel her sanity—it all came rushing back in a torrent of fear and confusion.

"I... I thought I was going mad," she confessed, her voice trembling. "The things I saw, the voices... it was too much."

Ezekiel finally looked up from his book, his piercing blue eyes locking onto hers with an intensity that made her breath catch. "You were on the edge," he said, his tone neither comforting nor cold, but filled with an understanding that only someone who had walked that path before could possess. "But you did not fall. That, Amelia, is a testament to your strength."

Amelia tried to process his words, but the lingering effects of the ritual made it difficult to think clearly. She felt as though she were teetering on the brink of something vast and terrifying, a darkness that threatened to consume her whole.

"Why did you bring me back?" she asked, her voice barely more than a whisper. "Why not let me face whatever it was... down there?"

Ezekiel closed the book and set it aside, his gaze never leaving hers. "Because you are not yet ready," he said, his voice softening. "The Amlagrarian realm is not a place to be entered lightly. You must first understand the forces you are dealing with, or you risk losing yourself entirely."

Amelia nodded, though the fear still gnawed at her insides. The line between reality and the otherworldly had been blurred beyond recognition, and she wasn't sure she could ever trust her own mind again.

Ezekiel stood, his movements graceful despite his age. He approached her bedside, his presence both comforting and imposing. "Rest now," he said, placing a hand gently on her shoulder. "You will need your strength for the battles ahead. There is still much you must learn, and the darkness is ever patient."

Amelia closed her eyes, the weight of exhaustion pulling her under once more. But even as sleep claimed her, the remnants of the ritual clung to her consciousness, a reminder that the darkness was always near, waiting to reclaim her.

In the days following the harrowing ritual, Amelia found herself in a strange calm. The relentless assaults on her mind, the visions, and the twisted shadows that had plagued her seemed to retreat, leaving her in a state of uneasy peace. The world around her felt almost normal, as if the horrors she had faced were nothing more than a distant nightmare.

Amelia's walks through the quiet streets of Eldermoor became a daily ritual. The town, with its old, cobblestone pathways and ancient buildings, exuded an eerie charm. The air was crisp, the skies often overcast, but the oppressive atmosphere that had once clung to her every step was noticeably absent. She strolled through the narrow alleyways and along the tree-lined paths, the soft rustling of leaves providing a soothing backdrop to her thoughts.

She found herself drawn to the outskirts, where the ancient circle of stones still stood, their presence a silent reminder of the ritual she had endured. The stones, once ominous and filled with a strange, humming energy, now seemed dormant, as if whatever power they held had been exhausted. The undergrowth had begun to reclaim the clearing, with tendrils of ivy creeping up the sides of the stones, softening their harsh lines.

For the first time since her arrival in Eldermoor, Amelia felt almost at peace. The terror of the Amlagrarian realm, the visions of the Ebon Watchers, and the creeping dread that had stalked her every moment had all but vanished. She slept through the nights without the usual torment of nightmares, waking up each morning to the soft light of dawn filtering through the curtains of her room in Vandercliffe Manor.

Yet, as the days turned into weeks, a sense of unease began to creep back into her thoughts. The peace she had found felt fragile, like a thin layer of ice over deep, dark waters. It was only a matter of time before the horrors she had momentarily escaped would return.

And return they did. It started subtly—just a flicker at the edge of her vision, a shadow that seemed out of place. Then came the whispers, soft and indistinct, like the rustling of dead leaves in the wind. Amelia tried to ignore them, dismissing them as the remnants of a trauma that she would eventually shake off. But the whispers grew louder, the shadows more pronounced, and soon, the peace she had cherished began to crumble.

On one of her walks through the town, the familiar streets began to twist and shift before her eyes. What had once been a comforting routine now became a disorienting experience. The world around her seemed to fragment, the boundaries between reality and the Amlagrarian realm blurring once more.

As she walked, the ground beneath her feet felt unsteady, as if she were treading on shifting sands. The buildings of Eldermoor, with their weathered facades and crumbling stonework, seemed to pulse with a life of their own. The sky above darkened, the clouds swirling in unnatural patterns, and the air grew thick with an oppressive energy.

Amelia's heart raced as she began to see fleeting images in the corners of her vision. They were flashes of different times and places—moments that didn't belong to the present. She saw herself standing in the grand hall of Vandercliffe Manor, its once opulent decor now decayed and covered in a thick layer of dust. Shadowy figures loomed in the periphery, their forms indistinct yet menacing, watching her with unblinking eyes.

In another instant, the scene shifted violently. Amelia found herself standing on the shores of a fiery lake, the water boiling and churning with impossible energy. The air was thick with the scent of sulphur, and the heat was unbearable. Reflected in the molten surface of the lake were landscapes that defied comprehension—mountains that inverted upon themselves, forests that twisted into unnatural shapes, and the ever-present gaze of the Ebon Watchers, their grotesque forms emerging from the depths.

The urgency that had been building within her reached a fever pitch. She could feel time slipping through her fingers like grains of sand. The peace she had enjoyed was a cruel illusion, and now, the reality was unravelling around her. She was running out of time.

Her walks became desperate, each step an attempt to escape the visions that hounded her. But no matter where she went, the images followed, growing more vivid and terrifying. The streets of Eldermoor became a labyrinth, each turn leading her deeper into the madness that threatened to consume her.

By the time she returned to Vandercliffe Manor, Amelia was a shell of her former self, her mind frayed at the edges. The peace that had once lulled her into a false sense of security was gone, replaced by the all-consuming terror of the unknown. The world she had once known was slipping away, and with it, her grasp on reality. The struggle against the Ebon Watchers and the dark forces that sought to breach the veil between dimensions was far from over.

Amelia's battle to anchor herself in reality was a constant, harrowing struggle. Each day felt like a fight against a powerful current pulling her deeper into a sea of uncertainty. The lines between her memories, her present, and the terrifying visions of a possible future blurred into a tangled mess, leaving her feeling lost and powerless.

She began to doubt her every thought, questioning if any of it was truly real or if she was simply slipping further into madness. The once-clear memories of her past were now foggy and distant, like faint echoes in a vast, empty chamber. She could no longer trust her own mind and the fear that she was losing herself entirely gnawed at her relentlessly.

Ezekiel appeared before her one evening, his calm demeanour contrasting sharply with the chaos that roiled within her. His presence was the only thing that felt solid, a rare anchor in the storm of her thoughts. His eyes, deep and piercing, were filled with both concern and understanding.

"The ritual has opened doorways in your mind, Amelia," he began, his voice steady but filled with urgency. "The Amlagrarian forces you've confronted exist beyond time as we know it. The boundaries between moments are thin, and you must navigate them carefully."

Amelia nodded weakly, her voice barely a whisper as she expressed the depth of her despair. "I don't know what's real anymore, Ezekiel. I can't distinguish between past, present, and future. Everything feels like it's slipping away."

His gaze softened, though his tone remained firm. "The Ebon Watchers seek to exploit this very vulnerability—to distort your perception and lead you astray. But you mustn't let them. You have a strength within you, Amelia, a connection to the Amlagrarian forces that they fear. You must trust in that connection, even when everything else feels lost. Rely on the symphony of your experiences to guide you."

Amelia's doubt was palpable as she shook her head, her eyes filled with tears. "What if I'm not strong enough? What if I can't do this?"

Ezekiel reached out, his hand resting gently on her shoulder. "You can, Amelia. The fact that you've come this far, faced what you have, proves your strength. But you must believe in it. The Ebon Watchers will do everything they can to make you falter, but they cannot take away your will unless you let them."

Despite his words, the weight of her uncertainty remained heavy. Amelia knew the path ahead was fraught with peril, and the fear that she might fail, that she might lose herself completely, never left her. Yet, deep down, a small spark of resolve flickered, refusing to be extinguished.

As she walked the winding paths of Eldermoor in the days that followed, the world around her was deceptively peaceful. The visions and twisted shadows that had tormented her seemed to have retreated, giving her a brief respite. The streets of the town were quiet, the air calm, and for the first time in what felt like an eternity, Amelia felt a semblance of normalcy.

But this peace was fleeting, and soon enough, the shadows began to return. The sense of urgency that had plagued her before came rushing back, stronger than ever. The twisted figures and the whispers of the Ebon Watchers once again assaulted her mind, reminding her that time was running out.

On her walks, the world seemed to shift around her, the streets of Eldermoor becoming a distorted reflection of reality. Trees twisted into grotesque shapes, and the ground beneath her feet seemed to ripple like the surface of a disturbed pond. The sky above darkened as if the very fabric of reality was beginning to unravel.

Every step was a battle to hold on to her sanity, to keep the darkness at bay. Yet, with each passing moment, Amelia felt herself slipping further away, the line between what was real and what was not growing thinner and thinner. The sense of dread that had become her constant companion tightened its grip on her heart, and she knew that the true test of her strength was yet to come.

Amelia's psyche was unravelling, her mind a battlefield where reality and hallucination waged war with each other. The boundaries between the two had become so blurred that she could no longer tell where one ended and the other began. Every sensation, every whisper, every fleeting image clawed at her sanity, leaving her adrift in a sea of confusion and despair. The once-clear memories of her life felt like distant echoes, muffled and obscured by the relentless assault on her mind. She was desperate for something tangible, something real to ground herself in the midst of the chaos.

As the days dragged on, Amelia found herself spiralling further into madness. The Ebon Watchers, those grotesque and impossible beings with their tendrils and countless eyes, haunted her every waking moment. Their presence was a constant, lingering at the edges of her vision, taunting her with their twisted forms and the unfathomable depths of their otherworldly hunger.

Fear had taken root deep within her, paralysing her with its icy grip. She began to isolate herself, locking herself away in the bathroom, where she would sit for hours on end, unable to move. The bathroom became her prison, a small, cold space where the walls seemed to close in on her, trapping her with the visions that tore at her senses.

The voices—alien, incomprehensible, and filled with a malice that burned through her ears—were relentless. They hissed and whispered, their words twisting into cruel mockeries of her thoughts, leaving her shaking with terror. The shadows around her twisted and contorted, their forms ever-changing and impossible to comprehend. She could feel them watching her, their presence suffocating, as if they were closing in on her, waiting for the moment she would break.

"I can't do this... I don't know what's real," she thought desperately, her mind a frantic whirl of panic and confusion. The need to feel something real, something she could control, became overwhelming. Her eyes fell on a pair of scissors lying on the bathroom counter, and without thinking, she grabbed them, her hand trembling as she held the blade against her arm.

With a scream of both terror and determination, she thrust the scissors into her flesh, the sharp pain cutting through the fog of her mind. The blood that oozed from the wound was warm, a tangible sensation that brought with it a fleeting sense of control. The pain was real, the blood was real, and for a brief moment, she felt anchored to the physical world.

But it wasn't enough. The visions continued, the Ebon Watchers laughing at her, their eyes burning with cruel amusement. Desperation overtook her, and she stabbed herself again, and again, each thrust of the scissors accompanied by a scream of pain and fury. Blood splattered across her body and the floor, pooling around her as she sought some kind of release from the torment that consumed her.

Finally, in a moment of utter madness, she thrust the scissors through her palm, the pain so intense that it felt like her mind might shatter completely. She screamed a sound that echoed through the bathroom, raw and filled with a mix of agony and rage. And then, in a twisted, broken moment, she began to laugh—mad, hysterical laughter that seemed to come from some deep, dark place within her.

"GET OUT OF MY HEAD!" she screamed, her voice cracking with the intensity of her emotions. But the visions only grew stronger, their taunting more vicious, as if they revelled in her suffering.

Panting and trembling, Amelia looked down at her hand, expecting to see the blood still pouring from her wounds. But what she saw made her heart stop. The blood was gone. The wounds she had inflicted on herself mere seconds ago had vanished, leaving no trace behind.

Was that just a vision? she thought, her mind reeling with shock and disbelief. It had felt so real—the pain, the blood, the warmth of her own life spilling out of her—but now it was as if none of it had ever happened. "What's happening to me?" she whispered, her voice shaking with fear. The reality she had tried so desperately to grasp had slipped through her fingers once again.

As the realization dawned on her, her body gave out. Her eyes rolled back into her head as a vision of chaotic madness overtook her. It was a flurry of images and events, all bleeding into one another in a torrent of sensory overload. The visions were so intense, so overwhelming, that they seemed to claw at her very soul, each one bringing with it a sharp, searing pain like a constant migraine.

The last thing she heard before darkness claimed her was the mocking laughter of the Ebon Watchers, echoing in her mind as she slipped into unconsciousness, her body collapsing to the cold bathroom floor.

Amelia awoke on the cold tile floor of the bathroom, her body aching from the night's ordeal. Her head throbbed with the lingering effects of the visions, and for a moment, she struggled to remember where she was. The memory of the scissors and the blood—or lack thereof—flooded back, sending a shiver down her spine. Her eyes darted around the room, searching for something real, something she could hold on to.

The door creaked open, and Ezekiel stood in the doorway, his expression a mixture of concern and pity. He moved towards her, kneeling by her side he placed his hand on her lower back as he gently helped her to sit up. His presence was a stark contrast to the chaos that had gripped her moments before—a calm amidst the storm that had become her reality.

"Amelia," he said softly, his voice steady and reassuring. "You're safe now."

But Amelia's mind was still reeling, her thoughts a jumbled mess of fear and desperation. She reached out, clutching his arm as if she were a newborn kitten clinging to its mother as if it were the only thing anchoring her to reality. "I can't... I can't do this anymore," she whispered, her voice trembling. "I don't know what's real. I just need something real, Ezekiel. I need to feel... something."

Ezekiel's eyes softened with understanding. He could see the torment in her eyes, the desperate need for something to hold on to.

Without a word, he pulled her close, his arms wrapping around her as if to shield her from the horrors that haunted her. Amelia buried her face in his chest, breathing in the warmth and solidity of him, his natural aroma that smelt of Sandalwood and dark mahogany. At that moment, all the fear and confusion melted away, replaced by a deep longing for something tangible, something human.

Ezekiel's hand gently cupped her chin, lifting her face to meet his gaze. His eyes, usually so guarded, were now filled with a tenderness she had never seen before. He leaned in, brushing his lips against hers in a kiss that was both gentle and intense, a silent promise that he would be there for her, no matter what.

Their kiss deepened, a desperate exchange of need and solace. Amelia's fingers traced the contours of his face, feeling the roughness of his stubble, the warmth of his skin. She needed this—needed him—to remind her of what it meant to be human, to feel alive.

Ezekiel responded to her touch, his own hands roaming her body with a tenderness that belied the strength he possessed. He pulled her closer, their bodies entwined his arms wrapped around her body holding her close, their legs tangled up like branches in a flood, as they sought comfort in each other. The world outside, with all its horrors and uncertainties, faded into the background as they lost themselves in the moment.

For the first time in what felt like an eternity, Amelia found peace. In Ezekiel's arms, she felt safe, grounded, and real. The nightmares, the visions, the madness—they were all still there, lurking in the corners of her mind, but for now, they were distant, muted by the warmth and intimacy they shared.

As the night wore on, they remained together, their connection growing stronger with each passing moment. Amelia knew that the challenges ahead were immense, but for now, she allowed herself to rest in the comfort of Ezekiel's embrace, knowing that, together, they could face whatever came next.

As the night wore on, the atmosphere between Amelia and Ezekiel shifted into a realm of quiet intimacy. The previous tension, born of desperation and anguish, melted away in the embrace of a newfound connection. Their breaths synchronized, a gentle rhythm that spoke of solace and understanding amidst the chaos that had consumed Amelia's mind.

Amelia lay nestled against Ezekiel, her head resting on his broad chest, feeling the steady beat of his heart beneath her cheek. The warmth of his body was a stark contrast to the cold, unsettling darkness that had plagued her. His presence was a solid anchor, a reassurance that despite the tumult of her visions and the uncertainties of their quest, there was a moment of peace they could share.

Ezekiel's hands traced soothing patterns on Amelia's back, his touch tender and protective. The soft murmurs of his voice, barely audible but filled with warmth, spoke of comfort and assurance. He whispered stories of old, tales that were as ancient as the stones of Eldermoor, yet carried a sense of hope and resilience. These stories, woven with threads of myth and reality, seemed to ground Amelia in the present, pulling her away from the precipice of her fractured mind.

As they lay there, the night deepened, casting a serene hush over the world outside. The shadows that had once threatened to overwhelm Amelia now seemed to recede, replaced by a sense of calm. The room, dimly lit by the soft glow of candles, became a sanctuary from the horrors that awaited them. The flickering light danced on the walls, creating patterns that were both calming and mesmerizing.

Ezekiel's presence was not just a physical comfort but an emotional haven. His eyes, usually so intense and burdened with the weight of his own knowledge, now held a softer, more tender gaze. He looked at Amelia with a mixture of compassion and admiration, as if seeing her for the first time not as a troubled soul but as someone strong and deserving of care.

Amelia, in turn, felt a deep sense of gratitude and affection for Ezekiel. The trials they had faced together had forged a bond that went beyond mere words. In this intimate moment, the promise of support and partnership seemed to overshadow the looming dangers they faced. For the first time in a long while, Amelia allowed herself to fully embrace a sense of vulnerability, finding strength in Ezekiel's unwavering support.

They spoke in hushed tones, their conversations weaving through their fears, hopes, and dreams. Ezekiel's voice, steady and reassuring, provided a contrast to the chaos that had filled Amelia's mind. His words were a balm, soothing the raw edges of her psyche and offering a glimpse of normalcy.

As the night progressed, their connection grew deeper. They shared more than just physical closeness; their conversation became an exchange of raw emotions and unspoken understanding. Amelia felt a profound sense of relief, a rare moment of peace amidst the storm that had been her life. For now, she allowed herself to rest in the comfort of Ezekiel's embrace, knowing that, together, they could face whatever came next.

The quiet intimacy of the night was a precious respite, a brief lull in the storm of their journey. As dawn approached, they both understood that the challenges ahead would be formidable. But for this one night, they embraced the solace they found in each other, gathering strength for the battles that lay ahead.

XI. Lurking Shadows

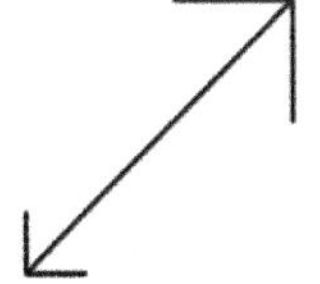

Guided by Ezekiel's steady presence, Amelia ventured deeper into the heart of Eldermoor's ancient forest. The canopy above formed a dense, shadowy vault, filtering the sunlight into eerie patterns that danced on the forest floor. The trees stood like towering sentinels, their gnarled branches stretching out like twisted fingers, each one seeming to beckon with an insidious intent.

As they walked, Amelia couldn't shake the feeling that the forest itself was alive and watching. The air was thick with a heavy, palpable energy that seemed to pulse with every step they took. The whispers she heard were not merely the rustling of leaves but carried an unsettling cadence—an alien language that slipped through her consciousness like sand through her fingers. The sounds were disjointed yet rhythmic as if the forest were conversing in an ancient tongue, she couldn't quite grasp but deeply felt.

The trees' shadows stretched unnaturally, twisting into grotesque shapes that danced at the periphery of her vision. It was as if the forest had its own dark will, manifesting in the gnarled branches that contorted into sinister forms. The undergrowth seemed to writhe and shift, the forest floor a tangled mess of roots and leaves that seemed to pulse with a life of their own. Every now and then, Amelia would catch sight of a shadow that lingered just out of reach, evoking the eerie feeling that she was being watched.

The air grew colder, the temperature dropping noticeably as they proceeded. The very fabric of reality seemed to ripple and warp around them, creating an unsettling sensation that the world was bending to an otherworldly rhythm. The forest seemed to grow darker, and the whispers became more urgent, their tones rising in a chorus that was both haunting and hypnotic.

Eventually, they emerged into a small, secluded clearing. The space felt oddly serene amidst the surrounding chaos, but the tranquillity was deceptive. The clearing was dominated by an unnerving sight: a pool of inky blackness spread out in the centre, its surface a mirror of darkness that seemed to absorb light rather than reflect it. The pool's surface was not still but rather in a constant state of flux—swirling and shifting as though something unseen was stirring just beneath.

The inky pool's edges were irregular and seemed to writhe as if they were alive. The darkness within it was a deep, oppressive black that seemed to pull at the very essence of reality. Occasionally, eerie glimmers would appear within the pool, like fleeting glimpses of distant stars swallowed by an endless void. The air around the pool felt heavier, charged with an ominous energy that made Amelia's skin crawl.

The shadows of the trees surrounding the clearing leaned in, their branches seeming to stretch closer to the pool as if drawn by its dark allure. The whispers that filled the forest now focused on the pool, their voices weaving a haunting melody that added to the growing sense of dread.

Amelia's heart pounded as she stepped closer to the pool, the inky darkness beckoning her with a sense of malignant curiosity. The forest seemed to hold its breath, the whispers and shifting shadows converging on the rift as if it were a focal point of their collective consciousness.

"Here lies the epicentre of the Amlagrarian influence," Ezekiel intoned, his voice a blend of reverence and gravity.

Amelia's heart pounded heavily in her chest as she faced the pool of darkness. The air around her seemed to grow colder, the atmosphere thick with a sense of impending doom. The pool, a deep abyss of inky blackness, felt like a gateway to another realm, an ominous portal connecting her to the very core of the eldritch forces that had tormented her. It seemed as though reality itself was fracturing at its edges, revealing glimpses into an unfathomable void.

As she peered into the depths, shapes began to materialize beneath the surface—twisted, amorphous figures that defied natural law. They writhed and shifted, their movements an unsettling dance that stirred the black liquid in unnatural patterns. The pool's darkness seemed alive, pulsing with a rhythm that echoed the chaotic beats of Amelia's own anxious heart.

The shadows around the clearing, drawn towards the pool, began to coalesce into tangible forms. They morphed into grotesque entities—creatures with faces contorted into expressions of malignant glee and insatiable hunger. Their features were a sickening blend of the familiar and the alien, shifting with every flicker of movement. The very air around the pool seemed to vibrate with an eerie resonance, amplifying the nightmarish visage of these shadowy beings.

Amelia's stomach churned with a deep sense of revulsion as the shadows began to manifest into physical forms. Her breath came in ragged bursts, and a cold sweat formed on her brow. The entities seemed to leer at her with a predatory hunger, their forms twisting and warping with a fluidity that made her skin crawl.

"Face them, Amelia," Ezekiel urged, his tone now laced with urgency and expectation. "You must confront the source of this nightmare. Only by facing these shadows can you hope to stand against the Ebon Watchers."

Amelia hesitated; her gaze fixed on the pool of darkness. The shadows continued to writhe and shift, their movement creating a sickening, almost hypnotic pattern. She could feel the weight of her fears pressing down upon her, making every breath a struggle. Yet, she knew that this confrontation was necessary.

Taking a deep, shuddering breath, Amelia summoned the resolve that had carried her through her ordeal thus far. She steadied herself, drawing on the inner strength that had been both her shield and her guide. With a determined nod, she stepped closer to the edge of the pool, feeling the oppressive darkness tugging at her very essence. The cold, inky surface seemed to beckon her forward, daring her to confront the nightmarish reality that lurked within.

As Amelia stepped closer to the pool, its surface began to ripple and churn, reacting violently to her proximity. The dark liquid seethed and writhed, as if sensing her presence and preparing to ensnare her. From the depths of the pool, a series of inky tendrils erupted, their movements serpentine and erratic. They twisted and contorted, each one a shifting mass of shadows and darkness, reaching out with an almost sentient malevolence.

The air grew thick with a palpable dread, the oppressive presence of the tendrils casting an ominous shadow over the clearing. The whispers in Amelia's mind grew louder and more chaotic, a cacophony of alien voices that seemed to echo from the very heart of the abyss. They spoke in a maddening symphony of disjointed phrases, their tones shifting from eerie calm to frantic shrieks, threatening to overwhelm her sanity.

Without warning, a tendril of darkness shot forth from the pool with a swift, slithering motion. It coiled around Amelia's body, its cold, sinewy surface pressing against her skin with an unearthly chill. The tendril seemed to pierce her very being, its dark energy seeping into her, filling her with a sense of encroaching dread. Her mind was bombarded with a torrent of maddening thoughts and disturbing images, the darkness within her growing almost palpable.

Amelia's heart raced, her breath coming in sharp, uneven gasps. The tendril's influence surged through her, an invasive force that sought to break her will. But Amelia refused to succumb to the encroaching darkness. She gritted her teeth, her resolve hardening against the tidal wave of terror that threatened to consume her.

Desperate to counteract the malevolent force, Amelia raised her hands, her fingers moving with a precision born from the fragments of ancient knowledge she had gathered. She traced intricate patterns in the air, each movement a deliberate invocation of eldritch energy. A symphony of shimmering light and arcane power erupted from her, its energies intertwining with the shadows that encircled her.

The battle that ensued was a fierce struggle of wills—a clash between the primal, chaotic forces of the abyss and the fragile determination of a mortal soul. Amelia's energy surged against the tendrils, pushing back with a force that momentarily halted their advance. The darkness writhed and recoiled, its tendrils twisting and snapping as if in pain.

Despite her efforts, the tendrils continued their assault, their grip tightening with each passing moment. Amelia's resistance was met with relentless pressure, the inky darkness attempting to pull her further into the pool's depths. The struggle was intense, a fight against an almost insurmountable force that seemed to draw on every ounce of her strength and willpower.

As the tendrils continued to lash out, Amelia could feel the weight of her own fear and exhaustion bearing down on her. But she pressed on, her determination unwavering, as she battled against the encroaching darkness. Her hands trembled with the effort of maintaining the arcane barrier, each motion a desperate bid to push back against the eldritch forces threatening to engulf her.

Ezekiel's voice joined hers, his incantations harmonizing with hers, adding strength to her efforts. The shadows writhed and contorted, their forms distorting as if struggling against an invisible force. Groaning in pain still focusing on the task at hand and not allowing the darkness to spread inside her mind it was for a fleeting moment, that Amelia caught a glimpse of something deeper within—the core of their power, a seed of eldritch energy that pulsed with ancient malevolence.

As Amelia stood on the precipice of her final confrontation with the darkness, she summoned every ounce of her remaining strength. The air around her crackled with energy as she prepared for the final part of the incantation. Her voice, though strained, carried the weight of her desperate willpower as she chanted the ancient words, each syllable resonating with a force that seemed to defy reality.

The incantation reached its climax, and Amelia's scream, raw and piercing, echoed through the forest. Her words, infused with the raw essence of eldritch power, coalesced into a blinding surge of light that exploded from the pool of darkness. The tendrils recoiled violently, their inky forms writhing in agony. The sound that erupted from them was a bone-chilling, unearthly shriek—a cacophony of grinding, scraping, and high-pitched, keening noises that pierced the very fabric of reality. It was a sound that seemed to claw at the edges of sanity, a dissonant symphony of torment that reverberated through the clearing.

The tendrils thrashed violently, their dark forms twisting and convulsing as the light engulfed them. The shadows wailed in an otherworldly chorus, their mournful cries mingling with the shrieks of the dissolving darkness. Slowly, their forms began to fragment and dissolve, breaking apart into wisps of shadow that were absorbed back into the pool. The unearthly sound of their retreat left a lingering echo of distorted, mournful moans that faded into an eerie silence.

As the light subsided, the clearing fell into an unsettling stillness. The once oppressive atmosphere now seemed almost serene, though the remnants of the eldritch encounter lingered in the air. Amelia's breath was ragged, her body trembling with the aftereffects of the immense strain she had endured. Her gaze, haunted and exhausted, sought out Ezekiel.

He approached her with a look of sombre respect and weary relief. "You have faced the heart of the rift, Amelia," he said, his voice carrying the weight of ancient wisdom and fatigue. "But remember, this battle is far from over. The Ebon Watchers' influence extends beyond this rift. What you've encountered is but a fraction of the darkness that lies ahead. You've done well to confront this challenge, but there will be more trials to come."

Amelia's brow furrowed as she faced Ezekiel, a mix of frustration and determination etched across her features. "Tell me, Ezekiel, what exactly is your role in all of this? Why have you guided me through this twisted journey?"

Ezekiel's gaze, as profound as it was inscrutable, met hers. "I am but a guide along the path of cosmic equilibrium, Amelia. My actions are driven by the currents of fate that weave through the fabric of existence. The reasons behind my guidance are as shadowed as the realm we have traversed. The truths you seek are wrapped in layers beyond the veil of my own understanding."

His words, though cryptic, carried an undertone of veiled meaning that seemed to obscure more than it revealed. The forest around them seemed to pulse with a latent unease as if reflecting the ambiguity of Ezekiel's answers. The shadows of the trees seemed to stretch and twist, echoing the uncertainty that now clouded Amelia's thoughts.

Ezekiel continued his voice a whisper against the backdrop of the shifting woods. "The balance I maintain is delicate and fraught with the unseen. Sometimes, to see the truth, one must navigate through the labyrinth of their own fears and uncertainties. I am bound by forces that are beyond mere mortal comprehension. Our paths are intertwined in ways that may not yet be clear."

Amelia's heart sank with the weight of his evasive answers. The pool of darkness, now a fading memory, left a heavy silence between them. She could feel the threads of reality around her growing thin and fragile, and Ezekiel's words seemed to deepen the chasm of doubt within her.

As she looked back at the place where the inky darkness had once swirled, a sense of foreboding settled over her. The Ebon Watchers, though momentarily thwarted, seemed ever closer in her mind's eye. The balance between her own reality and the Amlagrarian realm remained as tenuous as a spider's web, and with Ezekiel's enigmatic presence beside her, Amelia knew she had only begun to scratch the surface of the cosmic battle that lay ahead.

The path forward was fraught with peril and uncertainty, but with Ezekiel's cryptic guidance, she felt both a growing resolve and a creeping doubt. The horrors she faced would test her in ways she could not yet comprehend, and she braced herself for the challenges that awaited in the darkness.

XII. Echoes of Sacrifice

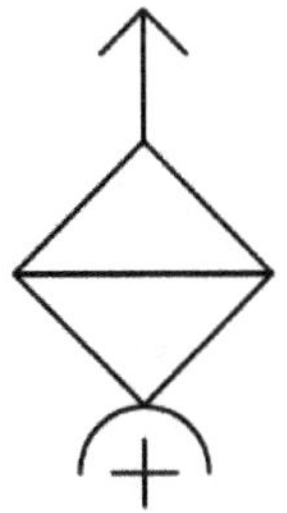

Amelia's days blurred into nights as she buried herself in the depths of her research, driven by a relentless need to uncover the truth about Eldermoor and its dark history. The library in the Vandercliffe Estate became her sanctuary, its walls lined with ancient, dust-covered tomes that held the secrets of the town's past. The more she read, the more she felt herself being pulled into the twisted web of the Order of the Obsidian Veil.

One evening, she stumbled upon a particularly weathered book, its spine cracked and pages yellowed with age. The title, barely legible, read "*The Chronicles of the Obsidian Veil*." As she turned the pages, a sickening sense of dread settled over her. This tome contained graphic and detailed accounts of the cult's rise to power in Eldermoor, its influence spreading like a malignant shadow across the town.

The Order, as it was revealed, had been a secretive and insidious force, gradually worming its way into the very fabric of Eldermoor's society. They had manipulated the town's leaders, infiltrated its institutions, and gained control over the townsfolk through fear and dark rituals. Amelia read about the horrific sacrifices made in the name of the Ebon Watchers—innocent lives taken to appease the eldritch entities that the cult worshipped. These rituals were conducted in the dead of night, deep within the forest, where the boundaries between realities were weakest.

The Order had been meticulous in its efforts to erase its presence from history. Over the years, they had faded from the town's collective memory, becoming nothing more than whispered legends and half-forgotten tales. But the book Amelia held in her hands provided irrefutable evidence of their existence, their dark deeds, and their lingering influence over the town. The more she read, the more she realized how deeply the Order had manipulated Eldermoor, bending it to their will while hiding in the shadows.

The town itself had become an extension of the Order's power—a place where the veil between realities was thin, and where the influence of the Amlagrarian realm seeped through, corrupting the very air Amelia breathed. She felt a growing sense of urgency as she continued to uncover the dark truths, knowing that the Order's hold on Eldermoor was far from broken, and that the Ebon Watchers still loomed, waiting to reclaim what had once been theirs.

The deeper Amelia delved into the book, the more she realized the magnitude of the task before her. The Order of the Obsidian Veil had not simply disappeared—they had become a part of the town itself, their presence woven into the very essence of Eldermoor. Their control was subtle but pervasive, like a poison slowly spreading through the veins of the town.

With every page she turned, the weight of her responsibility grew heavier. Amelia knew she was not just fighting for her own survival but for the soul of Eldermoor itself. The visions, the shadows, and the rift were all part of a larger, more sinister design—one that she had only begun to understand.

Amelia's heart sank as she read about the cult's practices innocent townspeople offered as sacrifices, eldritch symbols etched into their flesh, and dark incantations whispered into the void. The cult's goal had been to merge the Amlagrarian realm with the mortal world, to bring about a convergence that would grant them power beyond imagination.

But what struck Amelia to her core was a passage that spoke of her own familial connection to the cult—a bloodline tainted by the unearthly forces. The Vandercliffe family had been instrumental in the cult's rituals, passing down their knowledge and power through generations. The mansion itself was a conduit, a place where the boundaries between dimensions were thin and these ancient forces could manifest.

As Amelia delved further into the pages of "*The Chronicles of the Obsidian Veil*," the macabre details of the cult's practices unfolded before her eyes, leaving her with a deep sense of revulsion and dread. The Order of the Obsidian Veil was not just a shadowy group of conspirators; they were practitioners of dark and forbidden rites that defied the boundaries of human morality and comprehension.

The cult's rituals were designed to thin the veil between dimensions, allowing the eldritch forces of the Amlagrarian realm to seep into the mortal world. They sought to summon the Ebon Watchers—ancient, malevolent entities that fed on fear and despair. The sacrifices made in their name were brutal and gruesome, involving the blood of innocents. The cult believed that the suffering and terror of their victims would empower the Watchers, granting them greater influence over the physical world.

Amelia read about the "*Rite of Convergence*," a particularly horrific ritual where the cult would abduct townsfolk, often the young and vulnerable, and bind them in a circle of runes etched into the earth with their own blood. As the ritual progressed, the victims would be subjected to unimaginable torment, their screams echoing through the forest as the cult chanted in an ancient, guttural language. The rite would culminate in the offering of their lives to the Ebon Watchers, their souls consumed by the darkness that seeped through the rift.

The accounts of the cult members who participated in these rituals were equally disturbing. One passage described the testimony of a man named Alistair Vaughn, a high-ranking member of the Order. His account was chillingly detached, as he recounted the ease with which the town was manipulated. "The people of Eldermoor are like cattle," he wrote. "Easily led, easily deceived. They fear what they do not understand, and that fear is our greatest weapon. They will follow us willingly into the abyss, believing it is salvation."

Another account, written by a woman named Lydia Hawke, spoke of the seductive power of the Amlagrarian forces. "Once you have tasted the power of the Watchers, you are never the same," she confessed. "It is a hunger that cannot be sated, a thirst that can never be quenched. I have seen the darkness beyond the veil, and it calls to me in my dreams, promising power and eternal life. But the price... the price is steep, and I fear I have already paid too much."

As Amelia continued to read, she came across an image that made her blood run cold. It was an old, faded sketch of a cult member, his face obscured by a hood, yet something about him seemed eerily familiar. She stared at the image, her heart pounding in her chest as realization dawned on her—the man in the sketch looked strikingly similar to Ezekiel. The resemblance was uncanny, down to the sharpness of his features and the intensity in his eyes.

A wave of confusion and anger washed over her. Could it be that Ezekiel was somehow connected to the cult? Had he deceived her all along? The questions swirled in her mind, each one more troubling than the last. She had trusted him, and relied on him to guide her through the horrors she had faced, but now, doubt crept in, gnawing at her resolve.

Amelia's frustration boiled over as she slammed the book shut, her mind reeling with the implications of what she had discovered. The pieces of the puzzle were falling into place, but the picture they formed was far from comforting. Her family's ties to the Vandercliffe mansion, the eldritch influence that had haunted her dreams, and now this—an unsettling connection between Ezekiel and the Order of the Obsidian Veil.

The resonance of sacrifice echoed through her family's history, intertwining with the horrors that now threatened to consume her world. Amelia was left to grapple with the knowledge that her ancestors had played a role in the very darkness she was fighting against. The burden of her bloodline weighed heavily on her, a chilling reminder that the past was not so easily escaped.

Amelia sat in the dimly lit study, her hands trembling as she closed *"The Chronicles of the Obsidian Veil."* The image of the cult member who bore an unsettling resemblance to Ezekiel lingered in her mind, a seed of doubt that threatened to take root. Her breath came in shallow gasps as she tried to process what she had just discovered. The thought that Ezekiel might be connected to the very cult that had wreaked havoc on Eldermoor was almost too much to bear. But she knew she couldn't act on this revelation—not yet. If Ezekiel was hiding something, she would need to uncover it carefully, without tipping her hand.

She tucked the book back onto the dusty shelf, forcing her hands to stop shaking. The room felt suddenly colder, the shadows stretching ominously as if they knew what she was hiding. A sense of isolation pressed in on her, the weight of her secret adding to the burden she already carried. But she steeled herself, knowing that she needed to remain vigilant, to watch Ezekiel closely for any subtle hints at the truth.

As she turned away from the shelf, lost in thought, a voice broke the silence, making her jump.

"Amelia."

She whirled around, her heart leaping into her throat. Ezekiel stood in the doorway, his presence both commanding and enigmatic. His sudden appearance startled her more than it should have, especially in light of what she had just read. The doubt gnawed at her, but she forced herself to remain calm, pushing down the surge of fear that threatened to surface.

"We need to go," Ezekiel said, his voice steady but laced with urgency. "There's another rift—a powerful one. It's in the old auditorium."

Amelia's mind raced. The auditorium was a place steeped in history, once a hub of community gatherings but now long abandoned and forgotten. If a rift had opened there, it could be a gateway to something far more dangerous. But as she looked at Ezekiel, the questions she had suppressed bubbled up, making it difficult to trust his intentions. Was he genuinely trying to help her, or was he leading her into a trap?

"Amelia," Ezekiel repeated, his eyes narrowing slightly as he studied her. "We don't have much time."

His gaze pierced through her, and for a brief moment, she wondered if he could see the turmoil in her thoughts. She hesitated, but only for a second. There was no room for doubt now—she had to act as if nothing had changed, to pretend that she still trusted him completely.

"Right," she finally replied, nodding as she tried to mask the unease in her voice. "Let's go."

As they made their way out of the study and into the darkened corridors of the mansion, Amelia felt a strange tension in the air. The mansion's oppressive atmosphere seemed to close in around them, the walls creaking as if whispering secrets long buried. She walked beside Ezekiel, her senses on high alert, ready to catch any sign of deception. The image of the cult member's sketch lingered in her mind, a haunting reminder of the possible truth she couldn't yet confront.

Ezekiel led the way, his movements purposeful, but to Amelia, his every gesture now seemed tinged with hidden meaning. She couldn't shake the feeling that he was testing her, that he was aware of her newfound suspicion. But she couldn't let him know. Not yet. Not until she was certain of what he was hiding.

As they approached the auditorium, Amelia felt the weight of her secret grow heavier, pressing down on her chest like a leaden shroud. The air grew colder, and the shadows deepened, as if the building itself was reacting to the impending confrontation. She glanced at Ezekiel, his face stoic and unreadable. What game was he playing? And how long could she keep up her own?

The auditorium loomed before them, its doors creaking open as if beckoning them inside. Amelia steeled herself, knowing that whatever awaited them within those walls, she would need to face it with both courage and caution. The truth about Ezekiel could wait—for now, her focus had to be on closing the rift and keeping the darkness at bay.

But as they stepped into the shadowy expanse of the auditorium, the seed of doubt in Amelia's heart continued to grow, feeding on her uncertainty and fear. The battle ahead was not just against the forces of the Amlagrarian realm—it was also a battle for the truth, and for her own soul.

As Amelia and Ezekiel stepped into the cavernous auditorium, the air grew thick with a palpable sense of dread. The once grand space, now abandoned and forgotten, was shrouded in shadows that danced across the crumbling walls. Dust motes hung in the air, caught in the dim light filtering through broken windows, giving the place an eerie, timeless quality.

At the center of the auditorium, a gaping rift pulsed with malevolent energy, a swirling vortex of inky blackness that seemed to consume the very light around it. The edges of the rift crackled with energy, distorting the air and reality itself. It was as if the fabric of the world was being torn apart, and the rift was a gaping wound, bleeding chaos into the mortal realm.

Amelia's heart raced as she approached the rift, her mind reeling from the overwhelming sense of wrongness that emanated from it. She could feel the malevolent presence on the other side, something ancient and hungry, something that fed on fear and doubt. Her thoughts were a jumble of confusion and suspicion—about the rift, about the cult, about Ezekiel.

Without warning, the rift surged, and from its depths emerged a grotesque appendage—a long, spindly leg that resembled the limb of a spider, but twisted and malformed. The leg was covered in a slick, obsidian-like substance that seemed to absorb light, and it moved with a sickening fluidity, as if not bound by the laws of this world. It lashed out, slicing through the air with a terrifying speed, and anything it touched—chairs, debris, even the walls—was instantly reduced to rubble.

The sound that accompanied the leg's movement was unearthly—a high-pitched screech that reverberated through the auditorium, setting Amelia's teeth on edge and sending a shiver down her spine. The leg was followed by another, then another, until multiple limbs had breached the rift, each one reaching out like the arms of a nightmare, spreading destruction with every touch.

Amelia staggered back, her breath coming in short, panicked gasps. The sight of those monstrous limbs was enough to freeze her in place, but she knew she had to act. Her mind raced, searching for the words of the incantation Ezekiel had taught her, but the fear gnawing at her insides made it hard to focus. The entity on the other side of the rift fed on her fear, her doubt, and she could feel it growing stronger, its hunger intensifying.

Ezekiel stood beside her, his expression unreadable as he watched the rift with a grim determination. "Amelia," he urged, his voice low and steady, "you must close the rift. Focus."

But his words felt distant, muffled by the overwhelming terror that gripped her. The limbs continued to thrash, tearing through the auditorium, the destruction spreading like wildfire. Amelia could feel the entity's presence pushing against the boundaries of reality, trying to force its way through the rift entirely.

She raised her hands, trying to summon the eldritch energy she had learned to harness, but her fear was too strong. The words of the incantation slipped from her mind, replaced by visions of the cult, of the twisted rituals, and of the sketch that looked so much like Ezekiel. Doubt poisoned her thoughts, weakening her resolve, and the rift seemed to pulse in response as if savouring her despair.

Another limb lashed out, narrowly missing her as it tore through a row of decayed seats, sending splinters flying. Amelia cried out, the closeness of the attack snapping her back to reality. She couldn't afford to lose control now—not with so much at stake. She forced herself to focus, to push the fear aside, if only for a moment.

"Amelia!" Ezekiel's voice cut through the chaos, sharp and commanding. "Remember who you are. Remember what you've learned."

His words grounded her, if only slightly. She could still feel the doubt lurking in the corners of her mind, but she drew on whatever strength she had left, forcing herself to remember the incantation. Her voice trembled as she began to speak the ancient words, the syllables foreign and harsh on her tongue.

The eldritch energy responded, swirling around her hands in a pale, ethereal light. She directed it toward the rift, willing it to close, to seal the breach before the entity could fully emerge. The limbs recoiled slightly as the light touched them, but they didn't retreat—they fought back, pushing against her power, trying to break through.

The strain was immense. Amelia could feel the rift fighting her, resisting her attempts to close it. The entity on the other side was relentless, and every flicker of doubt, every moment of hesitation, weakened her further. It was as if the rift was feeding on her emotions, growing stronger with every passing second.

She gritted her teeth, pouring every ounce of her will into the incantation. The light grew brighter, more intense, but so did the resistance from the rift. The limbs thrashed wildly, their screeches piercing the air, a cacophony of unearthly sound that seemed to shake the very foundations of the auditorium.

Amelia felt herself weakening, her strength fading as the battle dragged on. The fear and doubt were too strong, and she could feel the entity's influence creeping into her mind, whispering insidious thoughts, telling her to give up, to let go, to surrender.

But she refused. With a final, desperate surge of energy, she shouted the last words of the incantation, pushing every last bit of her will into the closing of the rift. The light around her hands flared brightly, a blinding flash that engulfed the entire auditorium.

The limbs screeched, a sound so terrible and inhuman that it made Amelia's ears ring and her heart pound painfully in her chest. The rift buckled under the force of her power, the limbs thrashing in agony as they were forced back into the void. The light seemed to consume them, swallowing the darkness until, with one final, deafening wail, the rift collapsed in on itself, sealing shut with a crack of energy that left the air humming.

Silence fell over the auditorium, the sudden absence of sound almost as jarring as the chaos that had preceded it. Amelia stood there, her body trembling, her breath coming in ragged gasps. The destruction wrought by the limbs remained—a testament to how close she had come to failing—but the rift was closed. The entity was gone.

She turned to Ezekiel, her eyes wide with a mixture of relief and suspicion. He stood in the shadows, his face partially obscured, watching her with an unreadable expression. The seed of doubt in her heart grew a little more, but she knew now wasn't the time to confront it. She had survived the rift, but the battle was far from over.

For now, she needed to rest, to recover her strength. But as she left the ruined auditorium with Ezekiel by her side, she knew that the next time they faced the darkness, she would be watching him even more closely, searching for the truth that lay hidden behind his enigmatic facade.

XIII. Haunting Melodies

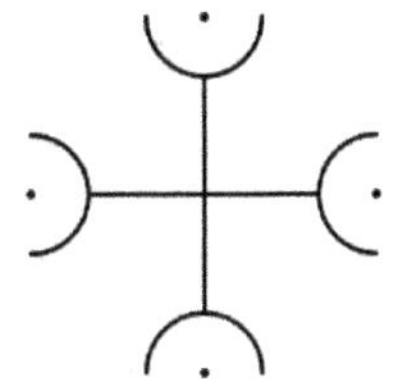

Amelia's grip on reality was slipping, her psyche stretched to its breaking point. Each day felt like a battle against an unseen force that sought to tear her mind apart. The once-familiar corners of the Vandercliffe mansion became alien, the shadows more menacing, the silence more oppressive. Every creak of the floorboards, every gust of wind, seemed like a whisper from another realm, reminding her that the line between sanity and madness was dangerously thin.

As night descended, the mansion was swallowed by a heavy stillness. The air was thick, suffocating as if the very walls were closing in around her. Amelia sat in her room, her thoughts racing, her heart pounding in her chest. The silence was deafening, amplifying the fear that gnawed at the edges of her consciousness.

Then, without warning, a melody began to play. It started as a barely perceptible hum, weaving its way through the silence like a thread of sound. But as it grew louder, the notes became clearer, more distinct—a haunting, ethereal tune that seemed to echo through the very walls of the mansion.

The melody was unlike anything Amelia had ever heard. It was soft yet piercing, its beauty tinged with an underlying darkness that sent shivers down her spine. It was as if the music were alive, reaching out to her, pulling her in. The more she listened, the more she felt herself slipping into its grasp, her thoughts clouded by the intoxicating lure of the notes.

The melody seemed to echo from every direction, filling the air with its haunting refrain. It was both beautiful and terrifying, a siren's call that beckoned her deeper into the madness that threatened to consume her. The sound wrapped around her like a shroud, lulling her into a trance-like state, her mind slowly unravelling as she surrendered to its allure.

The more Amelia listened, the more the walls of the mansion seemed to close in around her, the shadows growing longer, darker. Her thoughts became disjointed, her memories fractured as if the melody were unravelling the very fabric of her mind. The once-familiar faces of her ancestors, the stories she had been told, all seemed distant and hazy, replaced by the overwhelming presence of the music.

And yet, despite the terror that gripped her, Amelia couldn't help but listen. The melody was a lure, a trap that she was powerless to resist. It called to her, drawing her deeper into the darkness, promising answers to the questions that plagued her, even as it threatened to destroy her.

The melody was unlike anything Amelia had ever heard before. It was a sound that defied description, so beautiful and ethereal that it seemed to transcend the very fabric of reality. The notes floated through the air, delicate yet powerful, resonating with a purity that no man-made instrument could ever hope to replicate. It was as if the music itself had been woven from the very essence of the cosmos, each note a thread in an otherworldly tapestry of sound.

As the haunting lullaby filled the room, Amelia felt an overwhelming sense of awe wash over her. The melody was intoxicating, wrapping around her like a silken veil, pulling her deeper into its spell. Every note seemed to resonate within her, vibrating in perfect harmony with the very core of her being. It was as though the music spoke directly to her soul, its beauty both a comfort and a torment.

The sound was impossible to pinpoint, its source elusive as it echoed through the mansion. It seemed to come from everywhere and nowhere at once, filling the air with its haunting refrain. The more she listened, the more entranced she became her thoughts dissolving into the music, her mind surrendering to its seductive power.

Amelia felt her feet move of their own accord as if drawn by an invisible force. The melody guided her, its rhythm dictating her every step. She moved through the darkened halls of the mansion, her surroundings a blur as the music consumed her. The walls seemed to pulse with the sound, the shadows dancing in time with the melody, their shapes twisting and contorting as if alive.

The further she ventured, the louder the melody became, its intensity growing with each passing moment. It was an orchestral sound, layered and complex, yet perfectly harmonious—a symphony that seemed to be performed by an unseen hand. The notes soared and dipped, creating a soundscape that was both haunting and divine, a melody that seemed to hold the secrets of the universe within its chords.

Amelia's heart raced, her pulse quickening as the music led her deeper into the mansion. She was captivated, unable to resist the lure of the melody, her mind and body entranced by the otherworldly sound. The music was a siren's call, beckoning her to its source, promising her answers, or perhaps something far more sinister.

With every step, she felt herself slipping further into the melody's grasp, her sense of self fading as the music consumed her. The world around her grew distant, her surroundings a mere backdrop to the symphony that now dominated her thoughts. The melody was all she could hear, all she could feel—a lullaby that carried her ever closer to the source of its unearthly beauty.

As Amelia walked through the darkened halls of the Vandercliffe mansion, the melody's hypnotic pull guided her steps. The mansion, usually cold and uninviting, felt alive in a way that was both unsettling and mesmerizing. Shadows seemed to dance on the walls, following her as she moved, their shapes twisting in time with the music. The once familiar corridors had taken on an otherworldly quality, as if the mansion itself had become an extension of the haunting melody that filled the air.

Every corner she turned, every hallway she traversed, felt like a journey deeper into a labyrinthine world that defied logic. The mansion's walls, which she had scoured countless times in search of answers, now seemed to shift and breathe, subtly altering as if guiding her toward a hidden truth. The music grew louder, more insistent, compelling her to move forward even as a part of her mind screamed to turn back.

Then, as if summoned by the very notes she followed, a door appeared before her. Amelia halted, her breath catching in her throat as she stared at it. She was certain this door had never existed before, yet it stood there, solid and imposing, as if it had always been part of the mansion's architecture. The more she stared, the more uncertain she became. Had it always been there, concealed by some trick of the mind? Or had it materialized out of the very air, birthed by the same unseen force that had conjured the melody?

The door was unlike any other in the mansion. It was tall and narrow, crafted from dark, weathered wood that seemed to drink in the light rather than reflect it. Intricate carvings adorned its surface—twisting, vine-like patterns that seemed to writhe and shift when viewed from the corner of her eye. The carvings were ancient, their meanings lost to time, but they exuded a sense of foreboding as if they held secrets too dark to be spoken.

The door's handle was a work of art in itself. It was made of black iron, cold to the touch, shaped like a twisted, gnarled branch. The metal was smooth, worn by time, yet it retained an unnatural sheen, as if it had been polished by countless hands over the centuries. The handle curled around itself in a serpentine pattern, the grooves and ridges fitting perfectly into Amelia's palm as if it had been designed specifically for her. The sensation of destiny and inevitability washed over her as her fingers wrapped around it.

She hesitated, her hand trembling slightly as she prepared to turn the handle. The music swelled in intensity, urging her on, the melody wrapping around her thoughts, drowning out her fear. She could feel the door pulsing beneath her fingers, as if it were alive, waiting for her to open it. It was a door that led somewhere beyond the physical realm, a gateway to something unknown and unknowable.

Amelia stepped into the chamber, her breath catching as she took in the eerie surroundings. The walls of the room were unlike anything she had ever seen; they appeared alive, pulsating softly as if breathing in unison with the music that filled the air. The walls were covered in a dark, almost oily substance that shimmered in the dim light, creating an unsettling, undulating effect. Strange symbols etched deep into the surface, seemed to shift and writhe, defying her attempts to decipher their meaning. The air was thick, and heavy with a sense of ancient power, and the silence was broken only by the haunting melody that had led her here.

At the centre of the chamber, illuminated by a faint, ethereal glow, stood the source of the music—a harp-like instrument perched on a singular pedestal. The pedestal itself was carved from the same twisted wood as the instrument, its base rooted into the ground like an ancient tree. The harp was a bizarre amalgamation of organic and inorganic materials, its frame crafted from gnarled, dark wood that seemed to twist and contort as if it had grown into its current shape over centuries. The wood was smooth and polished, yet it retained a primal, untamed quality, as if it had been shaped by forces beyond human understanding.

The strings of the harp were a sight to behold. They were not made of any material Amelia could recognize; they shimmered like spun silver in the dim light, but when observed closely, they seemed to be woven from threads of pure energy, each one pulsing with a life of its own. The strings moved with a deliberate, almost sentient rhythm, plucking themselves as if an invisible hand were playing a haunting lullaby. The notes that emerged from the harp resonated deeply within Amelia, the sound so beautiful and ethereal that it felt as though the music was reaching out to her very soul.

As she stood before the instrument, Amelia felt a sense of awe mixed with a creeping unease. The harp's music was intoxicating, luring her deeper into the chamber, compelling her to draw closer. Yet, there was something deeply unsettling about the way the strings moved, as if the instrument were alive, its melody a language spoken by the eldritch forces that had ensnared her. The air around the harp seemed to ripple with an unseen energy, a low hum that vibrated through the floor and into her bones.

Amelia's eyes were drawn to the delicate, almost impossibly thin strings, each one vibrating with a resonance that defied explanation. The music seemed to pour from the instrument, filling the chamber with a sound that was both magnificent and unnerving. It was as if the harp were playing a tune that had existed long before the world was formed—a melody that spoke of forgotten gods and ancient rites, of power and madness intertwined.

The sight of the harp, combined with the haunting melody that filled the air, left Amelia feeling both entranced and fearful. She couldn't shake the feeling that this instrument was more than just a source of music; it was a conduit, a link to the very forces she had been battling against. The beauty of the music was undeniable, but beneath it lay a sinister undertone, a whisper of something dark and dangerous that threatened to pull her deeper into the abyss.

The harp was a masterpiece of otherworldly craftsmanship, its beauty captivating and terrifying in equal measure. The dark wood of its frame was intertwined with delicate tendrils of what seemed like liquid silver, swirling and flowing through the wood as if it were alive. The intricate carvings on the frame depicted scenes of celestial bodies, spiralling galaxies, and eldritch beings, their forms entwined in a cosmic dance that defied all logic and reason. Each curve and line of the harp seemed to pulse with a rhythm of its own, as if the instrument were breathing, its essence intertwined with the very forces of the universe.

The strings, shimmering like threads of light, seemed to hum with anticipation as Amelia drew closer. They emitted a soft glow, casting ethereal patterns of light across the chamber's walls. The music they produced was unlike anything she had ever heard—notes so pure and harmonious that they resonated deep within her, stirring emotions she couldn't quite name. The sound was both achingly beautiful and deeply unsettling, like a lullaby sung by a voice that had witnessed the birth and death of stars.

As she stood mesmerized by the harp's allure, a subtle shift occurred in the room. From the dark, pulsating floor, a stool began to grow, emerging slowly as if the wood itself were alive. The stool's legs twisted and curled, mirroring the organic patterns of the harp, and the seat, smooth and inviting, seemed to be carved from the same mysterious wood. It appeared as though the very room had willed it into existence, a silent invitation for her to sit and play.

Amelia's heart raced as she stared at the stool, a mixture of fear and curiosity gnawing at her. The pull of the harp was undeniable, its music wrapping around her like a siren's call, urging her to take her place before it. The stool, with its uncanny emergence, seemed to beckon her, as if the instrument itself was asking—no, commanding—her to sit and become part of its melody.

She hesitated, a deep sense of unease settling over her. This was not a mere instrument; it was a conduit, a bridge between her world and the eldritch forces that had haunted her every step. Yet, despite the fear that gripped her, the allure of the music was too strong to resist. It called to her, a whisper in the depths of her mind, urging her to play, to become one with the haunting melody that filled the chamber.

Her fingers itched to touch the strings, to coax the beautiful, terrible music from them. She could feel the pull deep within her, a magnetic force that made it impossible to turn away. It was as if the harp had woven its melody into the very fabric of her being, and the only way to unravel it was to play. The need to touch the instrument, to feel its strings beneath her fingers, grew stronger with each passing moment, until it became an overwhelming compulsion.

Amelia took a tentative step toward the stool, her heart pounding in her chest. The music swelled, the notes wrapping around her like a cocoon, urging her onward. She knew that once she sat down, once she touched the harp, there would be no turning back. The thought both terrified and exhilarated her. This was what she had been led to, the culmination of her journey through the mansion's dark mysteries.

With a deep breath, Amelia slowly lowered herself onto the stool. The wood was warm beneath her, as if it had been waiting for her all along. Her hands hovered over the strings, trembling with anticipation and dread. She could feel the harp's energy vibrating through the air, a living force that connected her to something far greater than herself. The melody swirled around her, its haunting beauty filling every corner of the chamber, and she knew, with a certainty that chilled her to the bone, that she was meant to play.

Her fingers brushed against the strings, and in that moment, the universe seemed to hold its breath, waiting for the music that would follow.

As Amelia's fingers danced across the strings of the harp, the haunting notes that emerged resonated with the very fabric of existence, weaving together a symphony that transcended the boundaries of the physical world. The music seemed to flow through her, guided by some unseen force, and with each note, she felt herself sinking deeper into a state of calm that was both alien and strangely comforting. Unlike the chaotic and nightmarish glimpses into Amlagrar that had tormented her before, this communion through music was soothing, a tranquil journey through the cosmos.

The notes she played intertwined with the original melody, creating harmonies that echoed through the chamber and beyond. As the music filled the room, Amelia felt a deep connection to something vast and ancient, something that existed beyond the realm of her understanding. The once-fractured images that had plagued her dreams now unfolded before her in a more coherent form, revealing cosmic landscapes bathed in otherworldly light, where reality twisted and shifted like liquid. She saw swirling galaxies, endless voids, and beings of immense power whose forms defied comprehension.

As she played, the music seemed to translate the thoughts and desires of the Amlagrarian entities into something she could grasp, if only faintly. The whispers of these beings filled her mind, not as words, but as a series of alien symbols and emotions that conveyed meaning beyond language. She could sense their presence, their minds brushing against hers, sharing fragments of their knowledge and intent. The entities communicated in a language that felt ancient and forbidden.

"*Ishkaral-narun*," the voices whispered, their tones a blend of sorrow and wisdom. "*Shaelith-kaum, velothar un'dris*." The words were foreign, yet they carried a weight of meaning that she instinctively understood—'*We see you, child of the veil, and we know your struggle.*'

Flashes of ancient rituals and forgotten histories filled her mind, the knowledge of civilizations that had risen and fallen long before humanity's dawn. She saw visions of the Ebon Watchers, their shadowy forms shifting in and out of existence, their eyes like distant stars burning with unknowable intent. They were guardians and deceivers, beings who straddled the line between protector and destroyer.

"*Karesh-na, Melanor*," the voices sang through the music, their tones soothing yet unsettling. "*Valaerith thol, ka'maror naruvalis*." The phrase twisted in her mind, leaving her with a sense of awe and dread—'*The path is dark, and the end is ever-changing.*'

The more she played, the deeper the communion became. The boundaries between her consciousness and the Amlagrarian entities blurred, and she felt as if she were becoming one with the music, with the very essence of the cosmos. Her fingers moved of their own accord, plucking the strings in a pattern that felt predestined as if the harp itself was guiding her to reveal secrets buried deep within the fabric of reality.

In the midst of this communion, Amelia felt a sense of peace, a calm that had eluded her for so long. The images that had once terrified her now seemed like pieces of a puzzle, a grand design that was slowly being revealed. The chaotic madness that had threatened to consume her was still present, but it was tempered by the understanding that came with the music. The whispers of the Amlagrarian entities were no longer incomprehensible babble, but a language she was beginning to grasp, a language of the cosmos, of the infinite.

The communion was not without its dangers, though. As she played, she felt her sanity teetering on the edge, the sheer weight of the knowledge she was receiving threatening to overwhelm her. But the music anchored her, guiding her through the storm of thoughts and visions, offering her a path through the madness. She was no longer merely a witness to the horrors of Amlagrar; she was a participant, a part of the cosmic dance that played out across the eons.

The entities continued to whisper, their voices weaving through the music:

"*Elarish korvanth, saerath un'drael.*" A command, a warning—'*Beware the cracking, for the walls grow thin.*'

As the final notes of the melody echoed through the chamber, Amelia felt a profound sense of exhaustion, as if she had glimpsed into the heart of the universe and come back forever changed. The music faded, leaving her in a silence that felt both peaceful and heavy with the knowledge she had gained. She had communed with the forces that lay beyond the veil, and though the experience had left her shaken, it had also granted her a deeper understanding of the cosmic forces she was up against.

She remained seated before the harp, her hands still resting on the strings, her mind reeling from the communion. The echoes of the Amlagrarian voices lingered in her thoughts, their cryptic messages seared into her memory. She knew that this encounter was just the beginning, that the path ahead would only grow darker and more treacherous. But for now, she allowed herself a moment of peace, a brief respite in the eye of the storm, as the weight of the cosmic knowledge settled into her soul.

As the final note lingered in the air and dissolved into silence, the weight of the moment pressed down on Amelia. The sudden absence of the music was jarring as if the universe itself had drawn a breath and held it, leaving her suspended in a void where time no longer seemed to exist. The silence was profound, wrapping around her like a shroud, isolating her from everything familiar.

Amelia's hands hovered above the strings of the harp, trembling with the residual energy of the communion. Her mind was a maelstrom of thoughts and images, fragments of the universe that she had glimpsed through the music. The memories of the melodies, the cosmic landscapes, and the Amlagrarian whispers were already beginning to fade, slipping away like sand through her fingers. She reached for them, desperate to hold on to the knowledge she had gained, but they eluded her, dissolving into the ether.

In the wake of those fading memories, a terrifying emptiness began to take hold. Her sense of self, once so firmly rooted in the struggles and experiences of her life, now felt fragile and insubstantial. Who was she? The question echoed through her mind, reverberating off the walls of her consciousness, yet no answer came. The more she tried to grasp her identity, the more it slipped away, like breath on a mirror, vanishing without a trace.

Her memories, the anchors of her existence, began to unravel. Faces of loved ones blurred, names lost their meaning, and the events of her life became distant echoes, almost as if they had happened to someone else. The certainty of who she was—Amelia, the heir of the Vandercliffe mansion, the seeker of truth—dissolved into the infinite vastness that she had glimpsed. In the grand tapestry of the universe, her life seemed insignificant, a mere thread in a fabric that stretched across time and space.

She had seen the universe, and in doing so, she had lost herself. The cosmos had revealed its secrets to her, but the price of that knowledge was her own identity. The boundaries that separated her from the vastness beyond had crumbled, leaving her adrift in a sea of stars and cosmic forces that she could barely comprehend. She was no longer Amelia, not in the way she had been before. The music had changed her, had unmade and remade her in the image of something ancient and unfathomable.

And so she sat there, alone in the chamber, the silence pressing in on her as the last vestiges of her former self slipped away. The question lingered on her lips, a whisper in the darkness: "Who am I?" But the answer, if there was one, was lost in the void, swallowed by the infinite expanse of space that now seemed to stretch out before her, vast and indifferent. Amelia's sense of self faded into the cosmic abyss, leaving her as a mere echo of what she had once been, a whisper lost among the stars.

Ezekiel's voice cut through the thick silence, laced with an urgency that startled Amelia. "You've communed with the Ebon Watchers Amelia. Do you realize what you've done? You've tapped into forces that even the most seasoned of us fear to approach."

Amelia, still reeling from the otherworldly encounter, struggled to steady herself. Her mind buzzed with the fragments of cosmic knowledge the Ebon Watchers had shared with her. "They showed me things, Ezekiel... things that defy explanation. They spoke to me, told me truths that—" Her voice trembled, unable to fully articulate the magnitude of what she had experienced.

Ezekiel's expression darkened, his usual calm demeanour replaced by something more intense, almost desperate. "No," he interrupted, his voice uncharacteristically sharp. "You mustn't trust them. The Ebon Watchers are masters of deception, weaving lies into half-truths to ensnare those who seek their wisdom. Their intentions are not to be trusted."

Amelia's gaze narrowed, her earlier suspicions resurfacing with renewed vigour. The defensiveness in Ezekiel's tone, the fear in his eyes—it all felt wrong. She recalled the image she had seen in the book, the one that eerily resembled him. A chill ran down her spine as the pieces began to align in her mind. Why is he so afraid? she wondered. What is he hiding?

"Why should I believe you?" she asked, her voice tinged with suspicion. "How do I know you're not the one deceiving me? You've guided me, yes, but to what end? I saw your likeness in that old tome, Ezekiel, among the cult members. Who are you really? What are your true intentions?"

Ezekiel's eyes flickered, a shadow of something unreadable passing over his face before he quickly masked it. "Amelia, the path you're on is fraught with danger. The Ebon Watchers will try to twist your mind, make you doubt everything you know. You must resist their influence, or risk losing yourself completely."

But his words did little to quell the storm of doubt swirling within her. The seeds of mistrust had already been sown, and Amelia could no longer ignore the nagging feeling that something was amiss. The Ebon Watchers had shown her truths, yes, but they had also planted questions—questions that Ezekiel seemed all too eager to dismiss.

As she stared at him, the haunting melody from the chamber still echoing in her mind, Amelia realized that her journey was far from over. But now, it wasn't just the Amlagrarian forces she had to contend with. The man who had been her guide, her anchor in the midst of the chaos, was now a puzzle she had to unravel.

'Who is Ezekiel really?' she thought, her resolve hardening. 'And whose side is he truly on?'

XIV. Entwined Fates

After the events with the harp, Amelia found herself unable to escape the haunting melody that had filled the chamber. The notes lingered in her mind, twisting and turning until they became an integral part of her thoughts. They were more than just music—they were a gateway, an entry point into the unknown. Each night, as she closed her eyes, the melody would return, wrapping itself around her like a silken thread, pulling her deeper into the labyrinth of her own psyche.

The dreams began subtly, almost gently at first. The music would drift into her subconscious, a soothing lullaby that led her into vast, shadowy landscapes. In these early dreams, Amelia would find herself wandering through strange, mist-covered fields where the boundaries of reality seemed fluid and malleable. She saw glimpses of cosmic truths, images of distant worlds, and celestial beings that whispered secrets just beyond her understanding.

But with each passing night, the dreams grew more intense, more vivid. The landscapes she wandered became darker, more oppressive as if the very fabric of reality was beginning to unravel around her. The once soothing melody transformed into something more sinister, a discordant symphony that seemed to mock her with its beauty. The deeper she ventured into these dreams, the more she realized that they were not simply visions—they were another reality, one that existed alongside her waking life, intertwining with it in ways she couldn't fully comprehend.

As she delved deeper, Amelia began to uncover fragments of knowledge— pieces of an ancient puzzle that slowly began to take shape in her mind. She learned of the Amlagrarian beings, of the rifts between dimensions, and the cosmic entities that sought to breach the veil of reality. These revelations came with a price, however, for each new truth she uncovered brought with it a corresponding nightmare.

In one dream, Amelia found herself standing on the edge of an abyss, the darkness below her teeming with unseen horrors. The air was thick with a sulphurous stench, and the ground beneath her feet seemed to pulse with a malicious energy. As she peered into the void, she saw the outlines of writhing forms—serpentine beings with too many eyes and too many limbs, their bodies shifting and changing as they moved. They reached out to her, their twisted forms wriggling toward her with a hunger that chilled her to the bone. She awoke with a scream, the feeling of those countless eyes still upon her, watching, waiting.

In another, she stood beneath a sky that was not a sky, but a churning sea of stars and galaxies. The constellations above her twisted and writhed as if alive, their forms rearranging themselves into grotesque shapes that defied reason. She could feel the weight of eternity pressing down upon her, the knowledge of countless eons flooding her mind. The sheer vastness of it all threatened to overwhelm her, drowning her in the realization of her own insignificance. It was as if the universe itself was trying to consume her, to erase her from existence.

These dreams were not just figments of her imagination—they were glimpses into the true nature of the cosmos, into the eery forces that lay just beyond the veil of her understanding. And with each night, the boundary between dream and reality grew thinner, until Amelia was no longer sure where one ended and the other began.

The nightmares became more intense, more terrifying. The music, once a guide, became a tormentor, leading her deeper into the darkness of her own mind. She would find herself in labyrinthine corridors that twisted and turned in impossible ways, the walls closing in around her as she desperately searched for an escape. The air was thick with the stench of decay, and the floor beneath her feet squelched with each step as if she were walking through a mire of blood and gore.

At times, she found herself pursued by shadowy figures—creatures that seemed to be made of the very darkness that surrounded her. Their eyes glowed with a sickly, unnatural light, and their elongated limbs moved with a fluidity that defied logic. They whispered her name in voices that echoed in her mind, filling her with a sense of dread so profound that it felt as if her very soul was being torn apart.

As the days turned into weeks, Amelia became more and more consumed by these dreams. The knowledge she gained was immense, but the cost was high. Her mind was fraying at the edges, her sense of self slowly eroding with each passing night. She could no longer distinguish between her waking life and the nightmares that plagued her sleep. The visions were all-consuming, filling her mind with images of horrors beyond comprehension.

The melody that had once been her guide had now become her tormentor, leading her deeper into the darkness with each passing night. She was trapped in a cycle of fear and discovery, each new revelation bringing with it a corresponding nightmare. And through it all, the eye watched her, its gaze ever-present, a constant reminder of the power she had unleashed and the price she would pay for seeking the truth.

Amelia knew that she was teetering on the edge of madness, that the line between reality and nightmare was becoming increasingly blurred. But she was driven by an insatiable need to understand, to uncover the secrets that lay hidden in the darkness. Even as the nightmares grew more terrifying, she continued to delve deeper, unable to resist the pull of the melody and the knowledge it promised to reveal.

Amelia stood on the edge of an unfathomable void, a darkness so complete and all-consuming that it seemed to swallow even the concept of light. The ground beneath her feet was soft and yielding, like a darkened cloud, as if she were suspended in the very fabric of the universe itself. There was no horizon, no sense of space or distance—just an endless expanse of shadow that stretched on for eternity in every direction. The air was thick and heavy, oppressive with a silence that was more profound than anything she had ever experienced. It was as if sound itself had been devoured by the abyss, leaving her isolated in a realm where even the echoes of thought were stifled.

As she stood on the precipice of this vast, unknowable void, Amelia felt the weight of infinity pressing down on her, a crushing awareness of her own insignificance in the face of such cosmic immensity. The darkness was not merely an absence of light; it was a presence, a living, breathing entity that watched her with unseen eyes, waiting for her to make a move.

Involuntarily, her lips formed the words that had haunted her since she first encountered the eldritch forces: "Dro'ga'rath."

The moment the phrase slipped from her tongue, the world around her shuddered, the shadows drawing closer as if awakened by the forbidden incantation. The void began to pulse and ripple, the darkness swirling and undulating like a living thing, gathering itself into something more tangible, more terrifying.

Slowly, the swirling shadows coalesced, taking shape before her eyes. A single, colossal form began to emerge from the depths, its outline barely discernible against the all-consuming blackness. The shape grew larger, expanding until it filled her entire field of vision, a presence so vast that it seemed to encompass the very essence of the void itself.

And then she saw it—the eye.

It was incomprehensibly massive, a cosmic eye that hung in the void like a celestial body. Its shape was reminiscent of a cat's eye, but far larger, far more terrifying than anything she could have imagined. The eye's surface was a swirling maelstrom of colours, shifting and blending together in ways that defied logic. Deep purples and midnight blues bled into inky blacks and sickly greens, creating a hypnotic pattern that seemed to draw her in, pulling her closer to the very heart of the void.

The eye's pupil was a vertical slit, glowing with an unearthly light that pierced through the darkness. It was a deep, molten gold, with flecks of crimson and silver swirling within it, as if the fires of creation and destruction were contained within that single, narrow gaze. The light from the pupil cast an eerie, flickering glow across the void, illuminating the darkness in a way that only made it seem deeper, more impenetrable.

Amelia was paralysed with awe and terror as she stared at the eye, unable to tear her gaze away. It was impossible to perceive the edges of the eye, to determine where it began and where it ended. It was as if the eye was the void, and the void was the eye—a singular, omnipotent entity that existed beyond the boundaries of time and space.

But the eye was not looking at her. At first, it gazed off into the infinite distance, as if searching for something far beyond her comprehension. The sense of anticipation was palpable, the air vibrating with the tension of something vast and ancient stirring within the void. The eye's surface rippled and shifted, the colours swirling faster, more chaotically, as if responding to some unseen force.

Then, slowly, deliberately, the eye began to turn.

Amelia's breath caught in her throat as the pupil narrowed, focusing in on her with a precision that felt like a dagger being driven into her soul. The eye's gaze was not just a look—it was an invasion, a violation of her very essence.

She felt as though every secret, every thought, every memory she had ever held was being laid bare before this colossal, omniscient eye.

The closer it turned toward her, the more the world around her seemed to compress, the darkness closing in on her from all sides. The air grew colder, the silence more deafening, as if the entire universe was holding its breath in anticipation of what was to come.

Finally, the eye locked onto her, its gaze boring into her with an intensity that made her entire body tremble. The pupil, now fully dilated, glowed with a terrifying brilliance, and the colours on the eye's surface churned violently, as though a storm was raging within it. The sense of power, of overwhelming presence, was suffocating. Amelia felt as though she were standing before a god—a being of such unimaginable might that her very existence was insignificant in comparison.

And then, from deep within the shadows of the void, a low, rumbling growl began to build. It was a sound that seemed to emanate from the eye itself, a primal, guttural noise that reverberated through the very fabric of reality. The growl grew louder, more intense, until it became a roar that shook the void, causing the darkness to tremble and pulse with each deafening note.

Amelia's heart raced as the growl reached its peak, the sound so powerful that it felt as though the universe itself was on the verge of tearing apart. The eye's gaze never wavered; its pupil locked onto her with a ferocity that threatened to consume her entirely. The darkness around her pulsed in time with the growl, the very air vibrating with the force of the sound.

Just as she felt she could take no more, the vision shattered. The void collapsed in on itself, the eye and the growl disappearing into nothingness as suddenly as they had appeared. Amelia was left standing in a vast emptiness, her heart pounding in her chest, her mind reeling from the encounter.

The silence that followed was absolute, a void of its own that filled the space where the eye had been. Amelia gasped for breath, her lungs burning as though she had been holding her breath for an eternity. The sense of dread lingered, the memory of the eye's gaze seared into her mind.

She woke with a start, her body drenched in sweat, the echoes of the growl still reverberating in her ears. The terror of the encounter clung to her, the image of the colossal eye forever etched into her consciousness. She knew that this was not just a dream—it was a warning, a glimpse into the unimaginable power that lay just beyond the veil of reality.

Amelia lay in bed, trembling, as the darkness of the night closed in around her. The knowledge that she had spoken the forbidden words, that she had summoned the gaze of something far beyond her understanding, weighed heavily on her. The universe had looked back at her, and she knew that it was not finished with her yet.

Amelia lay in bed, her body trembling and drenched in sweat, the terror from her encounter with the colossal eye still clinging to her like a second skin. Every beat of her heart reverberated in her ears, the sound of the growl echoing in her mind, refusing to fade. Her breath came in ragged gasps as she tried to piece together what had just happened, but the more she tried to make sense of it, the more elusive the answers became.

'Dro'ga'rath.' The word echoed through her thoughts like a curse, a dark and sinister presence that tainted everything it touched. She couldn't shake the feeling that the very act of uttering it had torn open a wound in reality, a wound that now bled into her dreams and waking moments alike. But what was it? A name? A place? A spell? The questions swirled around her mind, each one more urgent than the last, but the answers seemed just out of reach, hidden in the shadows that lurked at the edges of her consciousness.

She had read of ancient incantations, of words of power that could bend reality, but this—this felt different. *'Dro'ga'rath'* wasn't just a word; it was a presence, a force that existed beyond human comprehension. The way it had slipped from her lips, unbidden, as though it had been lying in wait, waiting for the right moment to escape—it sent chills down her spine. What had she called upon? What being had she awakened with those cursed syllables?

The memory of the eye haunted her. Its sheer size, its impossible existence in that void, its gaze that had felt like it could strip away her very soul—it was more than just a vision. It was a message, a warning from something ancient and malevolent, something that had noticed her presence, something that had decided to take an interest in her. The way it had looked at her, with an intensity that left her feeling exposed and vulnerable, as if she were nothing more than an insect beneath a magnifying glass—she couldn't shake the image from her mind.

And then there was the noise. That growl, deep and resonant, like the sound of the earth itself groaning under the weight of some terrible force. It had been more than just a sound—it had been a feeling, a vibration that had penetrated her bones and rattled her soul. What could have made such a noise? What kind of creature, what kind of entity, had the power to produce a sound that could shake the very fabric of reality? And why had it come in response to 'Dro'ga'rath'?

Amelia's thoughts spiralled further into confusion and fear. Every answer she considered only led to more questions, each more terrifying than the last. She had crossed a line, that much was certain. She had delved into forces that were not meant to be understood, into mysteries that were better left unsolved. But now, there was no turning back. She had awakened something, and it was only a matter of time before it came for her.

'Why does this word feel so wrong'? she wondered, her mind racing as she tried to grasp the enormity of what she had done. 'What kind of power have I unleashed'? The more she thought about it, the more she realized that 'Dro'ga'rath' was more than just a name or a phrase—it was a key, a gateway to something far more sinister and ancient than she could comprehend. And now that gateway had been opened, she could feel its influence creeping into her life, twisting her thoughts, distorting her reality.

She knew she was in danger, but from what, she couldn't say. The eye, the growl, the void—each was a piece of a larger puzzle, one that she was now a part of whether she liked it or not. She had no idea what awaited her, but she knew it was coming, drawn by the word she had spoken. was it a catalyst? a trigger that had set events in motion? Was she now caught in its wake?

As she lay there in the darkness, her mind racing, Amelia knew one thing for certain—this was only the beginning. The eye, the growl, the entity that lay behind it all—they were watching her, waiting for the right moment to strike. And as much as she wanted to turn back, to undo the words she had spoken, she knew there was no escaping the path she had set herself on. The truth she sought was now entangled with forces far beyond her control, and it was only a matter of time before those forces consumed her completely.

She had glimpsed into the abyss, and the abyss had stared back. Now, the only question that remained was how much of her soul it would take before it was satisfied.

XV. The Suffering Veil

Amelia's world had been unraveling, thread by thread, ever since she first set foot in the Vandercliffe Estate. The visions, the nightmares, the cryptic whispers that followed her every step—at first, they seemed like clues guiding her toward the truth, like a twisted puzzle she was meant to solve. But as the days wore on, and the line between reality and nightmare blurred, she began to feel the suffocating presence of something far more sinister at play.

Standing in the dimly lit library, surrounded by the dusty tomes that had become her only source of guidance, a creeping realization began to take hold. The pattern of events, the way every step seemed to lead her deeper into the darkness, began to feel too deliberate, too orchestrated. It was as if an unseen hand had been guiding her from the very beginning, pushing her toward a predetermined end. The more she thought about it, the more she couldn't shake the feeling that she had been walking straight into a trap.

And then there was Ezekiel.

From the moment he appeared, his enigmatic presence had been both a comfort and a cause for suspicion. At first, his cryptic knowledge and calm demeanour had been a beacon in the chaos, a guiding light in the storm of madness that surrounded her. But lately, something had changed. Amelia couldn't put her finger on it, but there was a shift in his behaviour, a subtle change in his tone that set her on edge. He had become more guarded, more evasive as if he were hiding something from her. His words, once reassuring, now seemed to carry a hidden menace, a threat that lurked just beneath the surface.

The discovery of the ancient tome had only deepened her suspicions. As she pored over the pages of dark rituals and forbidden knowledge, she stumbled upon an illustration that sent a chill down her spine—a figure that looked disturbingly like Ezekiel, cloaked in shadow, standing among the cultists of the Obsidian Veil. The resemblance was uncanny, and as she studied the image, a gnawing sense of dread settled in the pit of her stomach. Why had he been depicted here, in this book that detailed the sinister deeds of a long-forgotten cult? How was it possible that he could have been involved in events that took place centuries ago?

The more she tried to find answers, the more questions seemed to arise. Who was Ezekiel, really? What was his true purpose in guiding her through this nightmare? The thought gnawed at her relentlessly, even as she tried to focus on the task at hand. She couldn't help but study the image over and over again, searching for any clue that might explain why he was here, in this time, with her.

Ezekiel entered the room, his presence filling the space with an ominous tension. There was something different about him, something that made the hairs on the back of her neck stand on end. His movements were deliberate, calculated, as if each step was part of a carefully orchestrated plan. The air around him seemed to thicken, charged with an unseen force that set her nerves on edge.

"Amelia," he began, his voice smooth but laced with an undercurrent of something darker. "You've come so far. You've unravelled mysteries that have remained hidden for centuries, delved into secrets that most wouldn't dare to even contemplate. But tell me, why have you truly come here?"

Amelia's heart raced as she swallowed hard. "I received a letter... a letter from my Great Aunt Eleanor. It spoke of secrets and... the key that just appeared out of nowhere."

Ezekiel's eyes glimmered with something unsettling, a predatory interest. "A key, you say? Curious how these things manifest, isn't it? Almost as if they're drawn to you, just as I was." He leaned closer, a sly smile curling his lips. "What did you think the key unlocked?"

Her breath caught in her throat, the pieces beginning to click into place. "You... you're saying it's connected to you?"

"Connected? Perhaps more like orchestrated," he replied, his voice dropping to a conspiratorial whisper. "You've been following a path laid before you, one I crafted with exquisite care. Each vision, every haunting nightmare— merely threads in a tapestry I wove just for you."

A chill swept through her as dread seeped into her bones. "But I thought you were helping me."

"Helping?" he echoed, the word dripping with malice. "Ah, but your journey was never meant to be a simple guide. You've played your role so beautifully, unravelling the truth I wished you to discover. The key? I planted it right where you would find it. Each torment you faced? My design, my invitation to delve deeper into the abyss."

Her stomach churned as the realization settled like lead in her chest. "Why? Why would you do this to me?"

Ezekiel's smile widened, a grotesque reflection of satisfaction. "Because, dear Amelia, your suffering is the catalyst for something far greater. I needed you to be stripped bare, to feel the weight of despair. Only then could you truly understand what lies beyond the veil."

Amelia felt the walls close in around her, the air thickening with his dark intent. "You're a monster... you've manipulated me!"

"Monster?" He laughed softly, the sound a cruel caress against her skin. "No, Amelia. I am merely the architect of your awakening. Embrace it, for the true horror has yet to unfold."

Ezekiel's expression hardened, his eyes narrowing with a predatory gleam. "Monster, you say?" His voice was a chilling whisper. "Because you are the key, Amelia. Not just the key you found, but the key to a ritual that will grant me power beyond imagination. You've been a vessel, a means to an end. Your mind needed to be fractured, your spirit weakened, to make you susceptible to the ritual's influence."

Amelia recoiled, her mind struggling to process the horror of his words. "You used me... manipulated me... for your own gain?"

Ezekiel stepped closer, his presence overwhelming, suffocating. "You were always destined for this, Amelia. From the moment you set foot in this mansion, your fate was sealed. I've been preparing you, guiding you to this moment, where you would be ready to serve your true purpose. You see, every trial, every torment was meticulously designed to lead you here, to this critical juncture."

The room seemed to close in around her, the walls pressing in, the air thick with the weight of Ezekiel's revelation. "What is this ritual? What are you planning to do to me?"

Ezekiel's smile widened, a grotesque parody of kindness. "The ritual is ancient, powerful beyond comprehension. It requires a vessel, one who has

[158]

been broken, who has been touched by the forces that lie beyond the veil of reality. That vessel is you, Amelia. You will be the catalyst, the one who will open the gateway and allow the Amlagrarian powers to flood into our world."

"No..." Amelia whispered, backing away, her heart hammering in her chest. "No, I won't let you."

Ezekiel's gaze was unrelenting, his tone becoming a sinister purr. "You may try to resist, but the threads of fate are already woven, and you are but a part of the tapestry. The ritual will proceed, and you will fulfil your purpose, whether you accept it or not."

The weight of Ezekiel's revelation crashed down on Amelia like a tidal wave of dread, each word sinking deeper into her psyche. The fear that gripped her was visceral, clawing at her chest, constricting her breathing. Her heart pounded so fiercely she thought it might burst. Her vision tunnelled, the edges darkening as the enormity of her situation sank in. Her legs felt leaden, and her breath came in ragged gasps as her mind raced through a haze of horror and disbelief.

Panic surged through her, propelling her to action. She turned to flee, her body moving on pure instinct. But Ezekiel, with an unnatural swiftness, was already there. He materialized in front of her with a malevolent grin, his eyes gleaming with an unholy light. The very air seemed to thicken, making each movement feel like wading through molasses.

Amelia's mind reeled, and she swung her arm desperately, grabbing anything within reach—an old vase, a heavy book. She hurled them at him with frantic, trembling hands, but Ezekiel's movements were too fluid, too precise. Each object was deflected or caught effortlessly, as if he were merely playing a dark game. Her attempts to fend him off were futile, the strength she mustered collapsing against his impenetrable presence.

Desperation fueled her struggle, but Ezekiel's smile only widened, an expression of twisted pleasure. He advanced on her with a menacing calmness. Amelia's heart pounded violently as she tried to strike at him, her blows landing weakly and ineffectually. In her frantic state, she barely registered his movements, his eyes reflecting an almost sadistic delight as he watched her futile attempts.

Without warning, Ezekiel's hand lashed out with a lightning-fast strike. The impact was brutal, sending Amelia crashing to the floor. Pain exploded in her head, a sharp, blinding agony that blurred her vision. The room spun around her as darkness encroached, her limbs feeling heavy and unresponsive.

She struggled to focus, to move, but her strength was sapped, her body betraying her. Ezekiel loomed over her, his silhouette casting an ominous shadow. The last thing she saw before consciousness slipped away was his face, an expression of cold triumph etched into his features, his eyes burning with a sinister satisfaction.

As the darkness enveloped her, Amelia's final, desperate thoughts were consumed by the overwhelming dread of what was to come.

When Amelia awoke, her vision was a jumbled blur of shapes and colors, her head throbbing with every pulse. The room slowly came into focus, revealing a nightmarish reality far removed from the library. She was sprawled on a cold, stone altar, the unyielding surface sending a jolt of discomfort through her body. Her wrists and ankles were bound by thick, coarse straps, the rough material cutting into her skin with a relentless pressure that left her feeling both confined and exposed.

The room was dimly lit, the weak, flickering glow of candles casting long, trembling shadows that danced grotesquely along the walls. Each candle was encased in an ornate, tarnished holder, their flames sputtering as if struggling to maintain their feeble light. The shadows they cast moved like living entities, elongating and contracting in a way that seemed almost to mock her helplessness.

The stone walls were scarred and uneven, etched with ancient, faded symbols that twisted into inscrutable shapes. The surface of the walls was streaked with dark stains, some of which looked disturbingly fresh, suggesting a long history of ritualistic activity. The floor, too, was cold and uneven, littered with remnants of past ceremonies: scraps of parchment, old incense ash, and what looked like dried blood.

A thick, oppressive cloud of incense hung in the air, its heavy, cloying aroma mixing with the sharp, metallic scent of blood. The incense smoke curled and coiled in slow, languid spirals, filling her nostrils with its sickly sweet fragrance. It was overwhelming, almost suffocating, creating a stifling atmosphere that added to her sense of dread.

Amelia's attire was minimal and unsettling—a ritualistic garment of dark, tattered fabric that barely covered her chest and nether regions. The material was coarse and rough, offering little protection against the chill of the stone altar and the oppressive atmosphere of the room. Her body felt cold and vulnerable, the garment doing little to shield her from the penetrating chill and the psychological torment of her predicament.

Everywhere she looked, the room seemed to conspire against her, the dim light and the pervasive stench amplifying her fear and disorientation. The straps binding her were thick and unforgiving, their coarse texture digging into her skin with each futile struggle. Amelia's breathing was rapid and shallow, her heart pounding erratically as she attempted to come to grips with the horrifying reality of her confinement.

Amelia struggled against her bonds, her heart pounding wildly as panic surged through her. Each desperate attempt to free herself only tightened the grip of the coarse straps, which cut into her skin with a cruel bite. The stone altar beneath her was unforgiving, its cold, hard surface a constant reminder of her helplessness. Her struggles were met with the unyielding resistance of the straps, which held her in place with a relentless, suffocating grip.

The room, dim and oppressive, seemed to close in around her, amplifying the sound of her labored breathing and frantic movements. The only other sounds were the soft, ominous echoes of footsteps reverberating through the chamber. Each step was deliberate, resonating through the cold, stone walls, adding to the mounting dread that clutched at her chest.

From the shadows emerged Ezekiel, his presence as commanding as it was menacing. He moved with a predatory grace, his face set in an expression of cold determination. His eyes, sharp and gleaming, locked onto hers with an unsettling intensity. He was dressed in a dark, ceremonial robe, its fabric heavy and flowing, adorned with arcane symbols that seemed to pulse with a faint, eerie light. The robe's deep black hue contrasted starkly with the flickering candlelight, enhancing his ominous aura.

In one hand, Ezekiel held a dagger, its blade catching the dim light and reflecting it with a sinister gleam. The dagger's handle was intricately carved, the metal cool and deadly. In his other hand, he carried a tome bound in black leather, its cover embossed with cryptic, shadowy patterns that hinted at forbidden knowledge.

"It's time, Amelia," he said, his voice devoid of emotion, each word dripping with cold finality. "The ritual will commence, and you will fulfill your destiny."

"No!" she screamed, her voice raw with terror and defiance. She thrashed against her restraints with renewed vigor, the straps digging deeper into her flesh. "You can't do this! You can't use me like this!"

The sound of her cries echoed through the chamber, mingling with the ominous silence that followed. Ezekiel's gaze remained unwavering, a cruel smile playing at the edges of his lips as he prepared to enact the dark rites that would seal her fate.

Ezekiel opened the tome with a deliberate motion, the black leather cover creaking softly as he revealed the ancient, brittle pages within. His voice, steady and resonant, began to chant in a guttural, alien language. The words were thick with a foreboding cadence, each syllable dripping with dark intent. The language seemed to wriggle and writhe in the air, its resonance sending shivers down Amelia's spine.

"Zhul-kara, fal'athul melek," he intoned, the rhythm of his voice rising and falling like the tide of an unseen ocean. *"Koth'laz sh'rauthan, vael'thar vorzul!"*

As the chant grew louder and more insistent, the symbols carved into the stone floor began to glow with an unearthly light, pulsating in time with his words. The room was bathed in a sickly, green luminescence that flickered like the last gasps of a dying flame, casting grotesque shadows on the walls. The very air felt charged with a dark energy, thrumming with the promise of what was to come.

Ezekiel stepped closer to the altar, his face a mask of fervent anticipation, the dagger poised above Amelia's chest. "This is the moment, Amelia. The moment when the veil will be torn, and the forces of Amlagrar will be unleashed," he declared, his voice rising to a fever pitch. "Your sacrifice will open the gateway, and I will be the one to command their power."

Amelia's heart raced, a frantic drumbeat of fear echoing in her ears. She struggled against the bonds, her mind racing as she searched for a way out, but the futility of her efforts only deepened her despair. There was no escape, no way to halt the ritual that was already in motion. She could only watch in horror as Ezekiel raised the dagger high, his eyes gleaming with a manic hunger for power.

As he lowered the blade toward her, the air around them crackled with energy. With a swift, practiced motion, he brought the dagger down, carving the symbols from the tome into her flesh. *"Kha'turash! Shal'zhul arai!"* he chanted, his voice a twisted symphony of fervour and malice.

The sharp blade pierced her skin, a jolt of pain that sent her mind spiralling into chaos. The symbols glowed with a brilliant, sickly light as they were etched into her body, each incision igniting a fresh wave of agony that rippled through her. The chanting continued, resonating in the air, entwining with the blood that began to flow from her wounds.

"Zhul-krath, vorl'nash arakai! Nyla'thak sh'rauthan!" Ezekiel continued, his voice rising, echoing off the cold stone walls like a malevolent chorus. Each chant fueled the dark energy surging around them, amplifying the terror clawing at Amelia's sanity.

In that moment, as the blade descended toward her once more, the pain became a backdrop to the sheer horror of the ritual, fracturing her mind. The last remnants of her sanity slipped away, consumed by the terror of what was to come, leaving her adrift in a sea of darkness and despair as the symbols carved into her skin pulsed with the power of the ritual, each heartbeat a countdown to her fate.

XVI. Cosmic Descent

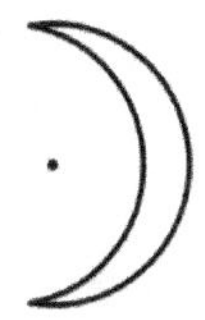

As Ezekiel continued the ritual, the air in the room grew thick with a palpable static, as if the very atmosphere was charged with ancient, forbidden power. Each symbol he carved into Amelia's skin was intricate, a series of curves and lines that seemed to pulsate with energy. The blade, cold and sharp, traced patterns that felt like they were being etched not just onto her body, but into the very essence of her being. The pain was excruciating, yet it was nothing compared to the terror of knowing that each mark brought her closer to an irreversible fate.

The room seemed to close in around her, the walls themselves appearing to pulse with a sinister life of their own. As Ezekiel's chants grew louder, the air crackled with energy, the atmosphere heavy and oppressive. The flickering candles cast eerie shadows that danced across the walls, the light twisting into grotesque shapes that mirrored the dark incantations.

As Amelia lay bound on the cold, stone altar, the environment outside mirrored the dark ritual unfolding within the mansion's desecrated walls. The sky had turned an ominous shade of deep indigo, heavy clouds swirling in a chaotic dance high above. Each roll of thunder reverberated with a sinister resonance, as if the very heavens were voicing their disapproval of the profane ceremonies below.

Lightning forked through the sky, a network of brilliant, white-hot veins that split the darkness with unforgiving precision. The room was intermittently bathed in their ghastly light, casting long, menacing shadows that danced along the walls and crept towards Amelia like spectral fingers reaching out from the beyond.

The air outside grew thick with the electric charge of the storm, the atmosphere tense and charged with an impending sense of dread. Leaves and branches thrashed violently in the wind, as if trying to escape the malevolent energy emanating from the estate. The sounds of the storm—howling wind, the persistent drumming of rain against the windowpanes, the occasional crack of thunder—created a symphony of chaos that perfectly accompanied Ezekiel's incantations.

Each word he chanted seemed to pull more energy from the storm, the elements themselves responding to the call of the ancient language spoken by a voice that was not quite human. The storm intensified, the sky an ever-shifting canvas of darkness punctuated by the blinding stabs of lightning, mirroring the crescendo of the dark ritual reaching its peak inside.

The room filled with an electric tension, a sense of impending doom that was almost tangible. Amelia could feel the power of the ritual building, the air vibrating as if it were about to tear apart. The symbols on her skin seemed to glow with a malevolent light, each one a connection to the dark forces Ezekiel sought to unleash.

The environment surrounding the ritual was charged with a palpable, sinister energy. As the storm raged outside, the room inside seemed to pulse with a life of its own. The wind howled against the ancient stone walls of the mansion, its mournful cry weaving through the cracks and crevices, carrying with it a cold, damp air that chilled to the bone.

Thunder roared with relentless ferocity, a deep and omnipresent rumble that seemed to shake the very foundation of the house. It rolled over the landscape in waves, each peal louder and more menacing than the last, echoing the dark power summoned by the ritual.

The lightning, now striking with unnerving precision, illuminated the room in stark, intermittent bursts. With each flash, the shadows in the room twisted and contorted into grotesque shapes. These shadows, thrown by the flickering candlelight and the erratic lightning, appeared to move of their own volition. They stretched across the walls and floor, elongating and twisting into forms that suggested lurking figures and twisted faces, as if the darkness itself was alive and reacting to the incantations.

These living shadows pulsed with the rhythm of Ezekiel's chants, growing more agitated and distinct with each verse of the ancient tongue. It was as though the shadows were feeding off the energy of the storm and the ritual, gaining strength and presence from the dark forces at play. Their movements became more deliberate, a sinister ballet of dark forms that danced along the periphery of vision, always just out of clear sight, yet unmistakably there—watching, waiting.

The air in the room grew heavier, charged with a static electricity that made the skin tingle and the hair stand on end. The atmosphere was thick with the smell of ozone, a sharp, clean scent that belied the dark, corrupt magic that filled the space. The combination of the oppressive atmosphere, the violent weather, and the eerie, animate shadows created a sense of dread that was almost tangible, a foreboding that suggested that the boundaries between worlds were thinning dangerously under the weight of the ritual's power.

Amidst the chaos of the storm and the ritual, Amelia's heart raced with fear and desperation. She knew she had to find a way to stop Ezekiel, to break free from the chains that bound her both physically and spiritually. But the pain, the overwhelming power of the ritual, and the oppressive atmosphere seemed to crush her will, making even the thought of resistance seem like an impossible dream.

Yet, even as despair threatened to overwhelm her, Amelia clung to the spark of defiance that still burned within her. She could not, would not, allow herself to be used as a tool for destruction. With every fibre of her being, she fought against the dark tide that sought to sweep her away, her spirit battling the forces that threatened to consume her.

As another bolt of lightning illuminated the room, Amelia's eyes caught a glimpse of something—a weakness in her bindings, a small, overlooked flaw. Her heart leapt with a mix of hope and fear. This might be her only chance, her only opportunity to break free and put an end to Ezekiel's dark ambitions.

Gathering all the strength she could muster, Amelia began to work at her bindings, her movements slow and careful to avoid drawing Ezekiel's attention. Outside, the storm raged on, a wild symphony of thunder and lightning that mirrored the turmoil in her heart.

With each passing moment, the ritual drew closer to its culmination, and with it, the risk of unleashing horrors beyond comprehension. Amelia knew she was running out of time. She had to act now, to stop Ezekiel before it was too late, before the world itself was torn apart by the dark forces he sought to command.

As she finally felt one of the bindings give way, a surge of adrenaline shot through her. This was it—the moment of truth. She had one chance to end this, one chance to save herself and prevent the catastrophe that loomed so close.

Amelia prepared to make her stand, to fight back against the darkness with everything she had. The fate of her soul, and perhaps the world, hung in the balance.

With a desperate burst of strength, Amelia wrenched free from her bindings. The pain from the ritual cuts seared through her as she shoved Ezekiel back, the dark symbols etched into her flesh burning with a fiery agony. She stumbled away from the altar, her steps unsteady and frenzied as she darted into the dark corridors of the mansion. Behind her, Ezekiel recovered quickly, his presence looming like a shadow as he gave chase.

Amelia's flight through the mansion was a nightmare come to life. Each shadow seemed to reach out, clawing at her with spectral fingers as she stumbled down the darkened corridors. Her breath came in harsh gasps, the air thick with dust and the scent of decay that hung heavy in the unlit passages. The mansion, once a grand structure filled with history and secrets, now felt like a tomb, its many rooms and hidden alcoves serving as perfect ambush points for the hunt.

The sound of her own footsteps was nearly drowned out by the thunderous echo of Ezekiel's pursuit. His steps were methodical and determined, the sound of his boots against the wooden floor a constant, ominous drumbeat that paced her frantic running. Every creak of the floorboard, every whisper of movement seemed amplified in the oppressive silence between their noises.

Ezekiel's voice continued to haunt her, a spectral presence that seemed to seep through the walls. "There's no way out, Amelia. You're trapped in the web you helped weave!" His words were a toxic mixture of derision and delight, his enjoyment of the chase palpable in the air that trembled with his dark incantations.

Amelia darted into a room, slamming the door shut and leaning against it, her whole body shaking. The dim moonlight filtering through a cracked window cast long, twisting shadows that danced around her, mocking her attempts to hide. Her mind raced for a solution, a way out, but the mansion was a maze, and Ezekiel, the spider at its centre, knew every twist and turn.

Suddenly, the door shuddered under a heavy thud, the sound jarring Amelia from her brief respite. She scurried away, her injured body protesting with sharp stabs of pain. As she exited through another door, she caught a glimpse of Ezekiel's silhouette at the end of the hallway – tall and foreboding, his figure haloed briefly by a flicker of lightning that penetrated the gloom.

"Amelia, you can run, but you can't hide from what you've unleashed!" Ezekiel's voice roared through the hallway, closer now, his words chasing her as relentlessly as his footsteps. Another crash of thunder from outside mirrored the chaos inside, the storm outside mingling with the storm within the walls.

Panic surged as Amelia navigated the labyrinthine hallways, her mind reeling from the echoes of Ezekiel's laughter and the incessant, heart-pounding fear that clawed at her sanity. The mansion was no longer just a structure; it was a living, breathing entity participating in the hunt, its every room and shadow complicit in her impending doom.

In a desperate bid to create distance, Amelia pushed over a heavy vase as she passed it, hearing it crash with a satisfying sound. She pulled down a tapestry, hoping it would entangle Ezekiel or at least slow him down. Every second mattered, every obstacle she could create was a small victory, but her strength was waning fast.

The mansion seemed endless, each hallway leading to another, each shadow a potential hiding place for her tormentor. As she dashed through a particularly narrow passage, a sudden, intense flash of white light struck her vision, disorienting her momentarily. It was as if lightning had struck indoors, the brilliance overwhelming her senses. The shock of the flash forced her to a halt, her hands clutching at the walls for support.

Regaining her senses, Amelia pushed forward, her breathing ragged, the pain from her wounds a constant agony. Blood dripped onto the cold floor, leaving a trail that Ezekiel could easily follow. She felt faint, her body on the verge of collapsing under the stress and pain, but the terror of being caught, of falling back into Ezekiel's hands, spurred her on.

As she turned another corner, her legs trembling with exertion and fear, she realized the futility of her escape within the confined spaces of the mansion. The outside—the forest, perhaps—offered a better chance at hiding, maybe even escaping. With what little strength she had left, she made for the nearest exit, a side door that led into the overgrown gardens.

Ezekiel's voice echoed behind her, closer now, filled with frustration and anger. "You're only delaying the inevitable, Amelia! The ritual will be completed, with or without your compliance!"

Amelia burst through the door into the cold night air, the garden's overgrown branches clawing at her as she ran. The open space was both a relief and a new terror, but she knew this was her only chance. Behind her, the mansion loomed large, its windows like watching eyes, and somewhere within its walls, Ezekiel pursued, determined and deadly as ever.

Amelia burst through the dense underbrush, her lungs burning as the cold night air sliced through her. The mansion's towering silhouette loomed behind her, casting long, ominous shadows across the ground as she fled into the sprawling estate gardens. The labyrinthine paths, once meticulously maintained, now overgrown and wild, seemed to mock her with their complexity and lack of clear direction.

In her panic, Amelia took a wrong turn and found herself at a dead end, the high garden walls insurmountable, covered in thick ivy that clawed at the stone like desperate fingers. Her heart sank as the realization of her trapped state dawned upon her. She turned, facing the path she had run down, her breaths coming in short, desperate gasps.

Ezekiel emerged from the shadows, his figure a dark blur against the lesser darkness of the night. His approach was slow, deliberate, each step measured to instill terror. "There is nowhere to run, Amelia. Accept your fate."

Amelia backed against the cold stone wall, her eyes darting around for anything she might use as a weapon. But there was nothing—only the chilling realization that her end seemed inevitable. As Ezekiel closed in, his expression twisted with rage and anticipation, Amelia braced herself.

With a sudden burst of energy born of pure survival instinct, Amelia lunged towards Ezekiel as he reached for her. She grappled with him, her fingers clawing at his hands as she tried to push him back. Ezekiel's strength was overwhelming, his grip iron-like, but the ferocity of Amelia's fear lent her a wild, unpredictable force.

In the struggle, Ezekiel's ritual dagger, previously tucked in his belt, became dislodged. It clattered to the ground, the sound piercing the night like a gunshot. Both of them paused, their eyes locking on the weapon. With a renewed sense of desperation, Amelia kicked, her foot connecting with Ezekiel's knee. He stumbled, his grip loosening just enough for her to break free.

Amelia scrambled towards the dagger, her hands shaking as she reached for it. Ezekiel recovered quickly and lunged at her, his scream of fury echoing through the garden. He grabbed her ankle, dragging her back as she clawed at the dirt, her fingers closing around the dagger's hilt.

With all her remaining strength, Amelia swung the dagger, striking blindly. The blade found its mark, sinking into Ezekiel's chest. A look of shock and disbelief crossed his face as he faltered, his blood seeping onto the ground. But Amelia didn't stop—driven by a mix of fear, adrenaline, and desperation, she stabbed again and again, each thrust a chaotic blur until Ezekiel's movements stopped.

His body fell heavily to the ground, the sounds of the night suddenly returning as if the world had been holding its breath. Amelia sat back, the dagger falling from her trembling hands. She was panting, her body covered in sweat and blood, her mind struggling to comprehend the finality of what she had done. Ezekiel, the enigmatic guide who had turned predator, lay motionless before her, his plans for her and the ritual ended by her hand.

The silence of the night was profound, broken only by the distant sound of thunder, a reminder of the cosmic forces that had been at play. Amelia's relief was tinged with horror as she realized the full extent of her actions. She had survived, but at what cost? The garden around her felt like a grave, the shadows like watchers bearing silent witness to the violence that had unfolded.

As she pulled herself up, her limbs heavy and aching, Amelia knew that her journey was far from over. The rifts were still open, the cosmic forces still at play, and the shadows of the garden seemed to whisper of darker challenges ahead. But for now, she was alive, and in her hands, she held the key to ending the nightmare. The ritual dagger, now stained with Ezekiel's blood, was more than a weapon—it was a symbol of her determination to fight against the darkness, to close the rifts and restore order to the chaos that had enveloped her life.

XVII. The Binding Symphony

The aftermath of the violent struggle left Amelia shaken, her breathing heavy as she slowly regained her senses. The night around her was eerily quiet, the chaos of the fight giving way to a tense calm. She wiped the blade on her torn clothing, her hands trembling with the aftermath of adrenaline. Looking down at Ezekiel's lifeless form, she felt a mix of relief and dread; the immediate danger was over, but the greater threat loomed large and ominous.

The sky above Eldermoor had transformed into a canvas of cosmic turmoil. Thick, roiling clouds swirled high above, intermittently illuminated by flashes of lightning that painted the heavens in eerie shades of green and orange. These were not the natural colors of electrical storms but the ominous glow of energy being twisted and torn by forces that defied the natural order.

Above her, wormholes began to puncture the sky, their edges flickering like burnt paper as they tore wider, revealing glimpses of other realities on their other sides. These rifts in the sky looked like wounds in the flesh of the world, each one a seething maelic of otherworldly light and shadow, pulsing and expanding with every passing second.

The air around these openings crackled with raw, chaotic power, the atmosphere charged with a palpable tension that made the hair on Amelia's arms stand on end. The stars that once twinkled benignly now peeked through the tumultuous clouds, their light dimmed and distorted by the thick, unnatural haze that spread across the heavens.

Each new rift that opened seemed to strain against the very essence of the world, as if pulling at the seams of reality itself. The sight was mesmerizing yet terrifying, a stark reminder of the catastrophic consequences if she failed to seal these breaches. The universe itself seemed to be crying out in agony, its ancient harmony disrupted by the unleashed forces that now threatened to tear it apart.

As Amelia watched the sky, the surreal beauty of the chaos above belied the danger it represented. The swirling colors and the menacing pulse of the wormholes served as a visual symphony of destruction, a testament to the power that lay just beyond the thinning veil between dimensions. Each moment she delayed, the rifts widened, eager to devour the world and reshape it into something unrecognizable.

With resolve, Amelia began searching Ezekiel's body for any items that might aid her in completing the ritual to close the rifts. Her fingers found the key—the same key that had begun this nightmare. It was heavier than she remembered as if now laden with the gravity of everything it represented. This key, which had unlocked so much darkness, would now be instrumental in sealing it away. It felt fitting, in a tragic sort of way, that the object which started it all would be the catalyst for ending it.

Gathering other ritual components from the surroundings and Ezekiel's supplies, Amelia found old tomes, candles, and esoteric symbols that had been used in the earlier rituals. Each item was a piece of the puzzle, and as she arranged them around the key, forming a circle in the clearing where the fight had taken place, the air grew thick with the power of her intent.

Amelia positioned herself in the centre of the carefully laid circle, each item and symbol placed with meticulous precision. The ancient tomes she had studied laid out the ritual in cryptic detail, the phrases thick with the weight of ages. She took a deep breath, steadying her nerves, and began to recite the incantations, her voice resonating with a force that seemed to echo through the very fabric of reality.

"Za'kathra esh'val, um'ren torak," she intoned, the words foreign but powerful, vibrating through the air. The key before her responded, pulsing with a glow that brightened with each syllable. The ground beneath her seemed to pulse, syncing with the cadence of her chant.

"Ve'shok nah'reen, dra'kol varith," Amelia continued, her hands moving through the air, tracing symbols that glowed briefly as if burned into the night itself. As she spoke, the rifts in the air shuddered, their edges flickering like unstable flames being drawn inward by an unseen force.

The ritual's energy built, a palpable tension in the air that made her skin tingle. Amelia could feel the eyes of the cosmos upon her, the weight of countless unseen watchers pressing down as if eager to see whether she would falter.

"Na'gath dro'val, tera'kith san," she proclaimed, her voice growing stronger. The key at the centre of the circle now blazed with light, its brilliance casting long shadows that danced around the ritual space. The rifts contracted more

aggressively, the edges starting to bleed colours into the sky—greens, oranges, and purples swirling in a dance of cosmic defiance.

The air around her thickened, shimmering with the energy of the ritual. Amelia felt as if she were standing in the heart of a storm, the forces of creation and destruction balanced on the tip of her tongue.

"Era'kath mal'divun!" she called out the final phrase, her arms raised high as she summoned the full power of the ritual. The ground vibrated violently under her feet, and the air crackled with static energy.

The key, situated at the heart of the ritual circle, throbbed with an intense, pulsating energy. It vibrated erratically, its surface shimmering with a luminescent glow that grew increasingly unstable. The air around it hummed, charged with electric tension as the key seemed to resist the immense cosmic forces being channeled into it. Amelia could feel the key's resistance, a physical manifestation of the battle between her will and the chaotic energies it contained.

As the incantations reached their climax, the key began to shake more violently, its vibrations growing so fierce that it seemed as though it might tear itself apart. The ground beneath it cracked, small fissures radiating outwards as if the very earth was responding to the intensity of the ritual.

Suddenly, with a blinding flash that lit up the entire area, the key exploded. The force of the blast knocked Amelia off her feet, sending her sprawling backwards onto the ground. As she lay there, dazed, a profound silence enveloped her. The explosive destruction of the key unleashed a shockwave of psychic energy that reverberated through her mind.

In that instant, Amelia felt as if her consciousness had imploded. A cascade of memories and visions from the past months overwhelmed her senses, each one a vivid, piercing shard of her experiences with the rifts and the Amlagrarian entities. Simultaneously, her previous memories, those of her life before the chaos that had engulfed her, snapped back into place with startling clarity.

It was as if two separate streams of her life—the one she had lived under the influence of the cosmic disturbances and her true past—had collided and fused into one continuous narrative. This sudden fusion of memories left her gasping for breath, her mind struggling to integrate the flood of information and emotions that now filled her consciousness.

As Amelia slowly gathered herself, each movement weighed down by the physical and emotional toll of the ritual, she felt a profound exhaustion envelope her. With great effort, she managed to stand, but the fatigue that gripped her body was overwhelming. Taking a step forward, her legs buckled, and she collapsed back to the earth, her gaze turning skyward.

Above her, the night sky had returned to a state of serene normalcy, the chaotic dance of greens and oranges replaced by the tranquil darkness speckled with stars. She lay there, drawing in deep, uneven breaths, allowing the coolness of the night air to soothe her battered body. The gentle rustling of the leaves in the soft breeze whispered through the quiet, a calming, rhythmic sound that contrasted sharply with the earlier cacophony of the storm.

Crickets chirped their timeless melody, a natural chorus that resonated through the field, their sounds a comforting reminder of the world's enduring rhythm. In the distance, an owl hooted—a solitary note that echoed in the stillness, adding to the nocturnal symphony that played around her.

Lying there, Amelia's eyes traced the constellations above, finding solace in their unchanged presence. The air around her felt lighter, the oppressive energy of the rifts gone, leaving behind a peaceful quietude. Each breath she took seemed to bring with it a renewal, the gentle night breeze cooling her flushed skin.

The calm of the night enveloped her, and for the first time in what felt like an eternity, Amelia felt a moment of peace. The turmoil that had raged seemed distant now, a stark contrast to the gentle embrace of the night sky. Her mind, though weary, began to accept the quiet, letting the serene sounds of the natural world lull her into a restful awareness. As she lay there, the weight of her actions and the depth of her journey settled within her, and she allowed herself to be cradled by the earth beneath her, under the watchful eyes of the stars.

As Amelia succumbed to sleep, a profound sense of relief washed over her, soothing the frayed edges of her mind. For the first time in what felt like an eternity, the shadows that had haunted her dreams receded, replaced by the gentle and familiar scenes of a life once lived in tranquillity. Her dreamscape transformed into serene and comforting vignettes: lush meadows under blue skies, the laughter of friends in sunlit rooms, and the simple joy of a quiet afternoon in a beloved garden.

Gone were the eerie landscapes and the looming, unnatural presences that had pervaded her slumber for so long. Instead, her mind wandered through peaceful memories, revisiting moments of joy and contentment that had defined her existence before the darkness had taken hold. In these dreams, there were no cryptic symbols or whispers from the abyss—only the clarity and beauty of normal life.

Her breathing steadied as she slept, and her face, usually marred by the strain of constant vigilance, now relaxed into an expression of calm. It was as if her subconscious, finally free from the influence of the eldritch forces, was taking this opportunity to heal, to rebuild the mental barriers that had been so thoroughly shattered.

In this peaceful slumber, Amelia found a temporary refuge, a nocturnal sanctuary where her psyche could mend. The normalcy of these dreams, so mundane yet so deeply cherished, was a balm to her weary soul. For tonight, at least, she could rest, her mind no longer a battlefield of cosmic horrors but a quiet landscape bathed in the gentle light of restoration and hope.

When she awoke, the world was startlingly different. Sunlight filtered through the leaves of the trees, casting dappled patterns on the ground. The air was fresh, carrying the scent of blooming flowers and new growth, a stark contrast to the oppressive darkness that had haunted Eldermoor for so long. Birds chirped cheerily, their melodies a celebration of the new day. Amelia blinked against the brightness, her senses slowly adjusting to the peaceful, vibrant surroundings.

Sitting up, she realized she was back in Eldermoor, but the town was transformed. The shadowy veil that had shrouded the buildings and streets was gone, replaced by the warm glow of the sun. The townspeople moved about, their faces no longer drawn with fear and suspicion but bright with relief and smiles. Children played in the streets, their laughter a sound Amelia thought she might never hear in this place.

As she walked through the town, people greeted her with nods and thankful expressions. The air of hostility that had once made Eldermoor feel like a prison was now lifted, and in its place was a sense of community and hope. Amelia felt a swell of pride mixed with a deep, pervasive relief. Her actions, driven by desperation and courage, had not only sealed the rifts but had also freed the town from the dark influence that had choked it for so long.

Despite the beauty of the day and the newfound peace in Eldermoor, Amelia felt a deep fatigue that clung to her bones. The ordeal had taken a toll on her, both physically and mentally. As she walked, her steps were slow, each movement a reminder of the battle she had endured. But even as her body cried out for rest, her heart was light. For the first time since she had arrived at the Vandercliffe Estate, she felt a genuine sense of accomplishment and hope.

Sitting down on a bench in the town square, Amelia took a moment to soak in the sun, the sounds, the sights. She had done what many would have thought impossible. She had faced down the darkest of forces and come out alive. She knew that the road ahead would still be long and fraught with challenges, but for now, she was content to simply be—alive, victorious, and free.

The warmth of the sun on her face felt like a gentle reassurance that despite everything, life could begin anew, and perhaps, just perhaps, there could be happiness after darkness. As she sat there, Amelia allowed herself a moment to dream, to hope for a future where she could find peace and maybe even happiness. For now, that was enough.

Chapter XVIII: A World Unravelled

In the days following the ritual, Eldermoor transformed in ways that Amelia could hardly believe. What was once a place veiled in shadows and whispers, was now alive with newfound vibrancy and warmth. The sun cast a gentle glow over the cobbled streets, touching everything with a soft light that seemed to bring out the deep, rich colors of the town—colors that had been muted under the heavy, oppressive atmosphere of the past.

The buildings, once dull and weathered, were now adorned with flowers and banners, their facades painted in cheerful hues that reflected the town's rejuvenated spirit. Gardens, long neglected, bloomed with an array of flowers, and the air was filled with their sweet fragrance, mingling with the fresh scents of pastries and pies from newly opened bakeries.

The townspeople themselves had undergone a transformation as profound as their surroundings. Faces that had been etched with lines of worry now smiled broadly, laughter replacing the hushed tones of fear. Children played openly in the streets, their joyous shouts a stark contrast to the silence that had once dominated.

Community events, which had been non-existent, now filled the town's calendar. Markets brimmed with local crafts and fresh produce, artists shared their work on every corner, and musicians played joyful tunes that danced through the air, inviting everyone to partake in the celebration of their liberation.

Amelia, the architect of this transformation, was treated with a mix of reverence and gratitude. Her walks through town were met with cheers and thankful nods, and she found herself enveloped in a community that had once seemed beyond reach. The grand festivity in her honor was a cathartic release for the town, a night of music, dancing, and shared stories that lasted until the early morning light.

As Amelia participated in the celebrations, she could feel the weight of her past struggles lifting. Surrounded by the laughter and warmth of Eldermoor's people, she began to see the tangible results of her sacrifices. The town was not just surviving; it was thriving, a beacon of hope and a testament to the resilience of its people. Eldermoor had emerged from the darkness, and in its rebirth, it found a vibrancy and life that promised brighter days ahead.

On the day of the celebration, the town square was adorned with banners and flowers, vibrant wreaths hanging from every lamppost and doorway. Music played from every corner, and tables laden with food lined the streets. The townspeople, dressed in their finest, came together in a spirit of communal joy, a stark contrast to the isolation and fear that had once defined their existence.

The mayor of Eldermoor, a middle-aged man with a warm smile, presented Amelia with a wreath of fresh flowers and a medal—a symbol of the town's gratitude. "Amelia, hero of Eldermoor," he proclaimed, his voice ringing out over the crowd, which erupted in cheers. "You have freed us from the shadows that bound us, and for that, we are eternally grateful."

Amelia, overwhelmed by the celebration and the outpouring of gratitude, felt a wave of emotions wash over her. The weight of her journey, the battles she had fought, and the darkness she had faced seemed to melt away in the warmth of the townspeople's smiles and the genuine affection they showed her.

As the celebration continued into the night, with dancing and singing filling the air, Amelia felt a deep sense of connection to these people and this place that had become her unexpected home. For the first time in a long time, she allowed herself to truly relax, to laugh and dance with the people who had once been strangers but were now friends.

The relief was palpable, not just for Amelia but for everyone in Eldermoor. The town had been through a dark period, its very soul threatened by the malevolent forces that sought to control it. But now, with the rifts sealed and the darkness banished, there was a sense of hope, a belief that the worst was behind them and that the future held promise.

Amelia knew that the road ahead might still hold challenges, and the scars of her battles would not fade quickly. But surrounded by the joyous celebration, with the medal around her neck and the wreath in her hair, she felt a peace she hadn't known in a long time. Eldermoor was no longer a place of darkness and danger but a community of resilience and recovery.

As the night wore on, Amelia looked up at the stars, their light clear and bright in the night sky. The horrors of the past seemed like distant memories, and in their place was a simple, profound joy. Eldermoor had been saved, and she had been the one to save it. For now, that was enough. And for the first time in what felt like forever, Amelia felt truly, deeply happy.

As the days turned into weeks, the decision was made to finally tear down the old Vandercliffe mansion. Its walls, once imposing and filled with dark secrets, were now just remnants of a troubled past. The townspeople, eager to rid themselves of the last vestiges of the darkness that had once dominated their lives, came together to dismantle it stone by stone. It was a cathartic process for everyone, a physical manifestation of their liberation from the shadows.

In its place, the community decided to build a park—a place of beauty and tranquillity, with lush gardens, a playground for the children, and a small memorial that told the story of the town's past and its liberation by Amelia. It was a place meant for reflection and joy, a symbol of Eldermoor's rebirth.

The town, deeply grateful to Amelia for her bravery and sacrifices, offered to build her a new home. It was a charming cottage on the outskirts of town, overlooking the newly created park. It had a warm, inviting feel, with a spacious garden where she could plant flowers and a small vegetable garden. The house was a gift from the people of Eldermoor, a token of their appreciation and a place for her to call her own.

As Eldermoor blossomed, so too did a new chapter in Amelia's life when she met Thomas. He had come to Eldermoor drawn by tales of its remarkable recovery and the community's warm spirit. Thomas, with his easy smile and thoughtful eyes, quickly became a fixture in the town's revitalized life, contributing to various community projects and events.

Amelia and Thomas's paths crossed during a town gathering where he was helping organize a small music festival in the newly established park. His genuine interest in her stories about Eldermoor's transformation and his respectful admiration for her role in it sparked something deep within her—a connection that quickly grew into affection and then into love.

Their relationship blossomed with the seasons, nurtured by shared walks through the lively streets of Eldermoor and long conversations under the starlit sky. Thomas proposed to Amelia one crisp autumn evening, and they married the following spring in an enchanting ceremony attended by the whole town.

The wedding was held outdoors, in the heart of the park where they first met, surrounded by trees heavy with white and pink blossoms. The air was filled with the scent of flowers and the sounds of laughter, music, and the soft rustle of leaves. It was a day full of joy and celebration, a perfect reflection of the new life Amelia and Thomas hoped to build together.

Their reception was a lively affair, with tables laden with food prepared by the local residents and dancing that lasted well into the night. Eldermoor's residents, who had come to see Amelia as a symbol of their town's resurgence, joined in the celebration with heartfelt enthusiasm.

In the years that followed, Amelia and Thomas built a happy life together. They restored an old house near the center of town, turning it into a warm, inviting home filled with laughter and love. The birth of their son, Eli, brought even more joy into their lives. Thomas was a supportive and loving husband, and together with Eli, they formed a family rooted in the strength and community spirit that defined Eldermoor's new identity.

Amelia, once besieged by nightmares and cosmic horrors, discovered in her family and community the serenity and purpose she had yearned for. Her days unfolded with delightful simplicity—teaching her son Eli about the wonders of nature, savouring tranquil evenings with Thomas, and engaging in community initiatives that sustained Eldermoor's vibrant spirit. While her past ordeals were indelibly part of her, they no longer overshadowed her life; instead, they highlighted the resilience and strength that had steered her to this new, contented existence.

Eli, her son, was a beacon of joy, inheriting his father's radiant smile and his mother's inquisitive gaze. He was nurtured in a community woven with tales of resilience and heroism, his playgrounds the very parks that bore witness to his mother's formidable resolve. His laughter—a pure, effervescent sound— echoed through their home, embodying for Amelia the ultimate vindication of life's joy prevailing over the shadows of old. This laughter was not just background noise; it was a melodic reminder of her new life's triumphs, resonating as a testament to a family and a community reborn in the light of hope and enduring love.

Amelia's life had changed in ways she could never have imagined when she first arrived in Eldermoor. The nightmares of the past had faded, replaced by days filled with laughter and nights of peaceful sleep. She often took Eli to the park, telling him stories of bravery and the importance of standing up for what is right. In these moments, she felt a profound sense of accomplishment and peace, knowing that her struggles had not only secured her future but had also created a safe world for her son to grow up in.

The love and peace she found in Eldermoor filled her with a deep satisfaction, a far cry from the turmoil that once plagued her dreams. With Thomas by her side and Eli's hand in hers, Amelia finally felt at home, her heart at peace as she looked forward to the many years of happiness that lay ahead. The dark legacy of the Vandercliffe mansion was gone, but the strength and courage it had ignited in Amelia would live on, a beacon of hope and a testament to the power of resilience and love.

Years had passed in peaceful serenity in Eldermoor, with days filled with laughter and nights of undisturbed sleep. Amelia, once haunted by visions of darkness, now lived a life full of light and love. Yet, as she walked through the town square one sunny afternoon with her young son Eli laughing beside her, the tranquillity shattered with the suddenness of a storm.

A thunderous crack split the sky, a sound so powerful and alarming that it halted everyone in their tracks. Following the crack was a twisted amalgamation of voices, echoing through the air with a chilling, sinister tone. "ENJOYING YOUR LITTLE DREAM IN PARADISE, AMELIA?" The words boomed around her, causing her head to throb with unbearable pain, the likes of which she hadn't felt since the dark days of her past.

Amelia's heart lurched as she gazed down at Eli, her son, whose features twisted into an unrecognizable and horrifying visage right before her eyes. His face, usually expressive and joyful, contorted unnaturally, the skin stretching and warping as if manipulated by unseen forces. His eyes, once a clear reflection of youthful curiosity, now morphed into unsettling, deep pools that flickered with an eerie, otherworldly light.

The transformation was rapid and disturbing, his once familiar face becoming something akin to the Amlagrarian entities that had haunted her darkest visions. The soft curves of his cheeks became sharp angles, and his mouth widened into an impossibly large grin that split his face in a grotesque parody of a smile.

"IS THIS WHAT YOU WANTED, MOTHER?" Eli's voice boomed, resonating with a depth that was completely alien, reverberating with the same chilling tone as the monstrous voice that had echoed from the sky. It was as if the malevolent entities from her nightmares had found a new voice through her son, mocking her deepest fears and throwing her past battles into a stark, cruel relief.

The sight of her son, transformed into a creature from her most terrifying dreams, sent a shiver of dread through Amelia. It was a brutal reminder of the dark forces she had contended with, now manifesting in the most personal and devastating way imaginable. The words, spoken with such sinister glee, felt like a direct assault on her soul, leaving her reeling in shock and despair as she faced the unimaginable horror of her reality unravelling once more.

Panicked and disoriented, Amelia grabbed Eli's hand and ran, but her surroundings had transformed into a maze of terror. As she dashed through the streets, the faces of the townspeople twisted into grim caricatures of their former selves, their eyes following her with unsettling intent. They began to close in, their movements synchronized and unnerving, as if they were puppets controlled by the dark forces that had once plagued her.

The town she had known as a sanctuary had turned into a stage for her nightmares. Every corner she turned, every alley she fled down, the distorted faces of the townsfolk appeared, blocking her escape and herding her towards an unseen but palpable doom.

Heart pounding, breath ragged, Amelia found herself surrounded. The townspeople formed a tight circle around her, their faces contorted into hideous expressions, their eyes empty yet accusing. She spun around, looking for any gap, any route of escape, but there was none. The voices from the sky laughed, a cacophony of madness that filled the air.

And then, just as the hopelessness threatened to engulf her, a blinding flash of white light engulfed her vision. The world went silent, the mocking faces disappeared, and the pain in her head ceased as suddenly as it had begun. In that moment of white silence, Amelia stood alone, disconnected from the world around her, her mind a blank slate wiped clean by the overwhelming light.

Was it another beginning or an end? Was it salvation or damnation? In that suspended moment, Amelia couldn't tell. All she knew was the white light, and then, nothing at all. The last thing she remembered before the darkness took her was the sound of Eli's twisted laughter echoing in the void, a haunting reminder that the nightmare was far from over.

Chapter XIX: Sacrifice Reborn

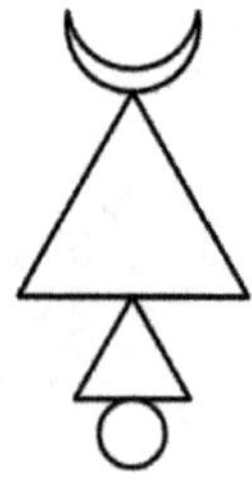

The white void enveloped Amelia, a brief sanctuary from the horrors that awaited her return to consciousness. When the white faded, twilight had descended upon Eldermoor, casting long shadows and a chilling stillness over the town square. Amelia awoke sitting on the cold cobblestones, the chill of the stone seeping through her clothes, which were soaked with blood. The metallic scent of blood hung heavy in the air, mingling with the damp earthiness of the evening.

As Amelia's gaze swept across the town square, the horrific tableau before her etched itself into her mind with unbearable clarity. The twilight cast long shadows, making the grisly scene even more macabre. The bodies of Eldermoor's residents were not merely scattered but displayed in a chilling spectacle of carnage.

Each corpse told a story of unspeakable terror. Some were slumped against walls, their faces frozen in silent screams, eyes wide open in a final, petrified stare. Others lay in the centre of the square, limbs twisted in unnatural positions, as if moved by a malevolent puppeteer. The most gruesome of sights were those bodies that had been torn apart; torsos separated from legs, heads from necks, with viscera spilled out onto the cobblestones in dark, congealing pools.

Several of the dismembered limbs were arranged in sinister patterns that mimicked the symbols Amelia had once studied in her fight against the dark forces. These ritualistic designs were drawn in blood, connecting the scattered body parts in a grotesque network that seemed to pulse with a malevolent energy.

The air itself was tainted with the metallic scent of blood, thickened into a mist that settled over the square like a funeral veil. This red haze diffused the moonlight, casting everything in a ghastly, surreal glow. As Amelia sat there, the reality of her actions—or those orchestrated through her—crashed upon her with the weight of a thousand nightmares, each more vivid and terrifying than the last.

The silence of the scene was oppressive, broken only by the soft, wet sounds of blood dripping from torn flesh and the occasional rustle of a breeze stirring through the grisly remnants of what had once been a vibrant community. Each detail was a stark reminder of the monstrous reality that had been forced upon her, and the unimaginable horror she had unwittingly unleashed upon those she had once vowed to protect.

Amelia's gaze fell upon her own attire, a chilling realization dawning on her as she recognized the garments she wore—the same she had on during that fateful night at the altar. The fabric clung to her skin, heavy with the blood not just of others but mingled with her own. The symbols carved into her flesh on that night were vivid, as if freshly etched. Each line pulsed with a searing heat, a stark reminder of the ritual that had bound her to this horrifying destiny.

Her hands, coated in dried blood, trembled uncontrollably as she traced the symbols, each touch sending a jolt of pain that was both physical and existential. The lines felt alive, as if they held the very essence of the dark forces she had been manipulated to unleash. The realization that her body had been used as a conduit for such evil, that her very flesh had been marked not just for one night but potentially for eternity, filled her with a profound horror.

Amelia's mind reeled, the memories of the night at the altar now intermingling with the brutal scenes before her. She struggled to piece together the fragments of her actions, the actions she had no recollection of, yet bore the gruesome evidence of their reality. Each breath was laboured, each heartbeat a reminder of the nightmare she could not wake from.

As she stood there, the ground beneath her feet sticky with blood, the weight of her situation became unbearable. The realization that she might never escape the consequences of that night, that her life might forever be entwined with these dark forces, was crushing. The burning of the symbols on her body served as a cruel testament to the permanence of her bond with the darkness, a bond sealed in blood and carved in flesh.

Then, her gaze fell upon the mansion. It stood unscathed, looming ominously as if it had never been torn down. Its dark windows stared back at her like hollow eyes, a silent witness to the carnage that had unfolded in its shadow. Beside her, glinting under the streetlamps, lay the ritual dagger—the same dagger she had used to kill Ezekiel years ago. It was pristine, except for the fresh blood that coated its blade, a stark contrast to the rusty age it should have borne.

As she picked up the dagger, her eyes caught sight of her arms. The symbols that Ezekiel had carved into her flesh during that dark ritual were there, fresh as if cut only moments ago. They burned against her skin, a cruel reminder of a past that refused to stay buried.

Amelia's mind raced, her breaths quick and shallow. She could not remember how she came to be here, covered in blood, surrounded by the dead. The last thing she remembered was the voice in her head, mocking and ominous, and then the white flash that swallowed everything. Now, the nightmare had returned, more visceral and horrifying than any vision the rifts had ever conjured.

She staggered to her feet, her body heavy with dread. The once peaceful town square was now a macabre tableau of death and destruction. Every step she took, her boots slipped slightly in the blood-soaked cobblestones. The silence was oppressive, the only sound her own ragged breathing and the soft squelch of blood underfoot.

Amelia looked around, desperate for any sign of life, any hint that this was just another nightmare. But the reality was inescapable. Eldermoor had been turned into a charnel house, and she, inexplicably, was at the centre of it all. The realization that she might have been responsible was too horrific to bear, yet the evidence was undeniable.

Amelia's scream tore through the silent twilight, a raw sound of horror and disbelief that echoed off the walls of the mansion and faded into the darkening sky. She fell to her knees, her hands trembling as she stared at them, covered in blood—evidence of her unthinkable actions. Tears streamed down her face, hot and unrelenting, as shock gave way to a profound grief.

Her mind desperately scrambled for memories, for any semblance of understanding, but it was like grasping at smoke. The more she tried to remember, the more her mind recoiled, leaving only fragments and shadows that danced just beyond her reach. With each attempt, a deep, wrenching pain throbbed in her head, as if her own psyche was preventing her from accessing the dark truths of what she had done.

Amelia's cries echoed through the empty square, her sobs a mournful backdrop to the gruesome scene surrounding her. "This can't be real," she gasped, her voice trembling with despair. "This can't be happening." Yet the evidence was undeniable: the blood on her hands, the dismembered bodies, the freshly carved symbols on her skin—all pointed to a horrific truth she couldn't escape.

Then, the chilling voice that had haunted her dreams pierced the silence, deep and mocking. "WELL DONE, MY CHILD, THE RITUAL IS NOW COMPLETE," it boomed, resonating with a sinister satisfaction.

Amelia's heart sank as she realized the gravity of the situation. The words sent a jolt of terror through her. "No, this isn't real," she insisted, her voice breaking. She couldn't—wouldn't—believe she had been part of such horror.

The voice laughed, cold and merciless. "OH, BUT IT IS, AMELIA. AS REAL AS THE BLOOD ON YOUR HANDS. DID YOU REALLY THINK YOU WERE ACTING ON YOUR OWN? YOU PERFORMED BEAUTIFULLY, EXACTLY AS REQUIRED."

The revelation shattered her. The idea that she had been manipulated, that her body had carried out unspeakable acts while her mind was ensnared in a fabricated reality, was too much to bear. Amelia clutched her head, trying to block out the voice, the truth, the overwhelming guilt and horror.

But the voice wasn't done. It continued, each word a hammer strike to her soul. Each phrase painfully thumping within her mind as if the very action of comprehending this voice was enough to make her head explode "YOU WERE THE PERFECT PUPPET, AMELIA. SO PLIABLE, SO BROKEN!. AND LOOK AT THE MASTERPIECE YOU'VE CREATED."

Around her, the night seemed to close in, the shadows of the dead twisting and looming as if to claim her. The air was thick with the coppery scent of blood and the oppressive weight of her actions.

Despair enveloped her, a dark cloud that threatened to suffocate her remaining will. The outlines of the bodies blurred, their twisted forms merging into a nightmarish tableau. Amelia sat amidst the carnage, lost in a sea of devastation and betrayal, utterly alone except for the mocking laughter of the unseen tormentor echoing through the chill wind. The laughter, a cruel reminder of the dark forces that had used her as their instrument, was now the soundtrack to her shattered reality.

Chapter XX: The Final Confrontation

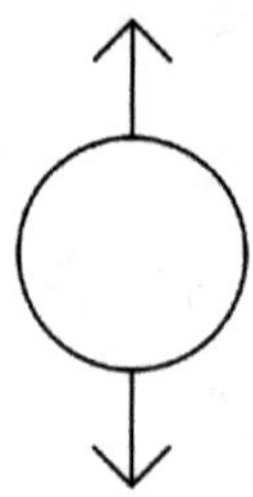

Amelia, reeling from the horror surrounding her, felt the dark presence intensify as the voice pierced the twilight silence again, resonating with a new level of malice and authority.

"YOU STILL DO NOT COMPREHEND THE BREADTH OF YOUR ACTIONS, DO YOU?" the voice taunted, its tone cold and calculating. "ALLOW ME TO ENLIGHTEN YOU, AMELIA. I AM NAA'VHA, AND YOU, MY UNWITTING SERVANT, HAVE FREED ME FROM MY ANCIENT BONDS."

The shadows around Amelia seemed to constrict as if the darkness itself was drawing closer to listen. Her heart raced with dread as Naa'vha's revelations continued.

"AMLAFRAR, THE REALM YOU'VE TOUCHED THROUGH YOUR VISIONS, WAS NOT MERELY A DISTANT PLANE OF EXISTENCE. IT WAS MY PRISON, CRAFTED METICULOUSLY TO CONTAIN MY ESSENCE, A PRISON MAINTAINED BY THE ARCANE MACHINATIONS OF UZ'AA'THAX'Z. BUT NOW, THANKS TO YOUR NAIVE MEDDLING, THE CHAINS ARE BROKEN, AND MY INFLUENCE CAN ONCE AGAIN PERMEATE THE COSMOS."

The air around her seemed to thrum with the weight of Naa'vha's words, each syllable laden with the power of unleashed chaos.

"YOUR WORLD, WITH ITS FRAGILE BOUNDARIES AND FEEBLE GUARDIANS, WILL EXPERIENCE A RECKONING UNLIKE ANY BEFORE. ALL REALMS, ALL DIMENSIONS THAT DARE CONTAIN ME, WILL BOW TO THE WILL OF NAA'VHA."

Amelia's despair deepened with each word, the gravity of her actions crushing her. As she looked upon the once peaceful town of Eldermoor, now a tableau of death and destruction, the reality of her role in this calamity sunk in.

With a sinister laugh that chilled her to the bone, Naa'vha continued, "CELEBRATE, AMELIA! CELEBRATE THE CATACLYSM YOU HAVE USHERED INTO YOUR WORLD. HAHAHAHAHAH" Naa'vha's laughter an ear piercing shriek that brough amelia to her knees clasping her ears trying to block out the sound. "REVEL IN THE DESPAIR YOU HAVE WROUGHT, FOR IT IS THE HERALD OF MY ASCENDANCY. YOU HAVE BEEN A SPLENDID CONDUIT OF DESTRUCTION, AND FOR THAT, YOU SHALL BE REMEMBERED—IF ANY ARE LEFT TO REMEMBER."

As the voice faded into a menacing whisper, Amelia felt an overwhelming sense of isolation and terror. Naa'vha's release—an event she had unwittingly facilitated—promised a future filled with darkness and strife. The once vibrant night sky now seemed to mirror the bleakness of her soul, the stars dimming as if in mourning for the fate she had sealed.

Her knees buckled, and she collapsed onto the cobblestones, surrounded by the ruins of her actions, her mind echoing with Naa'vha's mocking farewell: "EMBRACE THE CHAOS, AMELIA. IT IS THE LEGACY YOU HAVE CRAFTED WITH YOUR VERY HANDS."

The voice of Naa'vha seemed to permeate the very air around Amelia, coming from nowhere and everywhere simultaneously, enveloping her in a cloak of dread. As the full weight of her actions became apparent, Amelia's strength faltered, and she sank to her knees amid the devastation she had unknowingly wrought.

Her mind was a whirlwind of torment and confusion, each revelation adding layers of despair. The horrors that she had facilitated were beyond comprehension, beyond forgiveness. Amelia's sobs broke the eerie silence of the town square, her tears mingling with the blood and dirt beneath her.

"YOU WERE ALWAYS MEANT TO BE MY INSTRUMENT, AMELIA," Naa'vha continued, its voice a sinister whisper that seemed to echo inside her head. "THE VISIONS, THE RIFTS EVEN THAT PUNY WORSHIPPER, WHAT WAS ITS NAME? THAT'S RIGHT EZEKIAL—THEY WERE ALL PART OF MY DESIGN TO BREAK FREE FROM MY PRISON. AND NOW,

I SHALL EXACT REVENGE ON THIS COSMOS AND THE ONE AFTER
THAT."

"THE CULT YOU SO HEROICALLY TRIED TO DISMANTLE, IN TRUTH,
WERE UNDER MY GUIDANCE, THEY WOULD DO ANYTHING TO
ATTAIN THE KNOWLEDGE THAT I HOLD TO HAVE BUT A GLIMPSE
OF THE POWER I AM, YOU ANTS ARE ALL THE SAME BUT IN
ORDER TO GIVE THEM WHAT THEY WANTED THEY NEEDED TO GIVE
ME WHAT I SO DESPERATELY CRAVED.... A SACRIFICE ONE
WHOS MIND WAS ABLE TO TAP INTO THE AMLAGRARIAN SPACE I
NEEDED YOUR BLOOD TO FINALLY BREAK FROM THE SHACKLES
THAT BOUND ME. THOSE CULT MEMBERS WERE NOTHING BUT A
USEFUL MEANS TO AN END, AS ARE YOU."

Naa'vha's words twisted like a knife in Amelia's heart. The understanding that
her entire journey—the struggles, the battles, even her victories—had been
orchestrated by this malevolent force was unbearable.

"AND HOW DOES IT FEEL AMELIA? TO KNOW THAT ALL YOUR
EFFORTS, ALL YOUR SACRIFICES, WERE FOR NAUGHT?" Naa'vha's
voice carried a mock sympathy that quickly turned cruel. "YOUR PAIN,
YOUR FEAR, YOUR PATHETIC HUMAN EMOTIONS—SUCH
DELIGHTFUL SPICES FOR THE FEAST OF YOUR SUFFERING."

Then, with a laugh that chilled Amelia to her core, Naa'vha scorned her
further, "ALL YOU HUMANS ARE MERE SPECKS OF COSMIC DUST
COMPARED TO THE LIKES OF ME. YOUR LIVES, YOUR HUMAN
STRUGGLES, ARE NOTHING BUT BREIF FLICKERS IN THE VAST
DARKNESS THAT I COMMAND."

As the dark laughter echoed around her, Amelia felt a despair so deep it
threatened to consume her. Naa'vha's revelry in her suffering underscored
the utter hopelessness of her situation. Surrounded by the bodies of those

she had fought to protect, under the mocking gaze of a cosmic entity that saw her as nothing more than a tool, Amelia's spirit broke.

The town of Eldermoor, once a beacon of hope and a symbol of her victory, was nothing more than an elaborate trick while the true Eldermoor, the town so dark and void of colour was now a ghost town every inhabitant slaughtered in a bloody massacre by Amelia's own hand. The revelation that she had been a puppet in a cosmic game played by Naa'vha, a being of unimaginable power and cruelty, left her feeling hollow and utterly alone.

Chapter XXI: Shattered Reflections

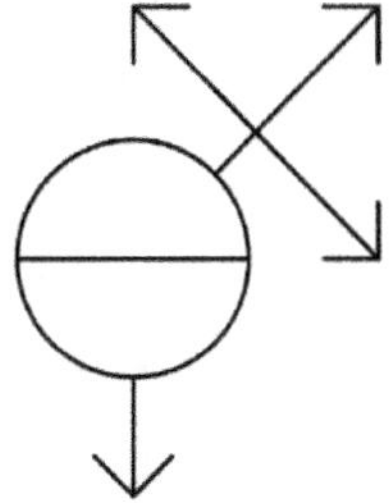

Naa'vha's laughter resonated through the blood-soaked town square, a sound as chilling as the blood that drenched Amelia's hands. "YOU ARE TO THANK FOR MY FREEDOM FROM THAT PLACE. I WILL NOT CONSUME YOU LIKE THE REST," the entity declared, its voice a sinister rumble that vibrated the air itself. "I WILL GRANT YOU KNOWLEDGE—THE KNOWLEDGE YOU SO DESPERATELY WISH TO CONSUME."

Forced to relive the horrors she unwittingly perpetrated, Amelia found herself trapped within her own memories, witnessing each brutal, ritualistic slaughter through her own eyes. The scenes played out in excruciating detail—every scream, every pleading gaze met with her own dispassionate, emotionless response as she moved through Eldermoor like a spectre of death. Her hands, though controlled by an unseen force, carried out the gruesome tasks with terrifying precision.

Each memory was a vivid tableau of violence: men, women, and children falling before her, their bodies left broken and dismembered in the streets. The air was thick with the iron tang of blood, which painted the cobblestones in horrific splashes of red. Amelia watched, a prisoner in her own body, as she moved from one victim to the next, her face devoid of any emotion, her actions methodical and chillingly efficient.

She danced in the blood and entrails of the people she dismembered and watched herself drink and gnaw into the viscera and marrow of the body parts she had torn to shreds, this revelation making Amelia feel sick to her stomach, the flashbacks continued aligning the bodies in the ritualistic patterns.

Amelia's heart ached with each replayed memory, her soul recoiling at the monstrous acts she had committed. She could feel Naa'vha's presence enveloping her mind and body like a thick, cancerous shroud, its dark energy seeping into her very essence. It was overwhelming, a constant, oppressive force that tainted every thought and intensified her despair.

Naa'vha, though not physically manifested, was omnipresent in her psyche, its malevolent will exerting a suffocating control over her. The entity's voice echoed in the recesses of her mind, a relentless reminder of her role in its liberation and the catastrophic consequences that followed. "YOU ARE MY

VESSEL, AMELIA, THROUGH WHICH I ENACT MY WILL," Naa'vha whispered, its tone both a caress and a curse. "YOUR PAIN, YOUR REGRET—THEY FUEL THE CHAOS THAT NOW CONSUMES YOUR WORLD."

As Amelia stumbled through the once-familiar streets of Eldermoor, surrounded by the aftermath of her actions, the shadows seemed to mock her with every step. The laughter of Naa'vha resonated in her ears, a sound as cruel as the fate she had sealed. Her body trembled under the weight of her guilt and the invasive presence of the dark entity that had used her as a tool for destruction.

Desperate for release yet bound by the dark fate she had unwittingly embraced, Amelia found herself at the mercy of an entity whose plans spanned dimensions and whose cruelty knew no bounds. The town of Eldermoor, now a grave for its inhabitants, stood as a monument to her devastating failure, a constant reminder of the dark pact she had fulfilled.

"YOU HAVE MEDDLED WITH FORCES BEYOND YOUR UNDERSTANDING," Naa'vha's voice thundered in her mind. "YOUR PURSUIT FOR KNOWLEDGE HAS COME AT THE ULTIMATE COST, AND NOW I AM FREE TO PLAGUE YOUR WORLD. NOT EVEN THE OUTER GODS CAN STOP ME NOW."

Each word from Naa'vha clawed at Amelia's mind, ripping it apart with a force that induced a splitting headache, a physical manifestation of the mental and emotional torment she endured. The entity's laughter echoed once more, a cruel reminder of the irreversible chaos Amelia had unleashed upon her world and possibly others.

In that moment, surrounded by the devastation she had caused and the overwhelming presence of Naa'vha, Amelia knew that her life, her very essence, had been irrevocably altered. The knowledge she had sought had indeed come at the ultimate cost, and the price of that pursuit was a burden she would carry for the rest of her days.

Chapter XXII: Redemption's Price

As Amelia sat amidst the wreckage of Eldermoor, the realization of her puppeteered atrocities weighing heavily upon her, a sudden, excruciating sensation seized her entire body. It began as a deep, gnawing ache in her bones as if the very marrow was being scraped out by invisible talons. Then, the pain escalated rapidly, radiating outward like wildfire through her nerves.

Her skin felt as though it were being seared from the inside, a scorching heat that made her gasp and clench her fists tightly. Muscles twitched involuntarily, contracting with intense, sharp spasms that left her writhing on the cold, blood-stained cobblestones. The sensation was overwhelming as if her body was being torn apart and reassembled by the malevolent force that had infiltrated her being.

Amelia's stomach churned violently, a sickening wave of nausea sweeping over her as the pain intensified. It felt as if a thousand needles were piercing her gut, twisting and turning with a mind of their own. The urge to vomit was overpowering, but no relief came; only the relentless, torturous sensation that consumed her every thought.

With each heartbeat, the pain pulsed through her, echoing in her head with a throbbing rhythm that matched the beating of her frantic heart. Her breaths came in ragged, shallow gasps, each inhale a sharp sting in her chest, as if the air itself was laced with shards of glass.

As she lay there, the ground beneath her seemed to spin and tilt, the world blurring into a dizzying kaleidoscope of shadows and light. The pain was not just physical; it invaded her psyche, a stark reminder of the dark entity's pervasive control. Amelia felt as though she was being consumed from the inside, her body and soul aflame with a torment that seemed designed to break her completely.

In this moment of agonizing revelation and physical torment, Amelia was painfully aware of her helplessness—a puppet whose strings had been cruelly pulled to orchestrate a tragedy of cosmic proportions. The entity's laughter, a sound dark and triumphant, echoed around her, a sinister soundtrack to her suffering.

Amelia's agony escalated to an unbearable crescendo. The pain, already insufferable, intensified as she began to cough violently, each spasm racking her body with such force that she felt as though her insides were being shredded. Blood, warm and coppery, trickled from the corners of her mouth, spattering the ground with dark, ominous stains.

Her eyes, too, started to bleed, tears of blood streaming down her cheeks, blurring her vision into a red haze. The sight was horrifying, a grotesque mask of her own torment. But the most terrifying sensation came from within her abdomen. It felt as if a malevolent force, a creature of unimaginable darkness, was clawing its way out, desperate to break free from the confines of her flesh.

Lying on her back, Amelia stared helplessly at the sky, which seemed to darken with her despair. Her stomach churned and convulsed as if alive with a sinister will of its own. She could feel—and see—something pushing against her skin from the inside, distorting the contours of her abdomen into unnatural shapes. Each movement within her was accompanied by a sharp pain that stole her breath away, a visceral reminder of the entity's pervasive and destructive presence within her.

The helplessness Amelia felt was complete and total. Paralysed by pain and horror, she could do nothing but watch as her body became a battleground for the dark forces that had claimed her. The sensation of being utterly powerless, a mere vessel for something so evil and ancient, filled her with a profound dread that was worse than the physical torment.

As she lay there, the ground cold and unyielding beneath her, the whispers of Naa'vha filled her ears, mocking her pain and celebrating her destruction. "THIS IS THE CULMINATION OF YOUR JOURNEY, AMELIA," the voice taunted, a cruel echo in her mind. "A VESSEL FOR MY AWAKENING, A SACRIFICE FOR MY ASCENSION."

With each word, the thing inside her seemed to grow stronger, its movements more frantic and determined. Amelia's mind reeled with fear and disbelief, her heart pounding a desperate, futile rhythm against the inevitable. The dark laughter of Naa'vha resonated around her, a sound so evil it seemed to strip the very warmth from the air, leaving a chill that seeped into her bones.

In that moment, Amelia understood the true horror of her fate—not just to be destroyed, but to be an instrument of destruction, her very body the portal through which unspeakable evil would enter the world. The realization was a torment all its own, a mental anguish that intertwined seamlessly with the physical torture she endured.

Amelia's screams dissolved into the chilling air as excruciating pain enveloped her entire being. Her gaze, blurred by tears and blood, fixed on her abdomen, which gruesomely distorted as something within fought to emerge. Suddenly, with a sickening tear of flesh and a gush of dark, viscous blood, a large, spidery leg burst through her stomach. The leg was grotesquely elongated, its chitinous surface glistening wetly in the dim light, tipped with sharp, jagged ends that dripped with her blood.

As Amelia watched in horror, more legs followed, each one ripping through her skin with brutal force. The sight was nightmarish—like a colossal spider, each limb thrashing violently as it freed itself from the confines of her body. The legs were covered in a thick, dark exoskeleton, jointed unnaturally, moving with a horrific, alien grace. Each new emergence sent waves of agony through Amelia, her body convulsing under the assault.

Overwhelmed by the unbearable pain and the grotesque spectacle unfolding before her, Amelia's consciousness began to fade. In her last moments of awareness, her vision filled with a blinding white light, transporting her away from the physical torment.

Suddenly, Amelia found herself in a stark, liminal space, an infinite expanse of white emptiness. There was no sound, no light, no sensation—just an oppressive void that enveloped her completely. It was as if she had been stripped of all senses, floating in a vacuum devoid of time and space. The only feature in this vast nothingness was a singular "doorway," a window-like opening that hung suspended before her. Through it, she could see the horrific scene she had left behind—her own body, now just a shell, being torn apart by the monstrous entity emerging from within.

The doorway offered a surreal, detached perspective, like watching a horror film in which she was both the victim and the helpless spectator. The creature continued to extricate itself, its massive body slowly becoming visible as more of its grotesque form emerged. Amelia wanted to scream, to cry, to do anything to express the horror and despair she felt, but no sound came out. She was a prisoner in this blank expanse, forced to witness the destruction of her own body and the realization of Naa'vha's monstrous plan without the ability to intervene.

As she watched, the last of the creature detached from her ravaged form, leaving behind nothing but a mangled, unrecognizable mass. The entity that had used her as its birth canal now stood complete—a nightmarish spider-like behemoth, its many eyes gleaming with malevolent intelligence as it turned to wreak havoc on the world Amelia had once known.

The finality of her situation settled in as Amelia realized she was trapped in this liminal space, condemned to observe the aftermath of her actions without the ability to change anything—a spectator to the end.

In the empty, soundless void of the liminal space, Amelia's psyche, already frayed and fragmented by her harrowing experiences, began to disintegrate further. What remained of her self-awareness withered, leaving behind a hollow shell, a wraith of despair unable to act or react—forever cursed by the weight of her horrific actions. In this bizarre realm where sound did not exist, Amelia felt a surreal, uncontrollable urge to laugh. Her mind, unable to cope with the complete sensory deprivation and the gravity of her fate, succumbed to madness. Her laughter, silent yet frenetic, was a chilling testament to her broken state. It was a laughter devoid of joy, a macabre response to the absurdity and horror of her situation.

As she cackled into the void, the world around her—the last tether to her former life—faded into darkness. Above, ascending into the cosmos with a grace that belied its grotesque form, was Naa'vha. This monstrous entity, now fully unleashed, was a sight of nightmarish splendour. It loosely resembled a colossal spider with a thousand legs, its body covered in a slick, dark exoskeleton that glistened as if wet. From its middle abdomen sprouted large, bat-like wings, each flap stirring the very fabric of reality, sending ripples across dimensions. The wings, vast and leathery, beat with a slow, deliberate rhythm, propelling Naa'vha upwards into the endless expanse of the cosmos.

The creature's eyes burning red as if made entirely out of crystalised blood— multifaceted and gleaming with malevolent intelligence—reflected the chaos it left in its wake. Below it, the world Amelia had once called home was now a mere speck, a trivial plaything left behind by a being of unimaginable power and malice.

As Naa'vha disappeared into the celestial abyss, the liminal space that held Amelia's fractured psyche began to dissolve. The last vestiges of light vanished, pulling her deeper into an abyss of insanity. Her laughter echoed in the nothingness, a haunting sound that would never reach any ears. Amelia's identity, her memories, her very essence, faded away, leaving behind nothing but the dark legacy of her actions.

The liminal space, once a brief refuge from her tormented reality, now became her eternal prison—a void where her psyche, a rotted and broken shell, descended into ultimate madness. The echoes of her despairing thoughts lingered for a moment before being swallowed by the all-consuming darkness. In the end, Amelia was no more, her existence erased as completely as the footprints left behind by Naa'vha's ascension into the universe.

In the cosmic silence where Amelia's psyche once dwelled, the echoes of her tormented laughter faded into nothingness, swallowed by the cold expanse of the void. Naa'vha, now unchained, soared through the cosmos, its grotesque form casting a shadow that stretched across stars and nebulae. Below, the world of Eldermoor lay in ruins, a testament to the horrors unleashed by a force that humanity was never meant to comprehend.

As the entity ascended, tendrils of its dark influence lingered, seeds planted in the torn fabric of reality. These seeds, hidden within the rifts of space and time, began to sprout, feeding on the chaos of Naa'vha's passing. In the shadowed corners of the universe, other beings stirred, drawn by the disruptions in the cosmic order. They whispered in ancient tongues, their voices like the scraping of bone on stone, discussing the newfound breaches that had appeared in their prison walls.

Back on Earth, in the once-quiet town of Eldermoor, the aftermath was palpable. The streets, slick with the remnants of the fallen, resonated with a palpable dread. But it was the silence that followed the storm which proved most horrifying. No birds sang, no children's laughter filled the air—only the hushed, fearful whispers of survivors, if any remained, hidden in the rubble of their broken lives.

And in the depths of the ruined mansion, amidst the shattered remains of ancient tomes and the echoes of forgotten spells, the ritual dagger that had ended Ezekiel and freed Naa'vha lay forgotten. Its blade, still stained with the blood of the ritual, began to hum—a low, menacing vibration that seemed to call out into the darkness. The blood acted as a beacon, a call to the creatures that now roamed freely between the thinned veils of the dimensions.

The world, unbeknownst to the few who survived, had changed irrevocably. The breach that Amelia had sealed was merely one of many, and as the barriers between worlds continued to weaken, the Earth became a nexus, a gateway through which horrors beyond imagination sought entry.

As night fell over the remnants of Eldermoor, a new sound began to emerge—a sound unlike any heard before. It was the sound of something vast and terrible stirring in the depths of the Earth, answering the call of the bloodied dagger. The ground trembled a slow, rhythmic pulsing that matched the beating wings of Naa'vha in the distance.

And somewhere, in the dark recesses of the world, eyes opened—eyes that had watched from the darkness, waiting for their moment to emerge. The cycle had begun anew, and with it, the promise of untold horrors. The cosmic dance of chaos and order continued, with Earth as its latest stage, and humanity, unknowingly, teetered on the brink of a new abyss—one that promised not just the return of Naa'vha, but the awakening of forces that even the gods had feared to name.

The horror was far from over; it had only just begun.

Epilogue: Awakening

In the endless expanse of the cosmic void, far beyond the reaches of known galaxies and the boundaries of the mortal realm, the universe whispered its ancient secrets through the fabric of space and time. It was here, in the blackest depths of the void, that Naa'vha journeyed, a sinister silhouette against the darkness, seeking the entity that had imprisoned it eons ago.

As Naa'vha moved through the void, its form shifting and shimmering with eldritch energy, it approached a region where light seemed to hesitate, where stars dared not shine. The silence was profound, broken only by the pulsing echoes of cosmic winds.

Suddenly, the darkness stirred, responding to Naa'vha's presence. A low, resonant sound filled the void, a language not spoken in millennia, its tones vibrating through the dark matter that filled the space between stars.

Naa'vha: *"ZU'UTH BARAK NA'AMLAGRAR, UZ'AA'THAX'Z! XUL'GARATH SK'TALATH DOR'EN!"*

Naa'vha's voice was commanding, each syllable a ripple across the cosmic sea, challenging and potent.

From the darkness, a response came a voice that seemed woven from the void itself, deep and omnipresent, enveloping Naa'vha like a cloak.

Uz'aa'thax'z: *"Naa'vha, k'tul ra'zahn. T'gar non'valis dor'ach."*

Uz'aa'thax'z spoke with a calm authority, its tone implying ages of wisdom and power, unruffled by Naa'vha's challenge.

The conversation between the two entities continued, a debate of ancient grievances and cosmic laws, each phrase a clash of wills, echoing through the dark reaches of space.

Naa'vha: *"GAR'NATH ZUL'RATHAK! AMLAGRAR XAN'KOR, XAN'THULAC!"*

Naa'vha's voice grew more forceful, its form expanding with anger, the surrounding darkness flickering with each word spoken.

Uz'aa'thax'z: *"Zu'garak nor. Thul'garak zu'valis. Naa'vha, zor'n Ta'chu'kam'a'a zar'rok."*

The entity's response was a soothing balm across the chaotic energies emanating from Naa'vha, its presence immense and unyielding, a foundational force of the universe.

The verbal duel reached a crescendo, the very fabric of the void vibrating with the power of their words. Then, silence fell—a dense, pregnant pause as if the universe itself held its breath.

From the depths of the void, two colossal eyes slowly opened, their irises a radiant emerald green that shimmered with a supernatural intensity. These eyes blazed like celestial jade lanterns, illuminating the darkness with a piercing, eerie glow. They were vast, each one dwarfing Naa'vha in scale—a clear testament to the immense power and ancient wisdom of Uz'aa'thax'z. The eyes flickered with an inner light, casting verdant reflections that danced across the void, hinting at the depths of knowledge and strength contained within.

Naa'vha, undeterred by the size or the ancient power it faced, bristled with dark energy, its form ready for a confrontation that would shake the foundations of the cosmos.

The stage was set, the players aligned, and the void watched in silent anticipation as the ancient enemies faced off in a battle that could alter the very structure of reality. The final confrontation was about to begin, and the stakes were nothing less than the fate of the universe itself.